"[With *Bad Juju*] Jonathan Woods has arrived fully fledged as a maestro whose collection seems like it must be his fifth or sixth book such is the assured tone...His ability to switch genres in the space of one story after the other is astounding. If you could image Poe, Paul Bowles, Chandler and the wondrous Robert Stone all contributing to a collection, *Bad Juju* would be it. The writing is of such a high calibre that I found myself reading the stories aloud to get the full flavour of Woods' artistry."—Ken Bruen, award-winning author of *The Guards*, *Blitz* and *London Boulevard*

[With *Bad Juju*] Jonathan Woods has laid down the gauntlet for gonzo noir in the 21st Century. His postmodern take on the genre is scorching the earth behind him."—Anthony Neil Smith, editor/publisher of plotswithguns.com and author of *Hogdoggin'*, *Yellow Medicine*, *The Drummer* and *Psychosomatic*

Bad Juju & Other Tales of Madness and Mayhem

Winner, 2011 Spinetingler Award
for Best Crime Short Story Collection

Praise for *Bad Juju*

"Quirky and disquieting, *Bad Juju* leaves you marveling at the imagination of Jonathan Woods. I want to read more."—Michael Connelly, author of the *Harry Bosch* and *Lincoln Lawyer* crime novels

"*Bad Juju* is hallucinatory, hilarious, imaginative noir."—*New York Magazine*

"*Bad Juju* delivers a dance of life and death that soars and plummets like Fred Astaire on methamphetamine."—*Booklist*

"These 19 tales of erotic or absurdist noir are lively, imaginative, sometimes parodic, often darkly funny, accurately likened on the back-cover blurb to opium dreams and Quentin Tarantino...all executed with enormous skill by a writer of formidable talent."—Jon L. Breen, two-time Edgar Award-winning critic, in *Ellery Queen Mystery Magazine*

"Unlike anything else you'll read this week. Or month. Or, probably, year...like a fever dream of noir."—Bill Crider's *Pop Culture Magazine.com*

"Violence, sex, and gonzo plot twists fuel Woods' diverting collection of 19 stories, most set in sun-and-blood-drenched borderlands. [The stories in *Bad Juju*] amp up the volume to 11... Throughout, a penchant for vivid imagery slaps the reader around like a boxing bag." —*Publishers Weekly*

"*Bad Juju* is a crazy group of stories...part Hunter Thompson, part Jim Thompson and all excellent."—*Crimespree Magazine*

Praise for Bad Juju

"Woods is the David Lynch of short crime fiction."—*Spinetingler Magazine*

"*Bad Juju* is unlike any noir I've read before...It's like Woods gave the whole crime [fiction] world a much-needed enema."—*Bookgasm.com*

"I'm delighted to recommend the stories in *Bad Juju*...These dark, often strange, eerily radiant stories add something special to the tradition of noir crime writing. Take note, Edgar Poe – there is life in the line you cast."
—Jay Parini, author of *The Last Station, Borges and Me* and *Robert Frost: A Life*

"Impeccable dialogue, wit, surprising plots—it's all here. Raymond Chandler and Dashiell Hammett would approve and be, I suspect, more than a little bit envious of these stories."—Ron Rash, two-time PEN/Faulkner Award finalist and author of *Serena, One Foot in Eden* and the Frank O'-Connor Award-winning *Burning Bright*

"First-rate noir is meant to alarm and horrify decent men like myself, and certainly I was quite shocked by nearly everything I read in *Bad Juju*. But Jonathan Woods' stories have everything you hope for from high-toned writing, so the gunfire, the stabbings, and the entirely mystifying sexual exploits are worth every minute. You'll finish this book feeling astonished, but with no regrets. Woods is the real thing, and once I've recovered I plan to read the book again."—Michael Dahlie, 2009 PEN/Hemingway Award-winning author of *A Gentleman's Guide to Graceful Living*

"*Bad Juju* is the product of a truly twisted mind, and I mean that in the nicest way. If you crossed the Coen brothers with Kurt Vonnegut, then threw in some Jim Thompson along with a couple of dollops of vintage Quentin Tarantino, you'd come up with a writer very much like Jonathan Woods."—Ben Fountain, award-winning author of *Brief Encounters with Che Guevara* and *Billy Lynn's Long Halftime Walk*

"*Bad Juju* is the wildest, funniest, scariest collection of stories I've read in a long while." —Scott Phillips, author of *The Ice Harvest, Rake* and *The Devil Raises His Own*

Bad Juju
& Other Tales of
Madness and Mayhem

Other Books by Jonathan Woods

Phone Call From Hell and Other Tales of the Damned

A Death in Mexico

Kiss the Devil Good Night

Hog Wild

Bad Juju
& Other Tales of
Madness and Mayhem

Jonathan Woods

Habent Sua Fata Libelli

Manhanset House
Shelter Island Hts., New York 11965-0342

bricktower@aol.com • NewPulpPress.com

Library of Congress Cataloging-in-Publication Data
Woods, Jonathan
Bad Juju
p. cm.

1. FICTION / Noir. 2. FICTION / Humous / Black Humor.
3. FICTION / Short Stories / (single author). Fiction, I. Title.
ISBN: 978-1-955036-85-6, Trade Paper

2025

To Dahlia

Contents

"I haven't laughed over anything so much since the hogs
ate my kid brother."

—Dashiell Hammett, *Red Harvest*

"Oh, there is nothing better than intelligent conversation except
thrashing about in bed with a naked girl and Egmont Light Italic."

—Donald Barthelme, "Florence Green Is 81"

The Dilapidated Isles

Jeff Walberg set down his bags and gazed out along the dilapidated dock. Across the looping water of the bay a line of picturesque palms was etched against the sky. Off the dock a figure splashed in the calm surface of the water, churning out a rapid if erratic Australian crawl.

Walberg squinted to make out the details. It's a naked woman, he thought. A stark naked woman. Her round white buttocks rolling from side to side recalled the hump of Ahab's famous whale. Or something less profound.

Reaching into the pocket of his seersucker jacket, he found the crumpled handkerchief and mopped his brow. The humidity was at 99 percent. He had a hard-on.

The swimmer finished her constitutional in a final violent lap and climbed up a rickety ladder onto the dock. Her nude body arched cat-like, as she shook off the water.

Leaning down, she swept off a white bathing cap just as the sun popped above a snarl of mangroves to the east. The new light burst on her blonde curls like a revelation. As she turned, it shimmered on an equally golden tuft of Brillo sprouting between her legs.

My god, thought Walberg. His mouth was as dry as a sand trap.

The unnamed goddess scampered across the dock and disappeared inside the giant silver-clad bird that rocked gently on the ebb and flow, its man-made wings spread in supplication to the newly risen sun.

When his erection had subsided, Walberg picked up his bags and walked down the ramp and out along the dock to the waiting pontoon plane.

Boxy and fish-scaled with shimmering aluminum plates, the aquatic aircraft suggested a simpler, but no less desperate, time. Walberg wallowed in a wave of retro-fantasy: Bogart looking sleazy as usual amid the flickering images of Beat the Devil; Hemingway aboard the Pilar hunting Nazi subs; Ava Gardner and Howard Hughes flashing their pearly whites for the paparazzi.

Walberg, an accountant, was going insane.

As he approached the plane, a man holding a wrench aloft, stepped from the shadow of one great wing. Walberg took two steps back.

The man looked at Walberg, then lowered the tool and began wiping it with a rag.

"Snuck up on me, pardner. You can't be too careful these days."

"Yes, you're right." What is he talking about? wondered Walberg.

The man thrust his hand forward, capturing Walberg's in a sissy grip. The hand was damp as a corpse.

"Ed Stone. People call me Eddy. Edie on the weekends. You doin' alright?"

Walberg grimaced.

"Too early for that question."

His teeth felt filthy. He quickly closed his lips.

His almost attacker's clean-shaven face was oblong and angular as a piece of heavy machinery. Threadbare khakis as soft as silk and faded almost to oblivion clothed him from head to toe. Vargas Moving & Storage was written in cursive across the front of his sweat-stained cap.

"You Smith?"

"Walberg."

"Ah. The last-minute booking. Susanne was taking bets on whether you'd actually show up."

"Why did she think I wouldn't show?"

"Well, pal, this ain't Club Med. Sometimes things can get a little dicey in the Islands."

"I've got lots of life insurance," said Walberg. "Where do I stow my gear."

Stone flicked his head in the direction of the bird.

"Suzanne'll give you a hand. And a handjob." Ed winked. "But sometimes she bites."

Teetering across the narrow undulating board stretched between the dock and the seaplane's open hatchway, Walberg wondered: Did he actually say handjob or am I dreaming?

The blonde, who at that moment appeared framed by the gunmetal edges of the doorway, left no doubt as to the answer. It was the same full-boned woman Walberg had caught sight of during her morning physical. Now she was dressed in a washed-out Betty Boop T-shirt, shorts that nibbled at her crotch and white Topsiders sans socks.

She grabbed Walberg and yanked him the last several feet through the hatchway. Taking his bags, she began to stow them in an overhead compartment.

"You must be Smith."

"Actually, it's Walberg."

She threw a flirty gaze back over her shoulder.

"I'm Suzanne, your air hostess. You want a hot towel? Or a handjob? How 'bout a drink? I make a mean Tequila Sunrise. Or we've got Mimosas. Daiquiris. We might even have a little ganja."

A torrent of words before Walberg could get his bearings. Or did you say "sea legs" on a pontoon plane?

"Coffee would be great," he faltered. "And the Wall Street Journal."

"Coffee coming up," she said brightly. "They cut off our Journal subscription at the knees. For nonpayment." She pretended to bite the air. Her teeth looked sharp. "You'll have to check out the views. Or polish your social skills interacting with us fellow fliers."

As Walberg took his first steaming sip of java, the prune face of an ancient mulatto appeared in the hatchway. He wore a white suit and Panama hat.

"Smith?" Suzanne asked, her head popping forth from the mini-galley.

The dark-skinned geezer seemed to nod in affirmation as he shambled to his seat.

Assisting him was a black-haired woman too young to be with such an old man.

Her skin was as pale and mottled as a clam sitting in its shell on a bed of crushed ice waiting for the hot sauce. Dark filaments fringed the upper lip of her oddly pretty face. The plunging V of her navy blue dress revealed an elaborate hieroglyph of tats across the tops of her breasts.

As she passed Walberg, her eyes looked straight ahead, avoiding his analytical stare. He wondered if she was also a Smith.

Three minutes later Ed Stone and another man, who stumbled and slurred his words, passed through the cabin into the cockpit. Suzanne slammed and secured the hatch door

"Seatbelts, everyone," she trilled. "No more drinky drinks till we're airborne."

Who was drinking? wondered Walberg. Surely neither Smith nor his goth companion was an early morning tippler. Then he realized there was liquor in his coffee. A lot of liquor.

That and the drone of the seaplane engines sent Walberg headfirst into the deep end of dreamland.

He awoke with Suzanne's lips on his.

"Oh! Mr. Walberg," she said. "Time to bring your seat up. We're just landing in the Islands."

The silver bird passed over a wide bay, then the docks, where a single tramp freighter was offloading containers, and finally above the rusting corrugated rooftops of Puerto Greenberg. In a moment they were above impenetrable rainforest, before curving back to the bay for landing.

The Smiths... Walberg had made them plural. The Smiths were met at the pier by a motorcycle with a sidecar. The orangutan-like driver wore a maroon zoot suit and pointy black shoes. His eyes peered from dangerous slits; his visage resembled a hillside torn by mudslides.

They stowed the old fart in the sidecar; hired a man to bring the luggage. Then Smith the younger hoisted herself up behind, hiking up her leg for Walberg to catch a glimpse of her black thong undies.

As the bike sped away, the muffler shook loose and clanked to the pavement. The engine roared and the motorcycle disappeared in a cloud of burning oil.

"We're staying in the Islands for a few days," said Stone to Walberg, grabbing his hand and pulling him across to the pier. "We'll see you around."

"Yeah, sure," Walberg mumbled distractedly.

Gazing shoreward, his eyes had come upon a young woman in a tight school uniform. She lolled on a bench at the crumbling seawall, her bare legs crossed, reading a novel in the shade of a scrofulous palm. Her cherry-red lips moved silently as she parsed the words.

Walberg had meant to ask Ed or Suzanne where they were staying, get a recommendation. But when he looked up, they were gone, including the palsied co-pilot, leaving Walberg on his own.

Walking both ways on the main street until the cheesy stores and bars gave out and exploring several side venues, Walberg determined there were only two hotels in Puerto Greenberg. El Hotel Miami and Hotel Paradiso. Someone had thrown a rock through the Paradiso sign, leaving a jagged hole. Taking this as an omen, Walberg checked into the Miami.

A sign on the front desk read Management is Out to Lunch. But when he rang the bell, which was broken and made a scratching sound, a paper-thin addict blew in from the back room. He unhooked a key and with his gray fingers slid it across the counter to Walberg. A mildewed leather tag read: room 13.

"It's the only room with a shower. Shiter's down the hall. $10.00 a night, $60 a week. Paid now. Let me know if you need some company."

In the room a pair of copulating geckos clung to the ceiling. Walberg lay on the bed for a while, but couldn't get a hard-on.

When he stood back up and started to arrange his stuff in the bureau, one of the knobs came off. He tossed it in a drawer. The ashtray on the table by the window was full of old butts. Some with lipstick. He decided he was hungry.

A crowd of raucous drinkers filled the Cantina Esplendido. Walberg stood at the bar with a rum punch and read the handwritten menu on the wall.

Suddenly Miss Smith appeared in the open doorway of the bodega. When their eyes met, she looked startled. A mutant sniffed out by the thought police. Blithely she walked over to him. They shook hands.

"You're Walberg, from the plane."

"Yes."

"I'm Always."

"Always what?"

"Always Divine."

"I'm getting confused," said Walberg. "Are you on valium?"

She scowled at him.

"It's my name. Always Divine."

Walberg wanted to say: Are you a Bond girl?

"Would you like a drink?" he asked instead.

"I can't," she said, placing her hand on his arm. "But come tomorrow for a barbecue." She hurried out.

"Cuando?" he shouted.

"Whenever."

She was gone before he could ask the location.

On the way back to the hotel after a plate of beans and sausage, Walberg bought a bottle of local rum. Several attractive hookers paraded past, but he passed them up for a drink in his room. He felt flushed.

Sitting on the sagging bed, he put a finger in his mouth, moving it along the gum line until he found the point of inflammation. The tooth moved; it was as loose as an old man's bowels.

What was going on? He'd just been to the dentist! Everything had been cool.

It was 11 a.m. when Walberg awoke to the sound of a loose hubcap clanging in the gutter. He lay for a while in the trough of the bed, trying to remember who he was. On the far wall a serious-looking inch-wide crack had opened in the night, running like a lightning strike from one corner of the ceiling down to the floor.

On his way out he mentioned the crack to the Chinaman sitting behind the check-in counter. The Chinaman rolled his shoulders in a dramatic shrug. Probably doesn't understand a word I said, thought Walberg.

He spent the day wandering the streets of Puerto Greenberg. The place was falling apart. Parallel and perpendicular had ceased to exist. Crumbling concrete, rusting sheet metal, insect-ravaged wood siding. Everyone he passed looked hot or angry in rayon shirts and tight pants.

A toothless Chihuahua bolted from a doorway and began humping Walberg's leg. When he tried to kick it away, the owner started a ruckus. A crowd gathered. Walberg fled.

He stopped for a cold drink and a shave in the main plaza. Afterwards, he saw himself in the barber's mirror: an uptight gringo in a button-down shirt. On the way back to the hotel, he bought two rayon shirts with aggressive prints in leftover colors.

Two notes had been left for him at the hotel desk.

One read:

Come at 9. We're roasting an entire pig. Tell the cabbie: World's End, on the South Road. Always.

The other, from Ed Stone, said they were drinking beer at the Stoned Iguana, if he wanted to drop by. Walberg changed into the shirt decorated with out-of-focus Havana street scenes in orange and verdigris.

Ed, Suzanne, and the co-pilot sat at the back of the bar near the pissoir. Overcome by sudden dizziness, Walberg collapsed into the fourth chair. His forehead felt like an electric hotplate left on too long. Surprisingly, the bottle of beer brought by the one-armed waiter was ice cold. Walberg rolled it back and forth across his brow.

"A touch of fever?" asked Ed. "Give it a day or two. Either it'll burn itself out or you'll be dead."

Walberg took a sip of beer; then stared morosely into the bottle. "I should have gone to the Galapagos," he said to no one in particular.

Suzanne passed him a smoldering spliff.

"Get a life," she said.

"Is it legal to smoke this stuff in public?"

"Just take a hit and move it on," said Suzanne.

Walberg did as he was instructed. The waiter arrived with another round of beers and shots of rum anejo.

"Telefono por Senor Walberg," the waiter said.

"Who the hell knows I'm here?"

Ed gave Walberg a noncommittal shrug. Suzanne sucked loudly on the roach. The co-pilot was in his usual never-never land. Walberg walked to the bar with the waiter and picked up the ancient handset.

"Hello?"

"It's me" came an urgent whisper. The voice belonged to Always. Next came an echo like bat signals bouncing off the walls of a vast steel pipe.

Always spoke again: "The man with the motorcycle. He scares the shit out of me. Bring a gun with you."

Before Walberg could even gulp, the line went blank.

"Hello! Hello! Fuck!"

What was he supposed to do now? Where could he acquire a gun?

Ed's arm came around Walberg's shoulder.

"Let's get some fresh air," he said.

Outside it appeared to be even hotter than back by the pissoir. Not even a cockroach moved.

"It was Always, wasn't it?" asked Ed. "Be careful, pal. You'll end up with two wheels in the ditch and your dick tied in a square knot."

"She told me to bring a gun," confessed Walberg.

"Where the hell are you going to find a gun?"

"I thought you might help me out."

"No fuckin' way."

Suzanne appeared beside them. She opened her purse and pulled out a semiautomatic weapon as sinister as a chunk of antimatter. She did a quick run-through, ejecting and inspecting the clip, cocking and firing on an empty chamber, reloading the clip. She handed the pistol to Walberg.

"You can borrow mine."

"How much?"

"Pay me in kind." Her hand brushed his crotch.

At that very moment the only cab that Walberg had seen in Puerto Greenberg slumped and wheezed up the street like a methadone addict in search of a fix. It stalled at the corner, just as Walberg climbed into the backseat.

"Where to?"

"World's End. On the South Road."

"You sure about that?"

"Yes."

"Have to charge you extra. No lights down that way. Sometimes there're bandits. Marxists."

"Here," Walberg said, handing the driver a twenty-dollar bill.

The driver folded the greenback into a tiny square and slipped it under his tongue, then cranked the engine. Nothing happened. After delving under the hood for cinco minutos, he tried again. The engine coughed like a smoker with terminal emphysema. Finally it caught.

Shortly they left behind the last light of Puerto Greenberg. But the road through the jungle remained two lanes of cement, not downgrading to gravel or mud. Someone had paid someone off.

The cab rounded a curve and shimmied to a stop, throwing Walberg helter-skelter against the back of the front seat. Caught in the headlights, a metal chain stretched across the highway between two posts. A sign hanging from the chain read World's End –Privado.

Walberg, his lip bleeding, clambered out of the cab. Without a moment to lose, the taxi backed and turned, backed and turned, its transmission screaming; then sped away, back toward Puerto Greenberg. The sky was full of stars sailing toward entropy.

At a slow jog Walberg started up the dirt track beyond the chained entrance. The blue-steel barrel of Suzanne's pistol, jammed into his waistband, rubbed irritatingly against his genitalia, already inflamed by some tropical rash.

After a mile or so, he came upon a single-story Caribbean-style plantation house facing the beach. There was no evidence of a barbecue in progress. The house was pitch black. Starlight revealed bales of razor wire unrolled in defensive thickets around the structure.

A fusillade from an assault rifle tore up the night, turning the banana leaves above Walberg's head into confetti. Walberg ate dirt.

"Don't come any closer," croaked a male voice. Was it Smith or the zoot-suited gangster? Where was Always?

As if in response, a hand lightly touched his shoulder. He turned his head. Always, in halter-top and jogging pants of some dark color, bent toward him, her pale skin like thick English cream.

"The old man...Smith...and the biker have taken over. They want me dead."

"Taken over what?" asked Walberg.

"The business."

"AAAhhh." Is it something illegal? he wondered. A ganja farm? Maybe a meth lab? Or just flaky? – exporting a homeopathic cure for cancer derived from tropical frog livers?

"Did you bring a gun?" hissed Always.

Walberg rolled sideways, pulled out the midnight black semiautomatic and held it aloft. A ray from the newly risen waning moon impaled the weapon.

In the next instant Always lunged forward and tried to wrest the pistol from his grip. Her teeth clamped onto the fleshy zone of his hand below the little finger. So unexpected was her assault, in a flash she held the pistol pointed at him.

Just then, Smith or the other man, attracted by the scuffle in the brush, opened up again with the high-powered automatic. Always's head exploded in slow-motion gore.

Holy shit! thought Walberg.

He began to crawl rapidly away from the plantation house clearing. Unable to find the road, he moved along the edge of the jungle abutting the sea. A thousand yards from the house, he broke from the jungle and began to run up the white sand beach. Barely a dozen loping strides later, he pulled up in excruciating pain. The spine of a sea urchin had pierced the sole of one of his Pumas.

Somehow he extracted it from his flesh in one piece. Then wrapped the wound with his handkerchief.

Limping like some dysfunctional Iraq war vet, he resumed his trek up the beach toward Puerto Greenberg. Dawn was a gray thought as Walberg entered the central business district.

When he retrieved his key at the Miami's front desk, the Chinaman handed him a note. It read Leaving today. Too bad it didn't work out. Suzanne

Walberg went back outside just in time to see the seaplane soar over Puerto Greenberg before heading stateside. He wondered when the next plane might arrive. Maybe he could book passage on the tramp freighter.

A three-legged dog hopped by. The town seemed more decayed and run-down than he remembered from the previous day. A man naked but for a Corona T-shirt slept on the pavement.

Walberg went into a small cafe that sold ice cream, coffees and tropical drinks. He ordered an espresso doble. Two of the whores from the other night on the street came in. They stood at the ice cream freezer, considering its contents and, obliquely, Walberg, as he sipped his coffee. He looked like a vagrant.

The one with black curly hair isn't half bad, he thought.

He appraised her ample tits, tight stomach and long firm legs. One of her eyes remained static. When she turned so the light from outside hit it, he realized the eye must be made of glass. She gave him one of those "check-it-out" smiles.

He looked away in embarrassment. Then down at his Rolex.

It had stopped working.

Incident in the Tropics

"That young man's staring at me," Marge says.

Ray Elrood, absent-mindedly perusing a set of female buttocks flouncing their way between two rows of plastic cafeteria tables, glances up at his spouse.

"Which young man?" he asks.

"Over there. In the soccer outfit."

Ray follows the trajectory indicated by Marge's nod. Across the aisle, a platoon of Latin youths is wolfing sandwiches and meat pies, slurping sweet drinks. They lounge provocatively; engage in macho shenanigans and repartee.

"They're all wearing soccer uniforms," he says. "Must be a local high school team stopping after the game."

"It's the one with the mustache. And the red bandanna."

Ray picks out the young man Marge means.

He looks about sixteen, smooth-faced except for a fringe of hairs curving in a half-moon above his upper lip. The accoutrement of some 1940s bebop hipster. His hair is jet and wiry, cut close to his skull. He wears the same black-and-gold T-shirt and sweatpants as the rest of the team, augmented with a bright red bandanna tied around his neck in the manner of a romantic poet. Gesturing dramatically, he concludes telling two teammates some wild-ass tale of seduction. They vie with each other in dissing its veracity. A mock tussle breaks out.

"He's not staring now."

"Well, he was," Marge says defensively.

"Ogling your tits, was he?"

"Don't be crude."

Ray scratches his chin. He's not sure whether Marge expects him to do something about the stranger's aggressive gaze. Perhaps slap him across the cheeks, demand satisfaction by dueling pistols at dawn. Ray's inclination is to drop the entire matter without further ado.

"Maybe we should head back to the tour bus," Ray says, glancing at his cheap plastic wristwatch. ("It is recommended," reads the cruise line brochure, "that no jewelry or expensive watches be worn while touring ports of call.")

"I need to use the bathroom," Marge replies.

Gathering up her oversized purse, she glances around, at last heading off to a far corner of the cafeteria. She strides like an alpine hiker at the mall.

On this, the fourth day of a ten-day cruise out of Ft. Lauderdale, Ray and Marge and a dozen other adventuresome passengers are on a day tour to the capital of the Republic. The day is waning. Marge has a bladder infection.

As Marge disappears from view into the bano mujer, Ray pushes away the plate with its abandoned sandwich crusts and brushes his shirt for crumbs. What I need, he thinks, is an ice cream cone. He pushes up to a standing position, looks again at the youth with the bandanna and peach fuzz, then meanders toward the dessert counter. His dick keeps hoping for another glimpse of the provocative buns.

He wanders around, licking the mango swirl ice cream, but the owner of the outstanding booty is nowhere to be found. He sits down just as Marge comes up.

"Where's the camera?" she demands, frowning at the ice cream cone.

"Half of this is yours," Ray says, waving the hand holding it.

"With your spit all over it? Gross! Now, where's the camera?"

Ray gives her a blank stare, his lips blow out a puff of air. Pfffff.

"You didn't bring the camera," he says, "because I wanted to take a picture of the bronze-horsed Hero of the Revolution and you said, quote, 'Oh fuck! The camera's sitting by my bed back on the ship,' unquote."

"I'm worried about you," Marge says. "You've totally imagined that little scene. It figures you'd contract some unusual form of Alzheimer's where you become delusional as opposed to brain dead." She tries to put her hand on his forehead. He pulls back.

"When I went to the john, the camera was sitting on the table directly in front of me," Marge says. "Now it's gone."

"I'm sure it wasn't here," Ray says. "I'm not that far gone."

"You wish," Marge says, "because you went to get ice cream and left the camera sitting here. And that hoodlum stole it."

"What hoodlum?"

"The one sitting over there with the faggoty mustache and the scarf. He's been eyeballing my Canon digital all afternoon."

"Him? The one who was checking out your mangos?"

At that moment, a woman with a management badge pinned to her pale blue polo shirt walks by.

Marge, still standing, addresses her with ferocity: "Senora. My camera's been stolen by that scumbag over there." Her words boom across the room. Her nod identifies the hipster-poet soccer player as the perp. His name, embroidered across the left breast of his soccer shirt, is Angel.

Marge is of the school of gringo travelers who thinks speaking in loud aggressive tones will overcome the impenetrable barrier between American-ese and the local lingo.

When she singles him out, Angel bounds to his feet. Anger suffuses his face like cheap Burgundy on a tan shirt. He accuses Marge of lying. Demands an immediate apology. All in Spanish. He's studied English in secondary school, but is too unsure of himself to speak it. His teammates crowd around, looking angry and nihilistic.

The coach pushes through the throng of testosterone.

"What the fuck's going on here?" he asks in perfect English.

"That boy stole my camera."

"Impossible. Why would a spoiled rich kid want to steal a camera from some fat gringa?"

Blows are exchanged. Marge uses her bag like a shillelagh. Ray swoops his arm across her chest and drags her backward. The cafeteria manageress steps between Marge and the coach, who promptly slaps the manageress in the face. She slaps him back.

Before things get too rambunctious, some kind of policeman in a faded blue uniform with frayed shirt cuffs edges through the tide pool of emotion.

"Mas tranquilo," he urges, his hands raising and lowering.

Turning to Ray, Marge asks: "What's he saying?"

"Something about tequila, I think."

"That doesn't make any sense."

"This whole thing doesn't make any sense. It's off the rails," admonishes Ray. "Let's just get on the van and get back to the ship." He looks again at his watch. "If we leave now, we can still make the first sitting for dinner."

"What about the camera?"

"Fuck the camera."

"Of course you'd say that. You didn't pay three hundred dollars for the latest model available only at the Vegas Electronics Show or online. As usual, you've got zero skin in the game."

"What do you mean, no skin? If we stick around here we're likely to have stilettos poked through our vital organs."

"I always knew you had a yellow streak."

"Hah."

He almost strikes her. Which is what she wants, so she can refuse him sex privileges back on the cruise ship. Relegate him to the couch in the sitting room of their suite. Even cut off his bar tab, which she pays for out of her mother's estate. Ray is presently unemployed. He holds his temper in check, gripping his hands into fists as if crushing a pair of fat water roaches.

Out of nowhere, two more cops appear. These guys are the real thing. Radiating menace.

The crowd grows nervous, restive. The Marxist slackers and hangers-on at the back peel away, suddenly remembering important appointments elsewhere.

"What's going on here?" the cop who looks like Ernie Kovacs in the movie version of Our Man in Havana says. Hard-billed Gestapo cap, algae-green fatigues with epaulets and a cluster of ribbons above one pocket. Shades. A large weapon in a flapped leather holster hangs at his waist.

This is Lieutenant Diablo Reiner.

"That young hooligan stole my camera," answers Marge. She gestures again at the youth with the lip fringe and bandanna. "And that man..." she wishes she could eviscerate the coach with the blade-like edge of her French-nail manicure job, "attacked me."

"She's making it up," the boy yells.

The other cop, in matching fatigues but without the fruit salad and wearing an Aussie snap-brim hat with one side turned up, backhands Angel in the mouth. Like in a comic strip, his head seems to fly in the opposite direction, then bounces back. Blood oozes from his split lip.

"How much is the camera worth?" Reiner asks.

"I paid three hundred dollars for it. U.S. dollars."

The cop licks his lips. It's a lot of money in a poor country contiguous to the Tropic of Cancer.

"And how do you know this person took it?"

"Because he's been staring at it the entire time we've been here."

Reiner looks sadly at the boy.

"Search him!"

The command is directed to both Sergeant Gomez in the outback headgear and the officer in the blue uniform, who's with traffic control. The latter grasps the young man's arms from behind while Gomez pats him down. A few coins and a condom in its foil wrapper are the only result.

"He must have passed it to a confederate," Marge says. "It's probably already for sale in the thieves market."

"Don't be making up shit," hisses Ray.

Marge takes a deep breath.

"And he was ogling my breasts," she says.

"Which must have been spectacular, senora, about thirty years ago." The Lieutenant says this in Spanish. Some of the remaining riffraff snicker. Others just blink their eyes. "Ah ha. Not only a thief but a sex maniac too," Reiner says in gringo-speak. "A bad hombre."

Before Marge can reply, their tour guide, a sassy full-breasted woman with a half-baked command of English, touches Ray's arm. Startled, he jumps.

"We must leave now to ship."

When he looks at her, Lieutenant Reiner's eyes carry a death sentence. He clicks his heals. "Not so fast. We have serious accusations that must be resolved."

"Their cruise liner departs at cinco y media. We have more than an hour's drive ahead of us to get there in time."

Reiner scowls at her.

"Get lost," he says. "Vámonos."

Sergeant Gomez takes over, placing his hands on the tour guide's shoulders and pushing her back into the scrum of teammates and onlookers. The rabble closes behind them like the high tide over the road to Mont-Saint-Michel.

"Wait a minute. We've...," Marge begins.

Reiner places his finger on her lips. He shakes his head.

"Silencio. Stop talking." His words are like the back and forth of a straight razor across a leather strop. "You must give written statements about this incident," the lieutenant says. "For that we will go to my office."

Ray's in a panic. We've got to amscray out of here, he thinks.

"Forget the camera," he bursts out. "If the kid stole it and you get it back, it's yours, officer. A gift. But we've got to leave. Get back to the ship."

For the first time Reiner focuses on Ray.

"If...?" he inquires with sloth-like slowness. "If he stole it? There can be no doubt in such matters."

"What I mean...," Ray says. He's not sure what he means. He just doesn't want to be there any more, in that cafeteria, in the capital of the Republic on a late Tuesday afternoon in mid-May.

Seconds later the tour bus pulls out of the parking lot without them. A viscous lump of fear settles at the back of Ray's throat.

"My name is Lieutenant Reiner of the Special Police," Reiner says. "Sergeant Gomez is bringing the car."

As if on cue, the motley assembly falls into tatters like smoke blown by a fan revealing a black Lincoln Continental oozing to the curb in front of the glass cafeteria doors. Sergeant Gomez shambles out of the front passenger seat and opens the rear door.

"Adalante," the lieutenant says, pushing an ashen-complexioned Angel through the hushed throng.

Marge looks at Ray. Her lips are as compressed and pale as twin slices of white peach flesh. She puts a hand over them as if she's about to burst into uncontrolled sobbing or vomit up her lunch. One of her beautifully manicured nails is chipped.

"Let's go," Ray says.

Soon they're hunkered down in the vast leather-bound backseat of the Lincoln. It's almost like prom night. Marge and Lieutenant Reiner sprawl on the couch-like banquette. Ray and the sergeant huddle on hard jump seats facing rearward. Between them, Angel flops on the floor on his stomach, a guppy out of water. A plastic restraint holds his wrists in the small of his back. The red bandanna is missing. Gomez's boot resides in the crook of his neck.

The pungent tang of fresh dog poop fills the air, and Ray has the urge to check the bottom of his shoe. Then he realizes the soccer youth has shit himself. Ray's own bowels gurgle like a drain clog on the move.

The car surges into traffic like some primeval cat prowling the chiaroscuro of the rain forest.

"You are enjoying your visit to our country?" Reiner asks. "Excluding, of course, this unfortunate incident of the camera."

"Swell," Ray says.

The conversation dies.

Waves of garlic and other more exotic spices emanate from Gomez. Despite the air-conditioning, the interior of the Lincoln is thick with sweat, stale tobacco, feces, and musk.

They pass through a business district, the sidewalks awash with pedestrians flitting in and out of the shops, bargaining vociferously with the street vendors. Then they turn and begin to climb a hill among more official-looking buildings. Acacia trees dazzle in full flame-yellow bloom. A blood-orange Poinciana explodes into view. Suddenly it begins to rain.

The headquarters of the secret police of the Republic is a squat frog-like building of green stone. On closer inspection, Ray realizes it's constructed of cement blocks covered in mold. A pair of guards in camouflage gear and armed with machine guns snap to attention as Lieutenant Reiner steps from the car.

The five of them, Reiner, Gomez, Marge, Ray and the alleged thief, mount the steps. Angel stumbles as if he's forgotten how to walk.

Inside, they climb ringing metal steps to the third floor. Gomez and two other cops, overwhelming Angel's feeble resistance, manhandle him down a side corridor toward the back of the building.

Lieutenant Reiner's office is a vast institutional gray space with windows on two sides. His desk is worn and unadorned. Marge collapses into a hard wooden chair in front of the desk, her hands covering her face. A larger-than-life-size photograph of the President of the Republic gazes down at her. The President's eyes are as vacant as the Dead Sea.

Ray walks to one set of windows. They look out onto a soccer field where, despite the pelting rain, two teams of men race and pivot back and forth chasing a mud-caked ball.

"Nice view," he says.

"Wasted when you're overworked," Reiner replies.

"I'll bet," Marge says.

A female secret police person enters the office through a side door. She doesn't bother to knock. Drab olive short shorts and slim-fitted military blouse. Combat boots with socks. Ink-black hair tied in a bun, pierced by a pair of chopsticks. A tiny gold cross hangs like a fallen climber between the foothills of her Sierra Madre breasts.

"Ah. Irena," Reiner says.

She carries a tray on which sit four cups of steaming espresso, a bottle of agua minerale con gas, and glasses, all of which she sets on the conference table.

Her bottomless brown eyes fixate on Reiner, then Ray. She gives nothing away.

"We'll be taking statements," Reiner says.

Irena collects a steno pad and pen from the credenza and sits sidesaddle at the end of the table, crossing her long bare legs. In a different venue, Ray would willingly tell her his life story; drop to his knees and perform cunnilingus.

Instead he throws himself into a chair at the table. Marge sits next to him. He pours them both a glass of water. She seems to be shaking. Small tremors every few seconds make her seem out of focus.

Reiner sits opposite them, with a clear view of Irena.

"Now then, Mrs. Elrood... ," Lieutenant Reiner begins.

"What are they doing to that boy?" Marge demands in a rush. "You've got to let him go!" She bursts into tears.

Ray gives Reiner an apologetic eyebrow roll. He touches Marge's shoulders. She shakes his hands away and starts digging in her carpetbag-sized purse, looking for a Kleenex.

At that moment Sergeant Gomez slips like a ghost into the room. He moves quickly to the Lieutenant, bends down and whispers.

The tip of Irena's tongue slithers between her lips. Her body twists and grinds as she seeks a comfortable position in the military-issue straight-back chair.

Suddenly, Marge screams; slumps sideways in her chair.

Is she having a stroke? Ray wonders.

Reiner throws a glass of water in her face. Marge shudders, uses the tail of her blouse to wipe her face and sits up. One side of her white silk blouse is soaking wet and you can see the nipple like an aroused prune. When she removes her hand from her purse, she's holding the missing Canon digital. She places it on the polished surface of the table. All eyes stare at the camera as if it holds the meaning of life and death.

"It was in my bag all along," Marge offers apologetically. "I totally forgot I put it there. You can let the boy go. I was mistaken."

"Even about the fact he undressed you with his eyes?" Reiner asks.

"I've got a very vivid imagination," she replies.

Ray nods in support of this admission.

"Please. Just let the boy go," Marge says.

Reiner: "I'm afraid it's too late for that."

"What do you mean?"

"Es muerto."

In an excess of emotion, Ray grabs the camera and with all his strength throws it against the wall. It splinters into jagged bits of shrapnel.

Marge is sniffling softly, her teeth worrying her lower lip.

Ray looks at Irena, who is staring down at her boots as though they belong to someone else. Lieutenant Diablo Reiner's voice interrupts: "But there is the matter of reparations...and justice for the family."

The room turns ice cold. Looking at Reiner, Ray imagines black membranous wings unfolding.

Ray feels his nads shrivel.

Bad Juju

I flew into Saint Hippolytus in an aging single-engine turboprop. As we made our final approach, the tarmac came up fast. Black and swollen as a dead dog's tongue remembered from childhood. Jungly foliage covered the landscape on either side. At the end were some mangroves and then the ocean.

I'd just read a three-paragraph story in the Financial Times about the Cessna Caravan being voluntarily grounded for landing-gear failures. In the next instant there was the twang of breaking metal components. As the front and one rear wheel scorched down onto the runway, the other side of the plane, missing the second rear wheel, fell sideways like a terminal drunk. When the fuselage hit the tarmac, the plane began to spin, propeller blade splintering, pieces flying wild-assed through the air.

Just before all this happened, I had glanced up from the Times article and read the words Cessna Caravan engraved on a cheap plaque screwed to the instrument panel. My seat was in the row directly behind the pilot.

Next thing we were spinning out of control, veering off the runway into the high grass. I could hear the howling of fire equipment. We pivoted one last time and lurched to a spine-jarring halt in three inches of water left by an earlier thunderstorm. When I pressed my face against the passenger window, I saw that the luggage compartment had split open, leaving a ragged line of suitcases strewn behind us. The captain kicked open the forward door. We bailed and ran.

When it was my turn, I judiciously kicked off my high heels before jumping into the pilot's arms. Smoke billowed from the engine that had scraped and sparked across the ground. Amazingly the other wheels hadn't given way. Running barefoot, I was quickly outdistanced in the dash for safety.

A sharp wind blew off the ocean. I tripped once, scrambled back to my feet and loped onward toward the terminal, my lizard clutch lost in the weeds. As I ran from the soggy grass onto the tarmac, I saw my Samsonite suitcase lying ahead, its shell cracked open like a blue crab on a crab-shack table on a hot Caribbean night. Caught by the wind, the money inside the suitcase, all US$4 million of it, spiraled upward and green-parrot-like swooped into the jungle.

I pulled up short and watched the final gust of greenbacks flap over the line of palmettos and coco palms twenty yards south of the runway. Then I blanked out for an instant.

Of course, this was all planned. I had twelve guys in the fallow rice paddy on the other side of the palm and palmetto windbreak scooping the greenbacks out of the air with butterfly nets. Estimated loss: maybe a hundred thou.

The only unplanned event happened when I walked into the airport terminal.

Inside, a crowd of on-lookers chaffed at the bit, held back by five or six barely eighteen-year-old camouflage-fatigued troopers hefting machineguns. Lieutenant Ariel Limon, fat, tanned and ghastly, stood in the forefront. Five years before half his face had been blown off by an IED allegedly planted by some shadowy Marxist cell. More likely by a disgruntled client who felt he'd not received good value for his payoffs. Now that side of his face was a white snarl of eyeless scar tissue.

As Ariel stepped toward me, he jerked a blue-steel military issue .45 from his flapped leather holster. The room suddenly became breathless. The ratcheting sound of the pistol being armed echoed like twin ball bearings dropped on a terrazzo floor.

"Anne Muldoon?" he demanded, knowing full well who I was. We'd met occasionally at government functions in years past.

I looked up from massaging a bruised ankle and flashed Ariel a fake smile. Bent over and wearing a low-cut camisole as I was, he had a great view of my tits. Big deal.

"Hi, Lieutenant. Hell of a close call. Guess I'm lucky to be alive."

He ignored my attempt at social repartee, his sole eye as scrunched and rugged as a hardscrabble field carved out of the jungle by some dirtbag campesino.

"Anne Muldoon. I'm arresting you for the murder of Tony Sanchez."

"You must be kidding," I said.

He wasn't. At a nod of Ariel's buzz-cut skull, two of his foot soldiers jumped forward and grasped my arms. They were so inept, I might have grabbed one of the machine guns and mowed the lot of them down.

I didn't.

My mind was already sorting back through the index cards of memory to the previous evening in Malibu Caye, when I'd last seen Tony "the Microbe" Sanchez. Then, he'd been very much alive.

Point of clarification: Tony's nickname wasn't a reference to the size of his dick, which was pretty average. It referred instead to his unwavering penchant to micromanage every frigging detail of his mostly shady businesses.

It started out as just another simple insurance scam. Tony would put in a claim for the lost money. The money that got blown out to sea. Meanwhile the missing money would go quietly into some privately owned businesses. Double your pleasure, double your fun. Tony agreed to pay me 25 percent of the missing money to set it up. I got 5 percent up front to cover expenses.

Now it had morphed into a murder rap.

As I hissed at Ariel, I realized the US$4 million was long gone. Slipped into someone else's pocket.

I needed to get Ariel to tell me whose.

"Let's get a drink. You can tell me all about Tony Sanchez's murder."

"You know the details better than I do."

"That remains to be seen."

Ariel's jaundiced eye coasted over the clusters of gawkers. His own toy soldiers watching his every move.

"This is no place to talk," he said.

He ordered his sergeant to clear out the upstairs lounge and secure the stairway.

In the upstairs bar, we took seats by the bank of windows looking out onto the tarmac. On the far side, smoke still wafted from the wreck of the Cessna.

A Mayan beauty, with skin the color of weathered cedar, brought a bottle of rum and two glasses. Then she went away; and we were on our own.

The first perfect sip of 1 Barrel took me by surprise. It always tasted smoother and more consoling than I remembered.

"Tell me about Tony," I said.

"A small caliber bullet through the forehead. Brain freeze."

Ariel tossed back two fingers of rum.

"Oh, yeah. And both eyeballs were slit with a razor. Some kind of juju trick. If the dead man can't see his killer, he can't say his name."

I wondered whether Tony's eyes had been razored before or after lights out. One way was a lot easier to take than the other.

Ariel reached his fingers into the flap pocket of his camouflage shirt, withdrew a shiny Zippo and set it on the table between us.

"You left your lighter at the crime scene."

It was certainly mine. Chrome plated with the initials A.M. engraved in Celtic script with a rising sun behind. Except I'd lost it more than two years ago about the same time I quit smoking.

"Is that all you have?"

"We've got your DNA all over his cock."

"No way. It takes at least two weeks to get DNA test results back from London."

He shrugged.

"So you were sleeping with him."

"Who's framing me?" I asked.

Ariel's hand caressed my leg.

Chances were all he wanted was to watch me make it with one or two of his crack Alpha Squad recruits. The video would get some laughs floating around the Caribbean rim.

And I'd never find work again. Except maybe as a hooker.

In the end, we settled on just a handjob, with my breasts showing. By then the bottle of 1 Barrel was two-thirds empty and I had no idea what I'd agreed to.

Ariel stood up and pulled at my arm. I looked around at the pool table. The multi-colored vinyl curtains separating the bar from the restaurant. The smoking remains of the Cessna across the runway. It was like an acid flashback.

I followed Ariel behind the bar.

His pistol belt was already hanging from one hand. He started to unbutton his pants. I could see he was rampant.

"Hey, pal. Give me the name first or it's no sweet patooti for you."

I put my hand over his eye and my tongue in his ear.

I heard him groan. As though I were torturing him. Cutting off his foreskin with a dull paring knife.

"Give me the name."

"Leroy Poe," he mumbled.

The lawyer.

My other hand pulled Ariel's handgun from the dangling holster. The rum had vaporized my synapses. I was running wildly out of control. Uncovering Ariel's single eye, I jammed the barrel of the weapon against it and pulled the trigger.

CLICK!

No ammo. I should have known.

As Ariel's hands grabbed my throat, I kneed him in the jewels as hard as I could. The next instant he was writhing on the floor like a dying insect.

Tucking the empty .45 in the top of my jeans, I catapulted over the bar; then dashed down the room, out the smudged glass doors and across the observation deck. A drainpipe descended at one end. I made for it, and hoisting myself over the railing, eased down the galvanized pipe to the ground.

There was still plenty of chaos out on the tarmac. Emergency vehicles parked at odd angles. Firemen, medics and security milling about.

Unobserved, I trotted in the direction of the garages for the emergency response vehicles, just beyond the terminal to the east. As luck would have it, a new silver-gray Mitsubishi Shogun was parked beside the garages, the driver's door open, its motor idling.

Moments later I drove the off-road vehicle hell-bent for leather through the airport exit and turned onto the main highway into Saint Hippolytus. No one was following.

I needed to find a hiding place as quiet as a grave to hole up in and figure out what the hell was going on.

Abraham Swallow was a second cousin twice removed on my mother's side. His job was caretaker of Death Shall Have No Dominion Cemetery, the original cemetery in Saint Hippolytus.

Nowadays most dead people in Saint Hippolytus were buried in the new cemetery called Happy Rest. This was because Death Shall Have No Dominion was just about full up. But somebody still had to mow the grass, whack down the weeds and pour poison on the fire ant mounds.

That's where Abraham Swallow came into the picture.

He lived in a puce-colored cement-block bungalow in a back corner of the cemetery beneath the electric-orange blooms of a Royal Poinciana. Since it was after one p.m., he'd already sucked down a couple of Belikin lagers with his rice and beans and fried plantains, and was thinking about a nap.

That was when I drove the SUV up the red-dirt road that meandered through the gaudy mausoleums and rococo tombs housing more than two centuries of the dead. With the recent summer rains, it was like driving with square tires on a carrot grater.

Swallow, sitting on the edge of the front stoop, watched my approach with wide-eyed dismay. I could have been the messiah or the devil's altar girl. In either case, I was trouble.

"Hey, Swallow," I said.

"Ain't seen you, cousin, since Uncle Luther died."

He stood up and scratched the back of his neck. He was decked out in a shapeless olive-drab T-shirt and the gray striped pants from an old suit.

"Bin a while," I said.

We drifted into the local patois. He asked after my mother, who'd been dead for the past seven years. As I stepped out of the Shogun, I pulled a pint of 1 Barrel from a plastic sack. A cheap trick.

We passed the bottle back and forth once or twice. Swallow excused himself and went in the house. He returned with a port-soaked cigarillo. I watched him make a scalpel-straight incision with his fingernail down one side, dump out the tobacco and roll a fat custom blunt from a scraggly handful of local herb. He lit it and took a deep toke.

"What chew want?"

"I need a new identity for the truck and a place to crash."

"I don' know, cousin. I'm not much for the heat."

He passed the blunt. I took some and held my nose. The acrid blue smoke burst out of my lungs. After the second puff, I began to mellow out.

"What's not to know? I need a place for tonight, a little time to clear my head. Then I'm outa here."

"You sure?"

"Just one night. Least you can do for family."

This last appeal put me over the top. We hid the Mitsubishi in an empty mausoleum. Then Swallow made me a plate of rice and beans doused with Marie Sharp's pepper sauce. We finished the pint of 1 Barrel and talked some more about family.

I asked Swallow if he knew where I could get some .45 shells.

"Might be I could help you out," he said. "Cost you two hundred dollars for a box."

All I had was a fifty, folded up in a gold locket dangling between my breasts. The locket also contained a tiny oval photograph of Tony.

Okay. Okay. So we'd been intimate for about six months.

I hated sleeping by myself. Scary dreams. Monsters under the bed. All that shit.

But that didn't make me a murderer. Or did it? Did a brown recluse kill her mate?

Swallow showed me a cot in a little room off the kitchen. He gave me a towel and a bar of soap. The shower was on an open cement pad out behind the house.

I knew he was watching while I soaped up, then let the water wash over me like a drug. After I came back to life, I hand-washed my clothes.

The rest of the afternoon I sat around naked, making lists. Seven capitals starting with the letter B. The last seven books I'd read. My last seven orgasms.

Swallow spent most of the afternoon changing the color of the Mitsubishi from silver gray to navy. It also got new plates and a cracked windshield. I gave Swallow the fifty bucks for the redo.

Dinner was canned tomato soup and some old fry jacks. I went to bed at dusk, still naked under a wonderful cotton sheet so old and soft it was like my own skin.

Tony kept getting in the way of sleep. He wasn't a half bad guy when he took his mind off his rackets. He liked to fish for amber jack and mackerel along the smaller cayes. Sometimes we'd tuck up on a moonlit sandy beach with a bottle of hooch, Tony playing old Bob Marley songs on a sway-backed guitar. Then fuck till dawn. Now all that seemed a long time ago.

Before I fell asleep on Swallow's cot, I hummed a few bars of "No Woman, No Cry" as my farewell to Tony. Maybe one day, there'd be payback. Right now I had to look out for my own ass.

I woke up with a plan on the tip of my tongue and tear tracks on my cheeks. The tearstains were easily washed away.

The plan was this: Get the drop on Leroy Poe. Apply enough violence to his person that he believed I would kill him unless he gave me my 25 percent of the missing money. With which in hand, I would split the scene.

Leroy Poe was your typical slimy organized crime lawyer slash businessman. He also happened to be the brother of the Attorney General.

When Poe, wearing mold-green micro-suede trousers and a scotch plaid silk golf shirt, face as round and red as a tomato with curly hair, came down the three front steps of his house in beautiful downtown Saint Hippolytus, I was waiting for him. The passenger-side windows of the Shogun rolled wide open.

His shiny black Daewoo was around the corner where I'd parked it, with two unconscious bodyguards slumped like lovers in the front passenger seat.

"Laissez le bon temps rouler," I said, pointing Ariel's ammunition-less .45 at him. When he didn't respond, I said, "Get in the fucking car!"

Poe complied, unhappily.

"Don't I know you?"

"We've met. When most recently, I can't remember."

I patted him down and took a nasty little Saturday night special from his pants pocket. In his briefcase he had a retractable stiletto, some cigars and a vial of coke.

As I said, your typical sleazy lawyer.

Next I backhanded him with the barrel of the .45.

There was a spray of blood but no scream. Poe fell sideways, retching. A tooth dropped into the plastic cup holder between the seats. When he recovered, he scrunched backward into the far corner, his face layered with fear and pain. Vampire-red saliva dripped from his mouth. The cheek was already turning black. It always amazed me what evil we did to each other.

"I want my million dollars," I said. "In the next 20 minutes."

"My office ... ," mumbled bruised lips.

"If this fucks up, you're a dead man." I shook the .45 at him. "Pow!"

"Use the alley entrance."

With a screech, we took off.

It was still early in Saint Hippolytus. A few women walking out for bread. The cafes catering to a desultory somnambulant crowd. Serving up johnnycakes and fry jacks, huevos rancheros, last night's leftover stew chicken, strong black coffee.

The smells made me hungry. I hadn't eaten yet.

The usual bums slept in the usual doorways.

The drains smelled like festering evil.

When a yellow ghost-dog materialized in front of my wheels, I instinctively whipped the SUV sideways into a utility pole. Hitting the pole was not part of the plan. My head slammed against the windshield. The tinkle of breaking headlight glass rose to my ears like the fizz escaping from an open bottle of agua mineral. This was just before things went black for a few seconds.

For a moment I was back in the apartment above the Chat Noir back on Malibu Caye, looking down at Tony's dead body. Black rings of dried blood smeared around each eye socket gave him a wild lemur-like look. The eyes themselves were split in twain as neatly as a filleted tilapia.

Then I zapped back to the Shogun in the here and now. My lip slit like the belly of a maggot; my head vibrating like a tuning fork.

Poe was trying to get out of the truck, but couldn't figure out how to unlock the door. No practical skills whatsoever.

I grabbed his collar and yanked him backward. His head thumped the steering wheel.

Throwing the SUV into reverse, I shot back from the pole.

A hive of high-octane bullets ripped through the space where we had just been, slamming like wood-boring bees into the wooden house abutting the sidewalk. If we'd been there, Poe and I would have been carpaccio.

Someone wanted us dead. Poe could get his brain around that.

I didn't wait for a reprise. Pitching and yawing in the ruts, we tore up an alley and around the corner. Two wheels, baby. A second spray of automatic weapon fire went wide.

I kept glancing in the rear view, but after a half dozen twists and turns, nobody seemed to be following. I pulled to a sudden stop next to a cement block wall painted the color of someone's rectum. A political statement or color blindness?

I looked at Poe, who appeared about as unhappy as anyone could without being dead. It's always a shocker when you find out your boss thinks you're expendable.

"We can't go to your office," I said. "They'll be waiting for us."

"Turn around and take New Gulf Road. I know a safe house."

I started driving again. Poe stared morosely at the dashboard.

"Your ass is grass, man," I said without looking at him.

"I know." After a long pause: "Maybe we can help each other out."

"I want my fucking money back." And I didn't trust him farther than I could throw a dead tapir. Which wasn't far seeing as how they weigh about 500 pounds.

"How did you know I was involved?" asked Poe.

"Ariel gave me your name," I said. "A precondition to a handjob he never got."

Poe's eyes burned for a moment as if I'd turned up the wick on one of those cheap plastic lighters.

"Who's orchestrating this cluster fuck?!" I shouted.

"I work for von Richter," said Poe.

The neo-Nazi Oberstgruppenfuhrer.

All this time I was careening like a madwoman through the narrow lanes and alleys of Saint Hippolytus. Past an abandoned factory protected by razor wire and some ancient rusting oil storage tanks, I swung the SUV down one last rutted byway, and we were there.

When we hit New Gulf Road, it was like a hallucination of a first-world highway heading straight to Hell. Two lanes of brand-new cement road disappearing into the endless tidewater swamps to the south. Lucky Saint Hippolytus itself occupied a gall-bladder-shaped volcanic extrusion older than the Bible.

The new mobsters had built their hideouts in those swamps, but their bars and nightclubs and bordellos and casinos were still in downtown Saint Hippolytus. Hence, New Gulf Road.

We sped along this dream highway, the Shogun's tires thumping on the uneven seams between the cement sections. Occasional unmarked turnoffs whizzed by in my peripheral vision: dirt tracks instantly swallowed by the seething tidal vegetation.

I looked at my watch. We'd been on the run now for thirty minutes. Pretty soon they'd have a helicopter up looking for us. We needed to hide the car. We also needed to get far away, as fast as possible. Tilt.

"Turn here."

We'd just cleared a long easy curve, like the outline of a classic pinup girl. I'm more a Jap manga type. Small-boned, quick and over-enthusiastic. With ash-black dyed hair and utilitarian tits.

The cutoff ID-ed by Poe was as nondescript as the others we'd passed. We bounced over the curb and slithered down a steep embankment into the maw of the mangroves. The private road looped through the swamp atop a low dirt levy connecting islands of higher ground overgrown with wild onion, sea grape, cocoplum and outbreaks of banana palms.

A shadowy hunting shack at the end of a dead-end turnoff brought to mind an illegal abortion clinic I'd once patronized in Mexico City. Alone, I'd taken the elevator to the eleventh floor of a crumbling half-empty building; then walked down a long ill-lit corridor to the door at the end, my stiletto heels tapping their way like two blind mice. I was nineteen.

Around the next bend, the view suddenly opened out. A low-slung post-mod beach house filled the foreground. Behind stretched the blue-green sea. An osprey took wing from a dead tree at the lower edge of the cleared area. An artificial beach of khaki-colored sand decorated the sea's edge.

There were no vehicles parked by the house. Did this mean the place was empty?

"Think there's anyone here?" I asked.

Poe looked at me like I was some new kind of idiot.

"Maybe," he said. "Maybe not."

"Only one way to find out," I replied, keeping the mundanities in play.

For whatever good it might do, I parked the Shogun facing back the way we'd come. But the dirt road was only one vehicle wide. Anyone driving in would block it like a cork in a bottle.

Clambering out of the truck, I stood stretching, feeling the morning's tension like nails hammered in my shoulders and back. When I was done with the Gold's Gym routine, I tucked the .45 in my waist and hefted instead the crass feather-light el cheapo, pissant mini-gun I'd taken from Poe's pocket. At least it had bullets.

Watchfully we approached the house, Poe walking slightly in front but not blocking my line of fire.

The beach house was constructed as a series of overlapping oblong boxes. The façade of each made from a variegated combination of glass and odd-shaped sandstone chunks fitted together like a puzzle. Underneath, a superstructure of steel I-beams were bolted to poured-concrete pilings. The land in front graded upward in a wedge to support the steps leading to the solid teak door.

Poe took a key from under the doormat and unlocked the deadbolt. I skipped inside, gun first, scanning wildly. A boxy shiny-white entryway with stairways spiraling up and down to other oblong boxes.

Directly in front of me, suspended from wires like a Calder-esque mobile, hung the moth-eaten remains of a Waffen-SS officer's uniform, including hard-brimmed cap, achtung boots and swagger stick. Thinking for an instant that it was an actual person, I dropped to one knee, pistol raised to fire.

"Relax, Muldoon. It's just a memento."

I looked at Poe.

"You figured out who I am."

"It came to me while you were driving. Anne Muldoon, Tony the Microbe's gun moll."

Well, I'd been called a lot worse.

"Whatever." I nodded at the uniform. "von Richter's?" I asked.

"Actually I think it belonged to his great-uncle. Deceased."

"I could give a shit."

"Let's get a drink," said Poe.

My instinct said: Check the house. My nerves said: Get a double. I followed Poe down a stairway to the lower floor. He seemed to know his way around.

We came into the main living arena, split into zones for lounging, eating and cooking. Which left the upstairs for fornicating.

The space was an oblong box with a perfect view. On the far side of the thick glass, a few whitecaps scudded across the undulating disquiet of the sea's surly surface.

Poe handed me a crystal cocktail glass. I put my nose to the rim and sniffed. Vodka.

I drank it off in one gulp.

When I heard a boot scrape on the stairway behind me, I knew I'd made the wrong choice back in the hallway.

"Drink up, ladies and gentlemen. I'm sure you've had a hell of a day so far."

von Richter! As I started to turn, a sharply colder voice continued:

"But if you turn around without dropping that little toy onto the floor, I'll cut you in half."

The Saturday night special skidded across the terracotta tiles.

Suddenly I felt as woozy as a Victorian heroine with the vapors. Maybe the double shot of booze on an empty stomach brought it on or the shitload of stress I'd been under in the last forty-eight hours. Or maybe it was the first symptom of a massive brain tumor. Whatever the cause, my head spun in the opposite direction from my body, a black fog rolled across my brain. I collapsed like a soggy condom.

"I'm sorry," I heard myself say. I was back at Malibu Caye. At Tony's flat. Tony lying there with a little worm of blood dribbling from a black nail hole in his forehead. Tony with a look of complete and utter surprise on his winsome face. Tony dead as a day-old scone.

But why was I sorry?

For myself? For poor dead Tony? For what I'd done? For the misplaced dreams and the roads not taken?

A photograph lay on the floor next to Tony's body. Next to the pearl-handled .22-caliber revolver with the initials A.M. engraved on a silver inset.

The photo was of two men, naked.

One of them was Tony.

You get the rest.

Screams echoed in my head. They were mine.

From out of pitch darkness, streaks of light lashed across my retinas. I opened my eyes. I was back in the present. Naked. On the beach to one side of the shoebox house. The sea breeze whipped my hair across my face. My hands bound in loops of rough sisal held aloft above my head, the rope looped over a tree branch and tied off somewhere behind me. My toes barely touched the sand.

A blond Aryan type with deeply tanned wind-scoured skin stood in front of me, hands on hips, watery blue eyes feasting on my nakedness: von Richter for sure. Behind him, Poe sat in a deckchair, his feet propped on a canvas valise as fat as a pregnant sow.

"What are we to do with you?" queried von Richter. "In other circumstances, I'm sure we could find some piquant diversions to pass the time. But your presence here puts everything in jeopardy. No doubt your friend Ariel is using every available resource to hunt you down."

He reached out his veiny hand and touched my left nipple. It hardened like a pink tessera. It was impossible to avoid his caress.

"Is that the four million dollars?" I asked, flicking my eyes in the direct of Poe and the canvas bag.

"How very astute."

"So it was you who murdered Tony," I said.

"Me?" von Richter laughed with genuine glee. "Did you hear that Poe? The little bitch thinks I killed her lover."

Poe just looked nervous. "I'll get the truck," he said. "We need to go quickly."

He pushed himself up out of the chair and, gripping the satchel, walked toward the Shogun.

"Yes, of course," said von Richter, his voice drifting on the wind gusts off the ocean. When his eyes focused on mine, they were as cold as a January morning on the Baltic Sea. "You must look deeper inside yourself to unlock the riddle of Tony the Microbe's murder."

That's when I remembered the razor in my blood-covered hands.

The explosion of a high-powered rifle split the afternoon into a million fragments. My eyes darted in the direction of the SUV in time to see Poe flail backward, then fall like a felled trunk of a mahogany tree.

von Richter curled into a crouch, a large ugly pistol suddenly in his hand. He lurched behind me, one arm wrapped across my belly. My flesh crawled. I felt the twelve below zero muzzle of von Richter's weapon against my head.

"Give it up, von Richter!" boomed an amplified voice. "There's no way out."

The thup-thup-thup of a helicopter filled the sky. I was afraid von Richter would pull the trigger in a panic, blowing my brains to kingdom come on a perfectly nice afternoon in the tropics.

But suddenly he burst away, running low and fast toward the seaward edge of the beach, zigzagging to avoid the sharpshooter's methodical sweep. His thin wiry physique sliced into the surf. Then he was through the tumbling spume and cutting across the billowing surface of the briny deep with a powerful Australian crawl, heading for one of the outlying mangrove cayes.

No further shots rang out.

The rhythmic thumping of the copter became the entire world. Sand swirled, stinging like tattoo needles against my skin. When the tumult of the helicopter's landing subsided, I opened my eyes to see Ariel and two of his camouflage-bedecked minions coming toward me. One of the latter used a Bowie knife to release me from bondage, while the other retrieved the valise from where it had fallen from Poe's grip.

Ariel threw an oversized military shirt across my shoulders. Buttoned, it hung to my knees.

In no time we were airborne: Ariel, me, the pilot, his two troopers and the satchel containing US$4 million.

I looked at Ariel. His face was as empty of emotion as a cigar-store Indian molested by stray dogs.

"What about von Richter?" I asked.

"My men will pick him up or the sharks will have a feast. We knew he'd taken the money. We just needed to flush him out of his hiding place. That was your job. There was a tracking device imbedded in the handle of my .45."

"Now you've got Tony's murderer and the money," I said.

"When I arrested you at the airport, I didn't have all the facts." Ariel pulled my lizard-skin clutch from beneath his seat and clicked it open. His fat fingers extracted the photo of Tony giving it up the ass. "Looks like a valid defense to me," he said. "But you still owe me a handjob."

Down Mexico Way

It's only eight in the morning, but already hot as Hades. Jack Niles stares helplessly at the cleavage of the bikini-clad bar girl, Ginny, as she leans over the beer cooler, filling it with longnecks. A skinny Mexican kid is vacuuming sand from the pool. Otherwise the pool area's deserted.

Everyone in the all-suites hotel is sleeping late. Ordering room service. Catching a lazy fuck or a few more zzzz's. The kids watching cartoons in the other room.

Jack's hand plays nervously with a cheap plastic lighter, depressing the starter mechanism a dozen times in rapid succession. All but once the flame blossoms from the metal nozzle. Out of a hundred flicks, how many times will it fail? he wonders. How many times did the space shuttle soar into the sky like a brilliant bird before the Challenger exploded in an inferno of burning metal and flesh? These days, only two things get Jack's blood up. Probability and chance.

The probability that out of the hundreds of companies listed on the NASDAQ, the SEC would pick his to investigate. Whether he has a chance of avoiding jail time.

Lighting a cigarette, the first of the day, he leans with his back against the bar, watching the Mex kid work the long aluminum pole that maneuvers the pool vac.

A man in floral trunks comes out through the glass doors from the lobby and crosses the empty concrete deck. Choosing a chaise lounge at random, he drops his towel and a paperback. Then continues purposefully around the pool toward the bar pavilion where Jack waits in the shade. The newcomer's skin exudes the rich walnut tan of a beach habitué.

As he comes up to the bar, his eyes meet Jack's with curiosity; then shift to Ginny. She gives him a cute bar-maidenly smile.

"Tequila Sunrise, sweetheart?" she asks.

"Sure thing."

Up close, Jack can just about count the hairs curling out of the man's ears. His eyes are gray and sad like a rainy December day in Dallas.

"And bring my friend here a fresh whatever-it-is he's drinking." He nods at Jack. "Bill. Bill Oaks. No relation to the dead protest singer."

"It's a tad early for me," says Jack, crushing out his cigarette.

"Lighten up, pal. You're on vacation, right?"

An avalanche of ice cubes plunging from a plastic bucket into a bin area behind the bar drowns out Jack's reply. Ray, the other daytime bar person, sets the bucket down and looks at Jack and the other guy.

"Bill. Meet Jack the gambler. He never drinks before noon."

"Surely an exception can be made."

"My wife doesn't like morning drunks," says Jack. "And she has the money."

Bill sips his Tequila Sunrise. Ice tinkles. How many ice cubes in a Tequila Sunrise? wonders Jack. Jack's mind races like the wheels of a pickup stuck in soft sand; he can't concentrate on anything.

"Say," says Bill. "Aren't you the CEO of that software company that went belly up in Dallas after the FBI raid? Some kind of SEC investigation?"

Jack's eyes glaze over. "Can't talk about it." He holds his palms aloft. They're like two soft white wings. "Lawyers," he adds as an afterthought.

The raw clank of coins colliding overrides the ice-striking-glass sound. It's Ray, jiggling the tip change in the pocket of his knee-length Abercrombies.

"Twenty says you can't guess how much money's in Ray's pocket plus or minus ten percent," says Jack, his eyes unglazing.

Bill cocks his head like a parrot, listening to the sound of the coins striking each other. Counting the dimes and nickels and quarters. He pouts his lips.

"You're on."

* * *

41

Two and a half hours and five Tequila Sunrises later, Jack Niles steers the Cadillac Escalade on to the cement causeway linking South Padre Island to the Texas mainland. His wife, in the white leather seat opposite, reaches out her fingers and squeezes his leg. Her given name is Jill. As in Jack and Jill. It still gets a laugh with strangers. Caught in the blasting stream of the air conditioner, her blonde hair sways across her austerely pretty face.

"Don't catch cold, hon," she says.

In the backseat Bill Oaks lounges sideways, the collar of his silk tropical shirt askance. "Hot back here," he says. Jack turns on the back seat blower.

The Escalade rolls like a sailor through the streets of Port Isabel. At last, just past the H-E-B supermarket, it turns onto the two-lane highway to Brownsville and Matamoros.

It's a dull dusty ride to the border. Bill Oaks, agent to the stars, regales Jack and Jill with strange tales from the Pacific edge. Mudslides and ecstasy parties in Malibu. A midnight run through the desert to Vegas— a famous starlet behind the wheel, naked except for a pink dog collar around her neck. The only difficulty arises when she sashays bare-assed across the lobby of the Bellagio and tries to check in without any luggage.

"So," ponders Jill. "What brings y'all to boring South Padre?"

"Just taking a breather. Step out of the fast lane." Then, after a pause: "Go some place where I won't run into anyone I know or who knows me."

"Been coming to Padre Island since I was a kid." says Jack. "Back when there was nothing but two lanes of cracked blacktop with a drawbridge out from Port Isabel. When a sailboat was going through the channel and the bridge was up, you just waited awhile." Flooring the gas pedal, he swerves the Escalade around a minivan that has pulled partway on the shoulder to let Jack pass.

The outskirts of Brownsville present a cluster fuck of dingy bars, taco joints, gas stations, junkyards and strip clubs, in no particular order. At the international bridge most of the traffic is coming north into the lone star state. They breeze across; on the Mexican side a mustachioed border cop in a green uniform waves them through. Under the bridge the Rio Grande glides by, brown and sluggish as a snake at midday.

Jack parks the car at Garcia's restaurant and gift shop and slips the private guard a hundred pesos. They catch a cab to the address Jack got from an old frat buddy.

"I don't understand why we've got to come to sombrero-land so you can gamble my money away," Jill says in a certain unmistakable tone, as the bare skin of her thighs squeaks across the vinyl back seat of the cab. "It's so damn hot away from the beach."

Jack looks at the photograph on the cab license, then at the driver's profile. They don't match up.

"You should have stayed at the beach, honey bun."

"Maybe I'll just find me a Mexican gigolo with a waxed mustache to fuck me silly."

"Suit yourself."

Bill is looking uncomfortable. "I'm not a gambler either. Just along for the ride."

"I'll bet," says Jill.

The cab drops them at a post-war palacio protected by a high wrought-iron fence. A buzzer opens the gate. The house is painted the same pink as a harlot's toenails. Several lemon trees and a fig fill the otherwise bare front yard. From the second floor balcony, a man in a dark suit watches them go up the tiled walk and disappear through the deeply shaded front door.

Inside a black man wearing a tuxedo serves drinks. You can play roulette, dice or poker. Jack leans over and turns up the leg of his cream-colored triple-pleated slacks. A rubber band around his ankle holds a roll of gringo bills.

He hands the money to the croupier at the roulette table.

In the meantime Jill has gotten hold of a drink. Something clear and lethal con hielo in a highball glass. While she and Bill watch, Jack loses the entire five thousand dollars in under an hour.

"Shit," Jack says, as the croupier rakes away his last pile of chips.

"Asshole," says Jill. "You did the same thing with your company."

After a brief scuffle, Bill manages to separate them. "Let's go in the bar and get a free drink," says Jack.

Jill and Bill and Jack, in that order, walk single file into the bar. It's in a separate room with heavy crown molding painted vampire red.

As always in these circumstances, an ample woman in a black negligee leans against the bar, fanning herself. She gives Bill the twice-over.

"You want something?" she asks.

"A drink."

A barman is slicing limes with a dull knife. He curses when the knife slips off the tough rind and cuts him.

They order cervezas. A dish of pickled jalapenos rests on the bar. Jack eats a jalapeno. After one bite, Bill drops his on the deeply polished wood. "Sensitive stomach," he says, and orders a Diet Coke.

Jill is sulking, her lips thrust out like a ripe seedpod about to burst.

"If the Escalade wasn't in my name, we'd have to walk home from here," she says. "I have absolutely no idea how I ended up married to you."

"Must have been my boyish charm."

"I must have been out of my mind."

"You always were a little light in the head."

"Listen, buster. I'm not the one that pissed away a hundred million dollar company and then cooked the books to cover my tracks."

"Shut the fuck up, Jill."

"Just great, Jack. Next I suppose you'll punch me in the face."

"Not if you shut up."

There is enough menace in his voice that Jill stops talking and takes a sip of her Corona. She looks anxiously up at the ceiling as if it might suddenly collapse.

A thickset man in a navy blue suit and white shirt enters the room. Two young men in thin-lapelled sharkskin jackets follow him. The older man's clean-shaven face is as dark and scarred as the earth. His nails are manicured. An immodest diamond ring circumscribes one finger.

The barman sets a frothy lime-green daiquiri on the bar in front of these expensive hands. One of the younger men sits at a table. The other leans against the wall. Apparently they aren't drinking. The man in the suit looks at Jill.

He introduces himself as Demetrio Sandoval. His English is accentless. "You're very beautiful," he says to her. She blushes.

"You're ten years too late, pal," she says and takes a long pull on her beer.

Demetrio looks past Jill to where Bill and Jack are standing against the bar. Jack is telling Bill about the eleven-foot hammerhead he caught off Port Aransas.

"Is your husband a gambler?" Demetrio asks.

"Jack's a loser."

"That's a tough situation to be in." Demetrio raises his hand. "Jack," he calls.

They exchange pleasantries. In the next moment they're into a game of liar's poker, using a pair of hundred dollar bills. It's all Jack has left -- his mad money for the coming week. He loses on the third round.

Demetrio drinks the dregs of his daiquiri and smacks his lips.

"How about a serious bet?" he proposes.

"I'm dead broke," says Jack.

"What've you got?"

Jack considers his doppelganger in the mirror behind the bar. His tongue curls over his bottom lip that is dry and chapped.

"An '05 Escalade. Silver."

"The fuck you do," squeals Jill, her voice cracking. She stares at Demetrio. "The car belongs to me."

Jill's mouth twitches.

"I need to pee," she says. Grabbing her snakeskin clutch, she strides out of the room. Jack and Bill and Demetrio watch her go.

"Now there's a fine piece of ass," says Demetrio.

"That's my fucking wife you're talking about."

"Fifty thousand U.S. or your wife. A fair exchange?"

Silence descends over the room. Bill raises an eyebrow. The barman polishes an already too clean glass.

"What shall we bet on?"

* * *

In the ladies room, Jill rucks down her black lace boybriefs and squats over the toilet. Of course the toilet paper dispenser is empty.

When Jill comes out of the stall, a woman in a beaded camisole is leaning over the sink adjusting her mascara. She's attractive in an undernourished borderland sort of way. Her cheeks are pitted with old acne scars. In the mirror her eyes glance in Jill's direction.

"What a day," says Jill, splashing water on her face.

"You need somethin' to pick you up?"

"Probably."

"Me to, honey."

The woman taps out two lines of blow on the black marble countertop. It's very pure. Jill leans on the countertop listening to her heart doing a wild tattoo.

Tears roll down her cheeks. She tells the woman about Jack, more than she could ever want to know. The woman makes a satirical remark about men and their equipment.

When Jill walks back into the bar, she's still feeling woozy. Demetrio is working on a fresh daiquiri. The two young men are gone. So are Jack and Bill.

"Jack and I made a bet," says Demetrio. "He said you'd be back in less than five minutes. 'A quick pisser,' he said."

"I must have gotten sidetracked."

"You don't belong to Jack any more."

A nervous smile quickens across her lips. "Where's your waxed mustache, ace?"

First Epilogue

A week after Jack gets back to Dallas, an acquaintance asks him about Jill. Is she visiting her mother, perhaps? He tells the woman Jill was swept out to sea while swimming at a beach known for its treacherous currents, its riptide.

Eventually the police take notice. Inquiries reveal no record of a gringa woman recently drowning in the Mexican coastal area Jack mentions. Jack is Jill's sole heir. Four million dollars worth.

Jack is arrested at DFW airport just as he's about to board a flight for Nassau. The charge is murder.

Second Epilogue

Five years later, a tall thin woman walks naked out of the sea. She stands alone on a stretch of tropical beach. Her face conveys an austere beauty, etched by time and the pain of childbirth.

At the edge of the beach she dons a terrycloth robe and walks through a grove of coconut palms to the glass doors of a sprawling postmodern beach house. The children are just sitting down to lunch. The boy, age four, is dark and sometimes cruel. The girl, a year younger, is an exact replica of her blonde mother. They're too excited to eat, despite the best efforts of the cook and the live-in maid.

The woman, whose name is Jill, is also excited. Demetrio's flight from Bogotá will be landing in less than an hour. Cancun airport is just an hour's drive north by armor-plated Mercedes.

We Don' Need No Stinkin' Baggezz

Univision Studios.
Mexico City.

Hola.

I wink at the studio audience. Then come to rest on the chair next to Raymondo. He slips a lit menthol cigarette between my lips. Leans back and crosses his legs.

It's great to be on your show, Raymondo. Thanks for having me.

A cup of coffee would be great. Black. Two sugars.

My earliest memory?

The click, click of the loom, as our mother, Margarita, worked through the long, cold winter of our gestation. Day after day sitting on the hard-packed earth, her hands moved back and forth, in and out, weaving wool blankets one homespun line at a time. Beautiful blankets, the gray of a rain-heavy sky. Geometric lines of red and yellow at either end, in the Toltec manner.

Our father, Juan, carried them seven kilometers into Valle de Bravo and sold them on the street.

What was it like in there?

Crowded. With five of us floating around in that salty inland sea that grew as we grew. Five identical males. Needless to say, there was a certain amount of jockeying for position. An elbow here, a kick there. I took the high ground at the top of my mother's womb. Strangely, during those months I came to see the world first through her eyes.

What did my father do for a living?

Whatever he could find.

Which wasn't much. It was a hard nine months. The eggs laid by our few feckless chickens froze in the bitter nights and turned black. Unusual rains rotted the corn harvest. One day my father appeared in the doorway.

"What is it?" asked Margarita.

"Another goat is dead."

My mother rose from her loom and we went outside. The goat lay like a ruptured and treadless tire in the dusty yard. A line of blood oozed from one nostril. A six-inch white worm wriggled from its anus.

"How will we ever have enough milk when the babies come?" moaned Margarita.

"Something will turn up," said Juan. "I'm going into town to look for work."

"God go with you."

He spat into the earth.

Of course, he found none.

He came home one morning just in time to see the last of us burp from between Margarita's loins. That was a sight: five bloody, howling grubs writhing on the floor, kicking our feet, our tiny penises like wasp stingers.

The next morning my mother found Juan hanging from the thorn tree at the edge of the yard. His tongue as black as a crow.

Raymondo's buxom assistant sits next to me and begins spooning sweet black coffee between my lips. The cigarette butt falls to the floor, where it burns a hole in the mint green industrial carpet before going out.

No, Raymondo, that wasn't the end of tragedy for us. You could say it was only the beginning.

How did we survive?

In the beginning, barely. Margarita set fire to her loom and our house of sticks, intending to throw herself and us on the pyre. But her nerve failed.

Somehow we trekked into Valle de Bravo where we joined a traveling carnival. We were an oddity. A freak show. Identical male quintuplets. We were right up there with the bearded lady, the sheep with two heads and the gargoyle man.

Four years later, in desperation Margarita fell in love with a drifter named Leon, who helped set up and dismantle the tents and rides. A sly opportunist, he told her they couldn't run off to Acapulco without money.

Then he told her about Don Silvester, a two-bit jefe mafioso. Childless and haunted by his desire for immortality.

She dressed us up in our Sunday best and took us to meet him.

"These are my five boys," she said. "They're fearless. And very loyal. They'll do whatever you ask them to do. They'll even kill for you."

Don Silvester fell in love with us. And we with him. We were to be his children that he couldn't otherwise have.

He paid Margarita a thousand pesos apiece.

She kissed each of us on the forehead and tweaked our little dicks. That was the last time we saw her. Unless you count the black-and-white photo of her in La Independencia a week later. Lying in a nameless cul-de-sac with her throat cut.

Our first hit?

I assume this is off the record, Raymondo. Ha, ha.

When the five of us turned eighteen, Don Silvester threw a huge party at his hacienda. He invited all his friends and most of his enemies. It was the wedding in The Godfather, only for real. Wine from Don Silvester's own vineyards in the Baja. Costa Rican anejo rum. Barbecued cabrito. Sexy girls and strolling mariachis.

Don Silvester introduced us to the crowd. Quinto, the youngest, Ernesto, Jorge, Justinian and me, Pepe. Almost everyone there had watched us grow up, but they hooted and applauded as though we were movie stars.

Then Don Silvester took me by the shoulder and we wandered amid the revelers. Through an opening in the throng, with a flick of an eye, he marked a man of medium height, in a medium-gray suit, white shirt and unmemorable tie with a medium knot.

"Javier intends to kill me," he said.

At dusk the celebrants disbanded. An ambitious whore enticed Javier to a lonely lane at the edge of the hacienda grounds. We leaped upon him, each thrusting a knife into his mortal flesh before he could cry out or draw his revolver. He lay bleeding to death in the dusty byway. I thought of the dead goat lying in our yard that other time just before we were born.

That was the first.

Thank you, Raymondo. I just tried to recapture the moment.

How many?

Between the five of us, I'd say three hundred fifty, mas o menos.

Remorse?

For what!?

They were all enemies of our stepfather. Every one of them wished him harm. To snuff out his life, steal his wealth, cut off his manhood and cram it down his throat, bask in the adoration of the common man.

Payback? Yes. I guess in the end that's what it was.

My lips are dry. Raymondo's assistant holds a glass of water to them. I take several sips, counting the moles on her largely exposed breasts.

What happened was this:

After kidnapping us from the beach in Acapulco where we were frolicking in the waves with our girlfriends, a rival crime cartel held us prisoner for three days. They kept us in a windowless latrine. We stank to Hell and back.

When Don Silvester refused to negotiate, they did it quickly. I don't blame him for that. If you negotiate with scum, you're finished.

Inside the bag I could still hear everything. But I couldn't see. The ride from Acapulco to Ciudad de Mexico was long and stifling.

The kidnappers burst into the private top-floor lounge of Don Silvester's nightclub in the Zona Rosa.

"You've no right to enter here," Don Silvester's voice boomed with menace. "If you're police, show me your badges."

To which the killers replied:

"We don' need no stinkin' baggezz."

Then they threw open the two burlap sacks. And out rolled our five severed heads. My four dead brothers and me.

Very funny, Raymondo. But there's no voodoo involved.

I wink at the studio audience.

I'm here today because of a miracle of modern science.

Truly I've enjoyed being on your show, Raymondo. I hope you'll have me back, God willing.

Adios.

The audience breaks into a fierce round of applause. The studio band slides into Raymondo's theme song. Two lab-coated attendants set my head back on the life-support machine and push me behind the curtain.

Ideas of Murder in Southern Vermont

May 20th is a good day to begin cutting the grass.
—*Old Farmers Almanac*

May 20. Ray, decked out in a faded Batman T-shirt, stands in comic book chiaroscuro, half in and half out of the dusky tool shed. The air is redolent with wood rot and grass cuttings. A robin struts across the greensward, a bushwhacked earthworm dangling like a miniature intestine from its beak. The sky is as blue as the eyes of a madman.

From the corner of his eye, Ray catches movement in the kitchen window twenty-odd yards away. A hand pulling aside the lace curtain. Baby blues peering forth. It's Gillian.

Too late to fade into his lair, Ray stiffens. The screen door swings wide and Gillian emerges onto the back porch. An apron disguises the skimpy details of her sundress, ordered from the Victoria's Secret catalog. Her reddish hair hangs in curlicues to her bare shoulders. A tropical fruit color taints her lips. Harlot, thinks Ray.

"Your lunch is on the table," she calls.

He waves at her, pretending he can't hear, his ears sealed with wax. His lips twist in the rictus of a smile. She smiles back at him. Fake as false teeth.

"I've got to go to the supermarket and the hairdresser's," she announces.

When Ray doesn't respond, she turns back into the house. Behind her receding derriere, the screen door smacks shut.

Stepping into the dim interior of the shed, Ray reaches down and gropes for the fifth of Old Crow hidden behind the gas can. Gasoline fumes slither up his nose like a flesh-eating amoeba, bringing a wave of nausea. He takes a long pull from the bottle. He knows that Gillian knows what he's up to.

After a second drink, Ray hoists up the waist of his belt-less khakis, reties the leather thongs of his deck shoes and strides across the lawn to the abandoned mower. It sits on the embankment above the drainage ditch that fronts the road. As he bends over to grip the starter rope, the screen door slams again. He turns his head to look. Everything is upside down.

Gillian descends the steps from the porch and walks to the Camry, parked at an angle parallel to where Ray crouches, futzing with the mower. Without the apron, the décolletage of the sundress is revealed in all its wantonness. The hem comes barely halfway to her knees. As she lowers herself into the driver's seat, the bleached-flour whiteness of her thighs momentarily flashes into view.

His groin tightening with desire, Ray looks away. He knows she's meeting someone in town.

In his mind he sees a dingy room, a shadow-cloaked divan. On it, caught in the glow of a cigarette tip, an unknown pair of lips nibble the crook of her neck, while a predatory hand plays with virtuosic aplomb up the keyboard of her thighs.

It's not clear to Ray how he and Gillian end up in the drainage ditch. She's beneath him. His knees dig inexorably into her bare arms, crushing them into the water and muck at the bottom of the ditch. Her head splashes from side to side trying to escape the pressure of his hands over her mouth and nose. Fear has turned her eyes into iridescent saucers. Mud and deep-green plants stain the paleness of her skin and the jaunty yellow design of the sundress.

Ray shifts his position, abruptly easing the pressure on Gillian's 112 pounds. She starts to sit up. But it's a trick from his high school wrestling team days. In the next instant he flips her over onto her stomach. His hands press downward again, mashing her face into two inches of runoff. She makes gurgling sounds, her body heaving and quivering. After a while she becomes as still as stagnant water. A sprig of watercress is entwined in her scum-streaked hair.

Ray's hands absorb the vibration of the mower, as it trundles moronically across the lawn. He squeezes his eyes shut to relieve the sting of oozing sweat. Opening them, he squints at the sun. 2 p.m. When he glances down, he makes the disturbing discovery that his pants and shoes are neither wet nor mud-stained. Instead, he finds himself thinking that Gillian should be getting home soon. He kills the mower and walks over to the tool shed for some additional distilled refreshment.

Ray's Ford F-150 is parked in front of the Paul Revere statue at the lower end of the Southbury commons. The red brick buildings of the college clutter the hillside. A summer school student in a lime green see-through camisole meanders by. Ray smokes a cigarette and watches her with psychosexual interest. He has no recollection of how he or the truck got into town.

Twombley's Tap Room is located in the Millard Fillmore Hotel— parking in rear. Ray turns down the alley. Behind and below the Fillmore East, as it's called by a few diehard hippies, is an open parking area covered in crushed stone. Wooden stairs of dubious pedigree wobble up to the ground floor of the hotel.

Ray sees the Camry in the third slot from the end. He wants to pretend it belongs to someone else. There's an open space right next to it, so he pulls in.

Rex, the afternoon bartender at the Tap Room, nods. Ray nods back, walks to the bar and shakes loose a cigarette. Rex lights it. This is not a pickup move. Anything between them happened when they were on the wrestling team together back in high school. As Rex pours a jigger of Old Crow, his eyes travel in an arc toward the back of the room. Ray squints in that direction. He's forgotten to put in his contacts.

But there's no mistaking Gillian's cascading tresses and shapely arms. A guy flaunting a straw Stetson sits on the reverse side of the same booth. Ray edges his drink down the bar until he can make out the cowboy's walrus mustache. When the cowpoke gets up to go to the john, he appears tall and lanky and dangerous.

Ray waits until the ranch hand disappears through the swing door to the pissoir. Then crosses from the end of the bar to Gillian's booth in a single bound. A Colt pistol with a pearl handle appears from somewhere. At the distance of twelve inches, it's hard to miss, especially when you pull the trigger five times. Blood spatters everywhere.

Dropping the gun, Ray turns and walks out of the bar. Rex nods again as he passes. No one moves to stop Ray's exit.

When the shots ring out, the cowboy pisses himself in the shoe. He stays in the men's room until a buddy gives him the all clear.

When he hears the Camry's tires on the gravel driveway, Ray opens his eyes. It's Gillian, back from town.

He's sitting in an Adirondack chair facing the setting sun. The empty Old Crow bottle is at his feet, but hidden in shadow. He stands and raises a hand.

"Ray, honey, help me out with these groceries. Then I'll make you a cup of tea."

As he walks toward her, he notes there are no bloodstains on his khakis. Maybe I should lay off the hooch, he thinks.

Gillian kisses him on the mouth. Her body pushes into his. As his tongue chases hers, she shoves him away; then does a half-assed pirouette.

"Do you like my hair?"

"Looks about the same."

"Ray, baby, how come you're always such a fucking romantic?"

She sets her grocery bag on the table, shaking her head. Next she puts on the teakettle to boil.

"Personally, I need a pick-me-up."

She waltzes into the dining room and comes back with a crystal tumbler half full of Cutty Sark, to which she adds ice. Gillian never has a drink, thinks Ray.

By now the teakettle is roiling and tooting. His stomach suddenly queasy, Ray chooses a mint teabag. An ill omen.

Ray sits at the table with its embroidered tablecloth made by some ancient relative of his or Gillian's. Gillian sets the everyday teapot on the table. The scent of the mint steeping rises like a Levantine ghost. She sets a cup and saucer in front of him and a pitcher of cream.

"I baked this morning. A chocolate cherry cake. Your favorite."

She puts the cake on the table. It's fallen in the middle, like a subsidence above an old mineshaft. She cuts a huge piece and places it on a plate in front of Ray. Gillian never bakes, goes through his head, as he swallows the first bite. Gillian is staring at him. Waiting for something to happen.

He carves out another large hunk of cake onto his fork.

He knows, of course, that it's spiked with a deadly poison that leaves no trace after five hours.

The things we do for love, he thinks, as he chomps on the second bite and goes for the third.

Drive By

The girl strolling past the Delta Omega Alpha house—from whence Earl Thigpen gazes out an upstairs window—is attractive in a bordello sort of way. Big chest, tight tank top, rayon miniskirt extra short. Secondary details obtrude: blonde, wide mouth framed in black cherry lip gloss, expensive handbag, long legs with a hint of five o'clock shadow, faux-panther Minolo Blahnik shoes. It's enough to make you pant and loll your tongue down to your chin.

Thigpen imagines she's on her way to her fancy sports car parked in the student garage.

"Y'all wanta get some lunch?" he calls out on a whim in his slow-as-molasses Mississippi drawl.

Her eyes roll vaguely in his direction.

"What did you have in mind?"

Holy cow! Thigpen thinks. A live one.

He leaps to his feet, leaning his barrel chest across the windowsill, his head thrust into a thicket of leaves from the live oaks shading the front yard of the fraternity. Behind him his flipped-over chair spins like a top on one leg; then crashes to the floor.

"Do you like French food?" he asks. Then: "Come in for a drink."

The woman, or girl, throws back her shoulders, tosses her golden tresses and saunters up the front walk.

"I hope you have some ice-cold beer, cause it's damn hot out," she says.

For an instant Thigpen stares at himself in the dresser mirror. Curly hair worn in a modified mullet. Last night's heavy drinking evidenced by swollen cheeks. Romanesque nose broken twice from playing fullback in high school. Eager brown eyes looking the worse for wear. His clothes are frat boy prep: blue oxford-cloth shirt with the sleeves rolled to the elbows, stained khakis, scuffed Docksiders.

Play it as it lays, he thinks, as he bounds down the stairs.

She's waiting on the front porch, with its six white-painted fake southern-style columns and rotting rattan furniture.

Thigpen sticks his head out the French doors.

"Heineken or Shiner?" he queries.

Her black crow-like eyes consider Thigpen as if he's a fat locust she might or might not choose to devour as an appetizer.

"Heineken," say her cherry-stained lips. "S'il vous plait."

Her French accent is as fake as a padded bra, but it's all the same to Thigpen, who's never been closer to Europe than a weekend trip to Atlanta for his brother's wedding. He ducks back inside and dashes down the hall, past the mug shots of former Delta Omega Alpha SMU chapter presidents, to the ramshackle kitchen.

The twin Heinekens he grabs from the beer cooler clink together like a pair of sterling ideas whose time has come. When he flicks off the caps, a puff of smoke erupts from each bottle like the denouement of a cheap magic trick.

He rolls each green-glass bottle, already foggy with precipitation, in a paper napkin and hurries back up the hall. It seems like it's taken an eternity to get all this done. But there she is sitting sidesaddle on the arm of the only Adirondack chair.

With a shit-ass grin to beat all shit-ass grins, Thigpen hands her one of the beers.

She draws it to her lips. For a second Thigpen thinks she's going to French kiss the mouth of the bottle. But she just takes a long deep swallow.

"My name's Earl," Thigpen says. "Earl Thigpen from Biloxi, Mississippi."

"Dandelion," she says, holding out her hand. "Pleased to meet ya." Her nails are the same deep purple as her lip gloss, but with little white edges the color of bass bait grubs.

"Is that a family name?" Thigpen asks to make conversation.

"Lord, I don't know." She pulls a handkerchief from her purse and uses it to mop her forehead. "But it sure is hot. Hot as Hades."

"You can say that again," Thigpen says.

A while later they're in Dandelion's silver Audi TT convertible. It drives like a wet dream. Thigpen can't take his eyes off the lushness of her inner thighs, as she pumps the clutch in and out, maneuvering the uber-beast through lunchtime traffic.

Instead of French food, they end up at a burger joint called Snuffer's on Lower Greenville.

"Sweet," the parking valet says, as he hops in and revs the engine.

"You take good care of my baby," Dandelion warns him. "No scratches and no joy rides. I wrote down the mileage."

The attendant gives her a mock salute and guns the Audi down a narrow alley.

"Asshole," Dandelion mutters. Then flashes Thigpen a big smile and clutches at his arm. "I'm hungry as a horse."

Inside, Thigpen slips the maitre d' a ten-spot. Instantly they're shown to an outside table with an umbrella. A waitress in a halter-top, camouflage capris and grease-stained Vans brings fresh Heinekens and a pair of flyblown menus.

Without looking at the menu, Dandelion orders them bacon jalapeno cheeseburgers, fried pickles and onion rings. The first round of beers are gone in less than 30 seconds. The waitress brings another.

"So," says Thigpen, "You're from ..."

"Daddy was in the oil business."

"Ah."

"Mama had a breakdown right after she gave birth to yours truly." Dandelion toys with a gold Zippo. "Never did recover. Daddy had to have her committed. After that there was a trail of gold diggers in and out of the master bedroom suite. Nearly broke my heart."

She looks wistfully at the traffic pounding up and down Greenville Avenue.

"Then you got your trust fund and moved to Dallas."

"I wish that were true, Earl. But Daddy's wells dried up a long while ago. I came to Dallas 'cause I couldn't bear watchin' him make a fool of himself any more."

"You're doin' graduate work at SMU?"

She laughs and starts a fresh beer, the deep green surface of the bottle heavy with moisture like meadow grass in early morning.

"Honey, I never finished high school. I was just killin' time in the library. Lookin' at magazines."

A giant question mark hangs behind Thigpen's eyes. What's up with this kitty?

Before Thigpen can come to grips with his cautionary intimations, the cheeseburgers and sides arrive. A flurry of activity descends around their table. Condiments and extra napkins are delivered. And, of course, more beers.

Thigpen and Dandelion dig in like there's no tomorrow.

When the last fried pickle is chomped, when the last onion ring is crunched, masticated and swallowed, Dandelion sits back and works a toothpick through her teeth with ladylike aplomb. When she's done, she flicks it off the deck into the parking lot.

Thigpen lights a cigarette he cadges off the maitre d'. Thigpen doesn't usually smoke but they've had six beers apiece and despite the grease and grilled steer he's feeling a little lightheaded.

"What if I told you I made all that up?" Dandelion asks.

"All what up?"

"You know. About Daddy and his oil wells and Mom goin' into the loony bin. Even about reading magazines at the library."

"Well ..." Thigpen ponders the burning end of his cigarette, the defaced wood surface of the picnic table. The phrase Jimmy loves L.D. pops out at him. Then: shit for brains.

"I guess I'd think you were a little bit dangerous. Like a moccasin hidin' in a clump of water hyacinths."

"Well, it's all true," she says. "Everything I've told you. As true as God's word."

Dandelion stands up, brushing crumbs from the front of her skirt.

"I need to pee."

As Thigpen watches her buxom long-legged departure, lust flares from his anterior hypothalamus, down his spine and into the tip of his dick.

When he takes a sip of beer, it's warm. He makes a face. Then realizes he desperately needs to take an elephant-sized whiz himself.

At the bathroom doors Thigpen waivers; then pushes through the one marked as belonging to the opposite sex. Dandelion and another woman with chapped lips and rosy cheeks are just finishing up a quartet of crystalline lines of coke.

Intimidated by Thigpen's abrupt arrival, the other woman grabs her purse and leaves. Dandelion offers Thigpen the tightly rolled greenback. Shaking his head, he pushes past her into one of the stalls, where he pisses vehemently.

Behind him Dandelion vacuums up the final line. When her hands circumscribe Thigpen's cock, he lurches sideways against the wall of the stall, scrawled as it is with femme-focused graffiti. His tumescence soars. She raises one leg like an egret, places the raised foot sheathed in a Minolo Blahnik pump firmly on the rim of the toilet bowl and mounts him. After a dozen or so erratic but energetic thrusts, he finishes, gasping for breath.

"Better than key lime pie?" she asks, adjusting her undies.

"Damn, sweetheart. I'd take that over key lime pie any day."

Thigpen looks in the mirror and sees a disaster. He slams on the water full blast and slashes his face, combs his wet fingers through his disheveled hair.

A waitress sticks her head in the door and raises her eyebrows.

"What's goin' on in here?"

"We were just leaving," Thigpen says.

At the cash register, he uses a credit card. Dandelion is already outside, retrieving her Audi. She checks the odometer, giving the attendant a look that could kill.

Hot damn! Thigpen thinks, as he saunters through the door and down the steps, hefting up the waist of his khakis and tightening the belt. Nobody's ever going to believe this.

As Thigpen tumbles into the passenger seat, Dandelion lays rubber. The valet attendant dives out of harms way. Gravel flies.

"WEE-HAH!" Thigpen yells, as they speed down Greenville.

"Let's get some drinks," Dandelion says.

"Whatever." Thigpen is ebullient.

Next thing, they're in this dark trendy bar called Black Velvet. At 3:30 in the afternoon it's deserted. The bartender appears stoned out of his gourd. Alt-rock cavorts from ceiling speakers.

Dandelion orders sippin tequila con rocas. For both of them.

"You a hunter, Earl? You know, camouflage duds, pump-action shotgun, the works?"

"We get some fine migratory birds down in Biloxi."

"I knew it. The moment I saw you, I said to myself: That S.O.B. gets his rocks off blasting away at poor defenseless creatures."

"That's one way of lookin' at it."

"You bet. But it's a different story over in I-raq. Over there it's man against man. Kill or be killed."

Thigpen takes another sip of tequila. Where is she going with this? he asks himself. And who cares...? Maybe I should get us a motel room.

"You ever killed anyone?" He waits for her to say "Earl." But she doesn't. She just looks at him with eyes like a surgeon's hands. Or a pair of stainless steel meat cutters in the Tom Thumb deli department.

Slice and dice. Thigpen knows he's in over his head.

But he can't help himself. By the third round, Dandelion's reliving Black Hawk Down frame by frame.

"Let's go back to the car," she says.

The light is beginning to attenuate with the westward decline of the sun. They walk in the deep shadows of a line of live oaks, next to an el cheapo Mexican restaurant. Neon lights come on in the windows. Tacos. Enchiladas. Ptomaine poisoning.

The Audi's parked on a side street.

When they get to it, she opens the trunk. Lying there on an old gray Army blanket in the dim trunk-light is an AK-47, clip in.

Wow, Thigpen thinks. But he doesn't say anything.

"Just point and shoot. Like a video camera."

"Tell me again..."

"My parents are dead. My brother's trying to kill me. Because I got everything."

"You mean the dried-up oil wells."

"They aren't dried-up. I lied about that."

"And your brother wants them."

"Yes."

"And you want me to shoot your brother."

"Yes."

"Why don't you do it yourself?"

"I'll show you why." She steps close and runs her hand up his fly. Fiddles with the top button. Thigpen closes his eyes.

The next moment, the hard point of her index finger taps his chest. His eyes fly open.

"Listen up, Earl. It's simple as pie. I drive by the café where Tim has a drink every evening at an outside table. You're in the passenger seat with the assault rifle. When I slow down, you blast him. Then we're outa there before anyone realizes what's happened."

"There's got to be another way. Maybe you should see a lawyer."

Her mouth closes over his, her tongue exploring the contours of his teeth. Her hand plays havoc with his genitalia. "Pretty please," she whispers.

When he opens his eyes this time, she's lighting a J.

"This'll chill you out," she says. She takes a deep drought and passes it.

Then they're back in the car with the AK-47 in Thigpin's lap, driving down the now dark side street.

Out of nowhere, headlights flash on bright. A car swerves in front of them blocking the street. The Audi's breaks squeal. A full-size pick-up zooms in behind, locking them in.

Bandidos, thinks Thigpen, as he slams into the padded dash. Luckily, the airbags don't deploy. Thigpen scrambles out of the car, only to be knocked to the ground by a knee to his stomach. He spews.

Dandelion screams bloody murder until someone slaps a piece of duct-tape across her mouth. Someone else punches her in the face and she slumps unconscious.

When Thigpen stops retching, the AK-47 comes into view, lying on the ground, a boot resting on top of it. Thigpen looks upward. In the light of a conveniently placed streetlight, the boot's owner is a young man whose features are almost identical to Dandelion's. Her brother, Tim.

"She's loony as a crack whore," Tim says. "Two days ago she escaped from the hospital in Amarillo where she stays out of trouble. Beat a lawyer unconscious with a crowbar, stole his Audi and drove to Dallas this morning."

Suddenly, Tim's booted foot flares out, catching Thigpen in the ribs. He groans and scrunches into a ball.

"You should be more careful about who you fuck with."

That's the last of Dandelion.

When he's sure all the vehicles are gone, including the Audi, Thigpen opens his eyes. Shit, he thinks. I could be dead.

He struggles to his feet. Nothing seems to be broken. He's still got his wallet.

Metal glints from the dark pavement, catching his eye. It's the crazy bitch's gold Zippo. He reaches down and pries it from the soft blacktop.

Its mirror surface is scratched and abraded. But in the glow of the streetlight, Thigpen can still make out on the Zippo's face the delicate etching of a dandelion in seed, its winged offspring breaking free into the breeze.

Slipping the lighter into the front pocket of his khakis, he starts walking back toward Greenville Avenue.

Maracaibo

"I'll have a salad," Yvette says.

"Have something substantial," Bill urges. "Who knows when we'll have a chance to eat again."

She considers the ceiling with a cross-eyed gaze.

"No, really," she says. "Just a salad."

The waiter pretends to write this down, though Bill knows he's completely illiterate. Can't even sign his name. Just an awkward X. You can tell by the way he holds the pen. Upside down.

Bill glances up at the waiter, then back at the menu.

The waiter waits, nodding his chin to some inaudible tune playing in his head. Something catchy, a fragment lodged in his brain from last week's carnaval. Women dancing bare-breasted on elaborate floats. Black men in gold lamé suits, top hats and canes strutting back and forth down Carabobo Street.

Patiently, the waiter waits for Bill to order. Pen poised upside down over his order pad. Each ticket in three parts, separated by sheets of carbon paper. Gallia est omnis divisa in partes tres, Bill thinks.

Bill is torn between the BLT and the carne asada with beans and rice and fried plantains. Finally he chooses the latter.

"Sorry," the waiter says. "Kitchen's out of plantains."

"How the fuck can that be?" Bill asks. "It's the national food."

Bill reaches for his water glass, which is beaded with nodules of precipitation. But his perspective is off. A gnat fluttering in the corner of his eye perhaps. Or the shitty lighting.

His fingers brush the side of the glass. It tilts. Falls. Spewing a swath of wetness across the tablecloth and into Yvette's lap. She screams and jumps from her seat. The waiter fumbles for his towel.

Bill puts his hands under the edge of the table and heaves upward. It goes over like a monstrous wave breaking on a placid shore. China, glassware, forks, knives, butter plate, breadbasket, floral centerpiece, the works, fly hither and yon.

In the aftermath of the explosion, a cacophony of voices rises like a mushroom cloud. Everyone in the room is talking at once about Bill's freak-out.

Throwing his napkin aside in disgust, Bill strides out of the dining room, leaving Yvette to make amends. Salaaming her apologies like some Arab princess who's parked her camel in a handicapped zone.

The lobby is deserted except for an old man nodding off in a tufted leather armchair. His skeletal hand holds a finely polished blackthorn cane. Bill slips the cane from the geezer's grip without incident. The old fart never even stirs. Bill hefts the dense hardwood shillelagh. A perfect affectation for the evening's frivolities, he thinks. He tucks it under his arm and continues his rapid pace to the heavy bronze and glass front doors.

Outside, the night is thick with fumes from the offshore oil derricks, rising like cruciforms above Lake Maracaibo's turgid waves.

Bill eases a 1,000-Bolivar note into the cupped hand of the parking valet. The attendant, encapsulated in an extra-tight pseudo-toreador outfit, weaves adroitly between two newly arriving autos to retrieve Bill's midnight-blue Lamborghini from its premier parking spot under the porte cochere. When he fires up the engine, it squeals like a stuck pig. Then settles into a deep and abiding rumble.

The valet holds open the driver's door, and Bill slips into the molded leather seat like a prick into a well-lubricated condom. The blackthorn cane goes behind the seats. Bill's almost feminine hand moves the stick shift in and out of gear with coordinated plunges and releases of the hair-trigger clutch.

His other hand clicks open a gold cigarette case previously ensconced in the side pocket of his Versace tux and retrieves an oval-shaped cigarette. The attendant scoops forward like an obsequious crab, holding a disposable lighter in his gigolo's fingers. The flame licks the tip of the cigarette. Bill draws deeply on the cancer stick, feeling the nicotine race through his blood with the speed of a greyhound after a fake rabbit.

Through the thick glass sheets forming the façade of the hotel, a flurry of movement becomes apparent. As Bill concentrates his gaze, the scene becomes clear. Yvette is at the forefront running as best she can in four-inch spikes, her party dress hiked most of the way up her delightful thighs. Behind rages a frenzied mob of diners bent on mayhem.

Bill revs the Lamborghini's mighty engine. His eye catches that of the valet.

"Get the passenger door," he barks.

As the attendant scurries into action, Yvette bursts through the glass and brass entry. At curbside she removes one stiletto-heeled pump and catapults it at the pursuing swarm. It soars like a ninja throwing star, catching the neck of the bare-shouldered blonde leading the pack. With a gurgling cry, the blonde stumbles, falls. The rabble roils over her like a berserk rugby scrum.

Yvette bounds around the Lamborghini and sweeps into the passenger seat, tucking her sequined dress beneath her perfectly proportioned haunches. The valet slams the door. The dull thud of heavy metal resonates in the humid air.

"Step on it, buster!" are Yvette's pithy instructions.

Bill obliges.

The Lamborghini blasts into the night, but not before a thrown champagne glass shatters on the rear bumper like a tiny supernova.

They cruise down the malecón fronting Lake Maracaibo where strolling lovers and trolling maricones rub shoulders in the rich purple light of early evening. Yvette tosses the other stiletto pump out the window; then squints into the vanity mirror, adjusting her makeup.

"You're such a fuck up," she says.

Bill's fingers tighten on the oak and leather steering wheel. A stand-in for Yvette's neck?

"The waiter was an idiot," he snaps.

"That's why you went nuts-oid! Because the waiter was an impoverished, illiterate dirtbag from Barrio 24 de Julio."

"And everyone was whispering about us."

"They were probably remarking on my serendipitous jugs."

There is no debate on that point.

Yvette turns on the radio and cruises the channels until she finds a tune that makes her hot between the legs. She cranks up the volume and begins to shimmy like the exotic dancer she once was.

"I want to dance 'til dawn," she says. "Then die."

Bill considers Yvette with a jaundiced eye. Is she suicidal again or just playing out some fantasy pilfered from an old David Lynch movie. But her lascivious Lambada moves are addictive. He begins to gyrate, his arms waving in the air.

"Yeah, baby!" he shouts.

The Lamborghini drifts into the on-coming lane. Scream of brakes. Blare of horn. Head-on collision avoided by a cunt hair.

Bill's forehead beads with oil and body waste, his intestines do a triple backflip followed by a grand jeté. His heart goes on vacation. I'm too young to die, he thinks, unaware that the fates have already taken his number. It's just a matter of time and place.

In the heat of near collision and almost death, Yvette pisses her panties. Except she's not wearing any. She scrambles in her purse for a wad of Kleenex. The scent of warm pee wafts on the night air.

"Don't ruin the leather seat!" Bill screams, scrambling for a cigarette.

Across town a car bomb explodes outside the U.S. embassy, killing two Marines and maiming a half dozen more.

The night is still young, though for Lake Maracaibo, rift with petrochemical pollutants and an exploding duckweed infestation, it may be later than you think.

Yvette and Bill believe they will live forever. Who can argue with that?

Yvette: "I'm hungry."

Bill: "I told you to order something more substantial than a salad."

"What are you talking about? We didn't even get started on our water glasses before you pulled that little table trick."

Bill grins sheepishly and pulls up at a taco stand. A stunning Latina woman in roller skates sails over to take their order. Her name is Leona.

"You've got great legs," says Bill.

Suspicion darkens her brow. Is this some kind of pickup line?

"Don't mind him," Yvette interjects. "He's legs crazy. But strictly a one-girl man."

"You hope," says Bill.

"You going to order something? Or just talk your heads off all night?"

"Talk's cheap," Bill says.

"So's the food," says Leona.

"Give me three tacos de puerco adobado." Bill says. "And a Polar negra."

"I'll just have a salad," says Yvette. "With the dressing on the side."

"You're starting with the salad thing again?" Bill grumbles.

"A girl's got to look out for her girlish figure."

"Jesus." Leona skates blithely away, the taut muscles of her calves and thighs rippling like the lash of a whip.

Bill watches her leggy departure, fascinated by the enigma of desire. An almond-sized knot of longing lodges in the back of his throat. He coughs discretely into the back of his hand.

Antoine's Pool & Billiards resides in a historic building that has seen better days. The brick exterior is covered with layers of intricate graffiti drawn by unknown Picassos of the barrio. A tin-roofed portico held up by Victorian cast-iron columns throws deep shadows on the interior through wide-open French doors. Inside, each pool table, like separate solar systems, has its own light source.

Bill and Yvette are playing modified eight ball. Bill is losing. And drinking steadily of the rum anejo. He smokes a Davidoff panatela. A ball teeters on the edge, but doesn't fall into the pocket.

"You've had piss-poor luck tonight," Yvette says. "Three ball in the corner pocket." She sights along her cue. Her hand draws back.

"At least I didn't lose my shoes," Bill says as he walks behind her, nudging her elbow.

Yvette is barefoot, the soles of her feet already as black as heavy crude. She shakes her ass at him. Then sinks the three ball.

"One more, baby, and you're history."

Bill motions for a fresh drink.

"You keep drinking like that, you ain't never going to get it up later."

"Piss off."

Using only the pressure of his hands, Bill snaps his cue in two; then walks over to the bar.

"Give me some ceviche," he tells the barman.

A soccer game ebbs and flows across the TV screen on a shelf behind the bar. Venezuela versus Bolivia. The players, spread across a shamrock-green field, mimic billiard balls spinning and colliding on the green baize of the tables. Bolivia scores. Yvette sinks the eight ball.

Bill is toast.

Tonight Yvette is getting under Bill's skin. So what else is new? While Bill sips his fresh drink, she scoots to the ladies room.

Tonight's the night, she thinks, as she squats over the smelly hole in the floor. If everything goes according to Bill's plan, we'll be on a flight to Mexico City in the morning. No more of Hugo Chavez's looney tunes. No more death squads. Left or right.

Back in the bar Bill keeps fiddling with his cell phone, checking the time. Pablo is late. Where the fuck is he? The bartender, Fidel, is asleep on his feet. Business is slow, dead even.

At last a familiar figure appears in the doorway, longish coal-black hair, white shirt, dark trousers. Pablo. But his mahogany complexion is bleached stark white, as if he's fallen into a vat of lime. He stumbles. Keels over at Bill's feet.

A crimson amoeboid stain spreads across the back of Pablo's white shirt, blood leaking from a mortal wound.

Holy shit! thinks Bill.

Fidel gapes over the bar.

"What's up with Pablo?" he asks.

"What does it look like?" Bill demands. "He's been stabbed or shot."

Fidel looks queasy, as if he might puke. He pours himself a brandy and shoots it back.

Just then Yvette walks up.

"What's up with Pablo?" she asks.

But Bill is already squatting down. He lifts Pablo under his arms, turning him partially over, resting his head on his knee. Blood dribbles between Pablo's lips. His eyes are vague, as if some insect from outer space has burrowed inside his brain and taken control.

Suddenly, Pablo jerks to a seated position, his mouth opens and he vomits. Clots of viscous blood spew across the floor. And a small leather bag soaked in magenta gore, its drawstring pulled tight.

As if he has achieved some final resolution of his sorry-assed existence, life swirls out of Pablo like an exhalation. He falls back into Bill's arms, stone cold dead.

"Well, I'll be damned," Bill says in amazement. He's never had anyone die in his arms before. He lowers Pablo's corpse to the floor.

"Live by the sword, die by the sword," says Yvette.

"What the hell are you talking about?"

"Pablo was not a nice person."

"But he served his purpose."

"Only because you weren't on the receiving end of his brass knuckles."

Yvette's knees crack as she bends down and reaches out for the leather bag. Bill slaps her hand away and scoops it up.

"Ow!"

When he releases the drawstring, more than a dozen jumbo rough-cut emeralds, like the multifaceted eyes of a greenhead fly, tumble into his palm. His hands are stained with blood from the bag.

"You're right, he was a bastard," Bill says. "But at least he delivered the goods come Hell or high water."

"And whoever punctured his tire won't be far behind," Yvette says, sucking on her teeth.

"Don't get nervous, pet."

"Most assuredly I'm not your pet."

Yvette takes a Beretta 9mm from her purse, confirms the clip is full; then ratchets a shell into the firing chamber.

"Keep an eye out, while we give Pablo a quick funeral," Bill says.

Together Bill and Fidel heft Pablo's cadaver into the alley and on the count of three hoist it into a dumpster. Fidel wheels a bucket and mop from the storage room and soaks up the pool of Pablo's blood.

Bill's Rolex shows 10 minutes to midnight. He stands behind Fidel, squeezing and releasing his shoulder blades. Fidel is as tense as an alley cat dropped in a cage of pit bulls.

"We've got a party to go to," Bill says gaily. "Take two aspirin and get some rest, pal. Everything'll look different in the light of day."

They zoom through midnight streets, where a light rain has left puddles capturing the red filigree flash of sudden brake lights, the neon yellows, crimsons, blues and purples of cheap pleasures and promises not kept.

A glistening black Land Rover 4 x 4 follows each twist and turn of the Lamborghini. Never too close, never too far behind. Yvette keeps looking back at the tailing lights. She spits through the open passenger-side window. The noxious fumes of fear waft from her armpits.

They're bound for the birthday party of the American consul, born at 12:13 a.m. fifty-seven years ago. Ahead, outside the consul's official residence, a line of expensive cars weave through a maze of steel & concrete anti-tank barriers and snarls of razor wire.

Security is extra tight after the earlier bombing of the U.S. embassy. Marines in full-combat gear flash light beams in the faces of the guests, bark incomprehensible questions, paw through car trunks and under seats.

They confiscate Yvette's 9mm, handing her a numbered claim ticket. When she starts to make a fuss, they threaten a strip search. Bill feigns a limp and they let him keep the blackthorn cane.

Yvette wonders if the young Lego-jawed Marine would be as good in bed as she imagines.

The consul's party spreads like pasteurized honey across the lawns of the official residence, which roll like black velvet down to the edge of

Lake Maracaibo. The main house is a blaze of light. Flickering tiki torches illuminate the ebb and flow of the guests.

Women, gorgeous and plain, stacked and flat-chested, lesbian and straight, mingle and collide like stars in a night fisherman's net. The men, all in dark suits, puff on Cohibas and talk money, whores and fast cars, not necessarily in that order. A mariachi band strolls and strums amid the throng.

Bill swoops up two flutes of champagne and hands one to Yvette. They tap glasses. Down the hatch.

"You know I'm crazy about you," he says.

Her shimmering cobalt eyes give him her reply.

Behind them, the tailing Land Rover disgorges three lugubrious travelers before being whooshed away by a valet. The driver's face is instantly recognizable as Agustin Rios, the gangster, flanked by two flunkies. He produces an engraved invitation. No one checks them for guns or similar paraphernalia.

Meanwhile, Bill and Yvette flit among the flotsam of guests and party crashers. Bill goes back to drinking rum. Yvette munches on chunks of iceberg lettuce provided by some hapless assistant to the salad chef. A DJ spins salsa tunes by the pool. A notorious female drunk sheds her clothes and dives in. When she climbs, dripping, up the chrome pool ladder, Bill hands her a towel.

Impelled by an instinct for survival at all costs, Bill glances behind. Light glints off the lapels of Agustin's sharkskin suit, as he repels toward them through the riffraff. Grabbing Yvette by the elbow, Bill spins her into the night.

Hand-in-hand they scoot to the bottom of the sweeping lawn. On a pier at the lake's edge, a clique of pleasure seekers waits to board a classic 1949 Chris Craft Sportsman bound for an oil rig a quarter mile out. There a famous Argentine dance band plies its vibes.

Just as the lines are cast off, Bill leaps aboard, pulling Yvette with him. She gives a B-minus imitation of a Marilyn Monroe squeal. They totter on the stern as the twin 120-hp Evinrudes rumble. Once they're safely in the cockpit, Bill bends her backward, a blade of grass in Lake

Maracaibo's fume-choked air, and kisses her deeply. The varnished mahogany decking of the motorboat shimmers like ancient gold.

Agustin rushes up to the edge of the dock, but comes up short. The launch is already twenty yards out. "Fuck!"

When the second launch, inbound, arrives at the shore-side dock, the trio of badasses leaps aboard with amphetamine-enhanced impatience. They elbow through the disembarkees. Eyebrows are raised. A foolish man steps toward Agustin, who knees him in the nads.

As the launch heads out to the oil rig, someone calls security.

Meanwhile, back at the rig, the band struts its stuff under the stars. The music is pure orgasm. Yvette goes wet between her legs for the second time that night. Bill's feet won't stand still. A dozen pairs of dancers swoop and glide across the rude planks of the rig. Overhead fog lights drape the scene in a talcish light, blanching the dancers to a corpse-like hue, the dancing dead.

The band transitions into a Joao Gilberto bossa nova tune amid scattered applause. The dancers just keep going, segueing into the new beat. This is serious business.

"They'll be on the next boat," Bill says.

"What shall we do?" Yvette says.

"Let's dance." Bill takes her hand and slow samba's onto the floor. There, things heat up. Yvette spins and gyrates. Bill moves with gravitas, a legacy of living in the Spanish tropics.

Suddenly Agustin splits through the audience. In his hand, a silver chrome Browning 9mm.

"I want the fucking emeralds," he shouts, shattering the rhythm of the band.

The mood changes from gay to tragic in a heartbeat. The crowd and the other dancers draw back in alarm. Only Bill and Yvette hold the floor. The band takes up a tango.

Bill and Yvette lock eyes. His right arm reaches around her back, pulling her close. Her bosom rises and falls with emotion. They begin to dance. Legs bent, torsos tight together. They move effortlessly. Slowly, then faster and faster.

"Stop!" screams Agustin. He levels the pistol at Bill.

As they swirl and swivel toward the gangster, Bill swings Yvette aloft, turning her almost upside down across his right shoulder. One long sumptuous leg points at the moon, her body is parallel to the floor, the other leg bends across Bill's chest. Her dress falls away. In the V between those stunning legs, she's naked as a jaybird.

Poor Agustin. It's as if he's never seen a quim before. For a split second, he's utterly distracted by this most hush-hush item of female anatomy.

Time enough for Bill to swing the blackthorn shillelagh in a withering overhead arc, slamming it full bore into Agustin's right temple. Skull bone cracks like an egg. Brain matter liquefies. Agustin sways; then

crumbles

down

dead.

Yvette continues her bare-assed flip, landing in a perfect split, just in time to snatch Agustin's gaudy 9mm as it spins across the planked surface. Blam. Blam. Good-bye bodyguards.

Bill pulls Yvette to her feet. The band breaks into a classic tango tune. Pugliese's La Yumba! With a wave to the onlookers, Bill and Yvette do a crossover tango walk to the waiting motor launch. Aboard, they disappear into the gloom of the vast lake, never to be seen again on the streets of Maracaibo.

Dog Daze

Cy looked up at me with his one huge wondering eye; then stuck his foot in his ear and began to scratch. A slow, languid scratch that seemed to use up all the time left in the universe.

When I first saw Cyclops at the pound, he already only had one eye. The other was a white sightless orb. A creature from Greek mythology half-blinded by some jealous demigoddess bitch he'd sniffed up too close and personal. The tag on his cage said his name was Jake, age 4. I didn't want a Jake. That name always made me think of the crappy sequel to the movie Chinatown. But I wanted this dog.

So I paid my hundred twenty-five dollars and renamed him Cyclops. According to the SPCA clerk, they'd found him wandering in a neighborhood of warehouse businesses and Korean restaurants. Dumped. "Get out of the fuckin' car!"

In that neighborhood it was a wonder he hadn't ended up as stir-fried japchae.

"What kind of dog is he?" I asked, taking his vaccination papers from the unbelievably long fingers of the volunteer SPCA associate.

"You've already adopted him and you don't know what breed he is?" In her eyes I was a walking pile of bat guano. Dr. No—you remember him—died buried under a couple tons of the stuff. In the book; not the movie. We don't get much call for bat guano at the BANK. That's why I always retool my deodorant during my lunch hour.

The BANK.

That's where I work as a teller and part-time junior assistant vice president.

If you bank at the Gulf Drive branch, I've probably processed one of your deposits or withdrawals. Does that sound right?

We're located in the only strip mall on the five point three miles of Gulf Drive. The rest of Gulf Drive is lined with mid-century homes and older, some of architectural significance. Many in significant disrepair. All with views of the Gulf of Mexico.

"So what kind of dog is he?" I repeated.

He was a brindle-colored creature, floppy-eared and stubby-legged, his hair cut Twiggy-short. He weighed maybe eleven pounds, stood nine inches tall at the shoulder, with a tail that curled into an elaborate quill. Cy's laid back nonconfrontational personality reminded me of the shrink my parents took me to back in high school. But I knew the shrink was faking it. Inside he was wound up tight as a virgin asshole.

Not Cy. Cy was 100% genuine.

The intern rubbed Cyclops behind one ear. "I'm not sure." She looked across two alleys of cages, a stray-cats-and-dogs Ramallah, to a tall skinny young man in a green T-shirt and jeans who was scrubbing out a cage.

"Larry," she yelled. "What kind of dog is this?"

He twisted the hose nozzle into the off position and looked at the dog I was holding up.

"What's his name?" Larry asked.

"Jake," said the pale-cheeked intern. Her skin exuded the scent, texture and absence of color of an albino rose petal.

"Cyclops." I said.

I wondered if she liked to fuck on her lunch hour. That would require some serious deodorant retooling. But the SPCA was too far away from the BANK where I worked. I'd end up spending too much time driving to and from fucking.

"Jake's a purebred Shih Tzu," Larry shouted above the sudden barking of dogs.

Cy and I stepped outside. It was a perfect Saturday morning in March with a breeze whipping off the bay carrying the tang of salted dead fish and marine oil. Clouds like the torn insides of a stuffed toy animal skidded across the sky.

Cy looked up at me and winked.

* * *

When Amber moved in, Cy and I had been living together for about four weeks. By then we'd established an acceptable working relationship. We took walks three times a day, a bath once a week, using the same lavender bath gel. Cy ate dog crackers mixed with water. I ate frozen chicken or steak dinners and drank sweet tea by the gallon.

Sweet tea was a habit from my student days in the Deep South. I'd quite smoking three or four times, but I could never get off sweet tea.

We both liked Law and Order and Nip and Tuck. Cy slept on the extra pillow on my queen-sized bed.

When Amber moved in, that became a problem because now Amber used my extra pillow. Cy tried two or three times to sleep on Amber's head. In response Amber locked Cy out of the bedroom. He sat by the door, barking.

As a compromise I moved Cy to a doggy pillow in one corner of the bedroom. He wasn't all that happy with my solution. But I told him he didn't have a choice.

Amber liked Cy well enough.

But after the pillow dispute they remained suspicious of each other. Cy was the old family retainer. Amber the blonde gold digger with the hot body.

Amber loved blow and giving blowjobs.

That's how we met: sharing a few lines laid out like runways on the chocolate Naugahyde dashboard of my Mustang, after which she brought me to the point of ecstasy. This happened at dusk in the far back corner of the H-E-B supermarket parking lot near the recycling dumpsters. Afterward we went to Al's N.O. Grill and sucked down fried oyster po'boys and Bud on tap.

But blow was expensive.

So a week after Amber displaced Cy on my extra pillow, I started siphoning small sums of cash into my front pocket rather than into my cash drawer at the BANK. This was facilitated by the fact that I handled mostly commercial deposits involving large quantities of cash and numerous small checks. Under these circumstances there was always room for discrepancies.

I became adept at fudging the numbers on deposit slips. Before taking a late lunch, I'd stash a couple of that morning's deposit slips between the pages of the paperback novel I was reading. Alone in the employee break room, with a meatball sub, chips and a Diet Coke spread out as camouflage, I'd ease the slips from between the leaves of text and carefully change a three to a two or a five to a four. Back at my teller station I pocketed the extra hundred bucks.

The BANK's privacy policy prohibited surveillance cameras in the break room or the bathrooms. And I was careful never to steal from the same account twice in the same week.

It was a bright June Tuesday around 1:30 when Mora, the head teller, barged into the break room. I was hunched over a deposit slip, pen poised like a tattoo artist. At the click of the door opening, my other hand flew willy-nilly, colliding with the meatball sub, sending meatballs flying. Tomato sauce dripped from my fingers onto the deposit slip. In the confusion, my pen fell to the floor and I kicked it under the table.

Mora stood at my elbow.

"What's that?" she asked.

"What?" I replied.

"That." Mora's plastic glitter-nail decorated index finger pointed accusingly at the soiled deposit slip.

"The receipt for my lunch?" I said without conviction.

"No, it's not. It's a deposit slip."

We both stared at it. Sweat poured from my armpits.

"It must have gotten caught in the pages of my book." A pocket edition of The Snows of Kilimanjaro & Other Stories with meatball lay next to the meatball-less sub roll.

"Bank documents are not permitted in the break room," Mora said. "You know that."

"It was an accident."

I dabbed at the tomato stain with a napkin imprinted with the sub shop logo. Mora grabbed the deposit slip, holding it aloft like a winning lottery ticket.

"I'm writing this up," she said and walked out.

That night I told Amber I was done with embezzling. Working at the BANK was a good job. The best I'd ever had. No way was I going to jeopardize that over her drug habit.

"I'll think of something," Amber said.

Her words followed me down the front steps like a curse, as I took Cy for his before-bedtime walk. Outside Cy stopped and stretched; yawned and gazed up at me. Then raised his leg and urinated. Not a care in the world.

A week later Amber and I lay in a sweaty, naked post-coital heap on the sisal rug in my darkened living room. Amber leaned sideways, picking sisal fibers out of her ass. The lights from occasional passing cars sent weird heffalump-ish shadows rummaging across the ceiling.

The weather had turned hot and steamy as a Chinese laundry. That's how it would be from now until mid-November. I'd cranked the window air-conditioning unit up to High but it didn't make much difference.

"There's this house on Gulf Drive," said Amber. "I've been watching it every time I drive you to and from the BANK. I think it's closed up for the summer."

"That's nice."

Amber's fingers ran playfully across my chest.

"No ... listen ... There's probably some really good stuff in there. Stuff we could boost and unload in one of those consignment shops."

I sat up, the tip of my dick tingling. It wasn't a sex tingle.

"You mean as in breaking and entering?"

"I'm sure the window locks are all rusted out from the salt air. And there's an overgrown camellia hedge between the house and the one next door. At night no one will know we're there."

"What about alarms, attack dogs, security guards, cops with guns?"

Just then Cy got up from where he'd been stretched out on the sofa watching the action and padded across the room to his water dish. He came over and stood next to me. His chin dripped water on my hand. I couldn't see his expression in the gloom of the unlit room but I knew he was rolling his one good eye.

"I don't know," I said.

"It'll be easy," Amber said. "Easy as pie."

It was a moonless night when Amber backed the Mustang into the broken shell driveway of the house she'd been scoping out. Camellia branches scraped the roof like fingernails on a blackboard.

"You see," Amber said, turning toward me. "We're completely hidden from the street and the neighbors."

"I can't believe we're doing this," I whispered.

She put her hand on my knee. "Everything's cool, baby."

I set the stepstool we'd bought at the hardware under the windows of a Florida room that looked off over the bay and climbed up. Amber was right. When I pushed up the old wooden window frame, the latch gave way with a splintering sound. I scrambled up and over the sill. It was hot as Hell in a ski mask, black sweatshirt and navy blue work slacks.

I carried two canvas sacks and a flashlight. We'd agreed I would take only small antique-looking objects. I made my first find in the sunporch: a bronze statuette of a naked nymph bolted to a crystal ashtray.

In the kitchen I scanned the countertops with the flashlight. They were bare except for an ancient toaster. I opened several cupboards, discovering only stacks of plates and rows of mismatched glassware. Amid a drawerful of rusted knives, I found several silver or silver-plated spoons. Into the bag they went.

My jitters had dissipated. I was into the rhythm of the thing now, moving silently from room to room in my black suede Vans. A Chinese-looking lamp base, a pair of Tiffany-style vases from the mantle, more silverware from the dining room sideboard, some old leather-bound books. Another bronze statuette in a western motif: an American Indian on horseback with drawn bow and arrow riding down a luckless buffalo.

One sack was full. I leaned it in the doorway to the front hall and started up the stairs. The third step groaned like an old harmonium under my body weight. For some reason I stopped dead in my tracks.

That's when I heard a shuffling sound. Like a zombie moving in the pitch-blackness of the upstairs hall.

Or a person!

In the next instant, the overhead light above the stairway snapped on. I slammed my eyes shut.

When I opened them seconds later, side-by-side shotgun barrels confronted me like twin black holes punched in the universe.

Gradually additional details filled in as the camera pulled back and upward. A pair of eyes as cold as blue-veined marble, hollow cheeks peppered with stubble. The maw of a denture-less mouth dripping with spittle.

The mouth closed.

Then opened again:

"Get out!"

I ran like a motherfucker.

After the burglary fiasco, I insisted Amber get into rehab. I couldn't afford to fund her monkey any longer, monetarily or emotionally. I'd been that close to getting my head blown to smithereens.

Nightmares of doing jail time haunted my sleep. Huge tattooed convicts, group showers, etc. You get the picture.

I went back to driving myself to and from work. Amber didn't get to use the Mustang any more during the day to cruise around looking for trouble. After she refused to sign up for a rehab program, I gave her a week to find someplace else to live. Cy got his pillow back.

On our walks Cy and I discussed the vagaries of women. More particularly, I ranted and raved about what a scary slut Amber was, while Cy listened patiently. When I finally stopped talking, Cy gave me a quizzical look. Then wiggled his tail like a cheerleader's pompom, as if to say: Jerk, I told you she was trouble from the get-go.

The next afternoon Amber started working at a gentlemen's club.

On the fourth day following my ultimatum, I came home from the BANK to find the dinner table set with plates and glasses, a bottle of wine and a bouquet of daisies. Amber, standing in the kitchen, lit a scented mood candle the moment I walked in the door. She wore an old Eurythmics T-shirt that had shrunk in all the right places. Tex-Mex takeout steamed on the kitchen counter: seared meat with jalapenos and onions, beans and corn tortillas.

"What's up?" I asked.

"I thought we should give it one more try."

"No way, José."

"I got beef fajitas. Your favorite."

"You've got three days left to find a new place. Then I put your stuff on the curb."

"You're such a Blue Meanie."

"I just want to work at my job at the BANK, hang out with Cy, lead a quiet law-abiding life."

Amber walked out from behind the kitchen counter. She was barefoot. In fact she was stark naked below her belly button where the bottom of the Eurythmics T-shirt ended.

"Oh, no," I said.

"Oh, yes," she said.

A while later, as I lay on the couch, my head cradled in Amber's lap, she explained about the guy she'd met at the tits and ass club where she'd started working. A wholesale diamond dealer drunk as a skunk. He had an office on the sixth floor of the old Bradbury Building downtown. A shipment of stones was arriving tomorrow worth over a hundred thousand dollars. A once in a lifetime opportunity.

"No, no, no," I said.

"Oh, yes, yes, yes," said Amber. "All you have to do is wait downstairs with the engine running. I'll take care of the rest."

At which point she put her face in my crotch and began performing CPR.

It was the nadir of the afternoon of the next day. Three-thirty. Everyone was asleep at their desks or sales counters. Only rich lesbians on the make cruised the mall department stores at that hour seeking desperate housewives with whom to perform lewd sexual acts.

I pulled my white '03 Mustang with the chocolate Naugahyde interior to the curb in front of the Bradbury Building. It was a six-story

Deco job with elaborate geometric tile work like the teeth of a hip-hop artist. The shoeshine guy inside the lobby slouched in the customer's chair, sound asleep.

The same Eurythmics T-shirt as the night before fondled Amber's chest. Hip-hugger jeans hung below. The front of her jeans bulged with an evil-looking 9mm.

"I'll be back in fifteen minutes. If you have to move, circle back around."

She leaned over and kissed me on the mouth.

"Wish me luck, chico."

I watched her walk silently across the lobby, her hips barely swaying, and go into the elevator.

I waited five minutes, the engine running. Then I slipped her into gear, moved my foot from the brake to the gas and pulled into the street. That time of day there were almost no other cars on the streets. In no time I was out of downtown and heading along Gulf Road. I pulled into the BANK and went inside.

The head teller looked surprised. I'd called in sick that morning.

"I couldn't stay away," I said.

Next morning's Caller-Times carried the story of a shootout during an attempted jewelry holdup. There was a picture of a woman's bloodstained body. A cloth covered her face. Her T-shirt advertised a band called the Eurythmics.

After that Cy and I just hung out and drank Corona. On the weekends we might go to the beach. The dog days of August were just too hot to do anything else.

Looking for Goa

One

The exact location of Goa is a question that has plagued scholars for centuries. Some believe it resides like a black freckle on the subcontinent's right nipple. Others point to a small protuberance on the Buddha's right testicle, noting also the similarity between Goa and gonad. Still others delimit a ragged sweep of Indian coastline abutting the Arabian Sea midway between the Gulf of Klambhat in the north and Cape Comorin at the southern tip. In any case, Portuguese adventurers stumbled upon it in the fifteenth century and refused to let go for the next 450 years.

Two

Over the summer I pulled off a series of bank heists among the lesser-known burgs of North Jersey, using a Dick Cheney Halloween mask and a Browning .45 I inherited from my father, a World War II vet. He gave it to me as he gasped his last emphysemic breath inside an oxygen tent at the Sioux Falls, South Dakota, VA hospital.

He started smoking after he made his first landing on some god-forsaken rock in the Pacific. As his platoon slogged up the beach, they came upon a Jap trooper leaning against a shattered palm tree, his guts hanging out like an exploded party favor. He was moaning in Japanese, a goner for sure. But when the G.I.s walked past him, he pulled out a revolver and shot dad's best buddy in the back of the head. Splat. Kind of a mini Pearl Harbor. Then the Jap keeled over dead.

Dad took his pal's dog tags and the pack of Luckies in his shirt pocket. From that day forward it was three packs a day until the afternoon he handed me the .45, made a gurgling sound and expired.

I never took up smoking myself. A nasty, dirty, purposeless habit. Kind of like life. Who needs a double dose of that?

Like I said, me and Marge, my partner in crime, had taken up bank robbing. We'd both been unemployed for over a year and were tired of eating beans out of a can.

The first four or five jobs went down smooth as silk. We netted almost sixty grand apiece. No one was hurt. And the cops didn't have a clue, since neither of us had any priors.

Then came the last one, which ran right off the fuckin' rails.

It all started when I pistol-whipped a teller who wasn't stuffing the cash fast enough into the canvas sack I'd thrown at her.

The security guard took umbrage with my rough treatment of the gentler sex. Anger pulsed through his paltry brain faster than common sense. Deciding I was distracted by the money, he went for his 9mm where it lay on the floor in front of him. He'd tossed it there at Marge's request moments after we made our grand entrance, shouting obscenities and waving our weapons aloft.

"Drop the fuckin' gun, asswipe!" But Marge forgot to scoop it up.

Now Marge, standing on the bank manager's desk surveying the scene through the slit eyes of her Martha Stewart mask, caught the guard's movement. Without the slightest hesitation, she squeezed off a round. Your marksmanship doesn't have to rival Natty Bumppo's when you're using Black Talon hollowpoints. Half the guard's face ended up smeared like pepperoni pizza across the nearest plate glass window.

The tellers found a whole new level of motivation to slam that cash into the canvas sacks I'd provided.

I walked over and looked down at the dead guard.

"Jesus, Marge," I said. "Why'd you have to do that?"

"It was him or us," she said.

Three

After the hold-up fiasco, we hid out in a sixth-floor-walkup shotgun flat in Hoboken, New Jersey.

It was too hot to leave town. And too hot to stay. The cops were everywhere. It was the dog days of summer and the apartment had no air conditioning.

The bar where Yo La Tengo first played was just around the corner. When I went out, every guy in a nylon Just Do It wife beater and navy blue watch cap was an undercover cop. I was so paranoid, I could barely make it down to the corner deli. The gook running the produce store next to the deli had to be CIA. Or maybe NSA.

Thank god I wasn't some raghead with an expired student visa.

Taking a murder rap was never part of my plan. All I'd wanted to do was stick up a few banks, pistol-whip the occasional teller, and stockpile enough loot so I could move to Costa Rica and open an ice cream parlor.

Now all I wanted to do was disappear. Like acting out a movie script written in lemon juice.

The apartment belonged to a writer friend of mine named Eric who'd gone to Greece with his girlfriend for the summer. Frisky fucking on the white sands of Mykonos, etc., etc. Knowing I was out of work and living in a cardboard box, he left me the key.

I sat on his Salvation Army couch gnawing my knuckles.

"Your nerves are eating you alive," Marge said.

"Thanks for the heads up."

"You need to chill before you get a cerebral hemorrhage."

"We're dead. Finished. Don't you see that, Marge? We'll never get out of Jersey alive."

She jumped up, pulled out her .357 magnum and started waving it like a drunk with a whiskey bottle. Her eyes flared like Fourth of July sparklers.

"We'll go out in a blaze of gunfire. Dead coppers everywhere. We'll make a video and send it to Oprah. You and me sitting here at this coffee table, eating vegetarian and talking about self-realization. Marge and Bill. The new age Bonnie and Clyde."

Luckily the doorbell rang. It was Looney Tunes, the meth addict from down the hall. I let him in.

He was constantly on the move. A blur. Like the Roadrunner.

He pushed past me: "Marge, baby."

They hugged. A tad too long and a tad too close for just friends. When they stepped apart, I could see Tunes had a hard-on. I'd heard that shit he injected made you a regular satyr until you crashed.

"Hey, Tunes," Marge said. "We got to get Bill unstressed 'fore he blows a gasket."

Tunes began to tap out an impromptu soft shoe. "Why don't we do it in the road...," he sang.

Pissed for every good reason and none at all, I walked into the bedroom and slammed the door. I sat on Eric's bed. A stack of books sprawled across the night table. I extracted a coffee-table-sized volume and opened it. The title page read *Palaces of Goa*. Inside were dozens of pictures of gaudy, otherworldly palaces built by Portuguese adventurers and merchant princes from the spoils of the East. For a brief time I was transported far, far away from the hollow streets of Hoboken.

Four

When I came out of the bedroom several hours later, Marge informed me it was my turn to go down to the deli for supplies.

"Get some egg salad," Tunes said.

"And some of that dark Russian rye bread," Marge said.

Taking a $50 from one of the bags of loot, I started down the narrow treacherous stairs. It seemed as though the building was deserted. In the dozen or so times I'd been up and down, I never saw anyone either on the stairway or down the asshole brown corridors that faded into shadows as murky as an abortion clinic in the Bible belt. I was wearing Vans, so I hardly made a sound. Just an occasional squeak when I pivoted too fast.

At the second floor I pulled up short, confronted by the ratcheting sound of a door chain unhooking. Click-click went the deadbolt. The door across from the stairwell opened. A woman teetered forth.

Plastered was my first take.

Then I realized she was wearing some kind of metal braces on her legs. One hand held a metal cane. Her eyes met mine and she took my breath away. They were the deep purple of pokeweed berries ripening in the vacant lot across the street. Without the slightest hesitation, I dove into them.

When she smiled, her face shimmered like an angel caught in a ray of heavenly light. Long perfect nose. Creamy brow. High cheekbones, angular and resolute. A moss green T-shirt hugged her twin guavas. Definitely kick ass.

"Did I surprise you?" she asked.

"No. No. I was on my way out to the deli. You're the first person I've met since I moved in the other day. Up on six."

"I didn't hear anyone moving in," she said.

"It's a furnished sublet," I said. "I guess you hear all the comings and goings?"

"With these fucking things, I don't get out much." One of the metal braces creaked when she moved. She blushed. "Excuse my French."

"Hey, no problemo." My eyes just kept eating her up, like some high school freshman with a crush on the homecoming queen.

"Do you always stare at women you meet in hallways?"

"Can I buy you a beer?" I asked, fixating on the ancient tile floor. "My name's Bill, by the way."

She gave me one of those is-that-the-best-you-can-do looks.

"Alice," she said. "And thanks for the offer. But I was just going down for the mail."

Suddenly I had this vision of the two of us living by the beach in one of the broken-down palaces of Goa. Meeting some swami who performed a miracle so she was no longer crippled.

I shrugged it off and started to descend the final circuit of stairs. There was no point in involving Alice in my personal nightmare.

"Do you play Monopoly?" she called after me. "I'm always looking for someone to play Monopoly."

Five

The torrid dog days rolled on like a tepid sea upon a tropical shore. I was as stir-crazy as a cat on a hot tin roof.

Marge kept slamming back the tequila and going off to the bedroom to boff with Tunes. I slept on the couch wearing earplugs and an eye mask.

Somewhere in there I started going down to Alice's to play Monopoly. She was cutthroat, and I usually ended up in bankruptcy. I always brought a six-pack of ice cold Heinekens from the deli. But the alcohol didn't affect her concentration. After the game, we'd talk about life and stuff. And finish up the beers.

I was in love. But I wasn't sure about Alice. She was very cautious. Because she was a cripple, everyone always tried to take advantage of her.

When we ran out of things to talk about, we watched gangster movies on her Direct TV hookup. They always ended badly.

"How come you never talk about yourself?" asked Alice.

"Boring," I said.

"I'd be interested."

I realized suddenly that she was falling for me. I couldn't let that happen. It was too dangerous.

"This is where I came in," I said, climbing to my feet.

Alice didn't stand up.

"Will you come and play Monopoly tomorrow?"

"I think I'm tied up for the rest of the week. But I'll call you."

"I don't have a phone."

"Well..." I backed toward the door. Then turned, twisted open the dead bolt and ran out like a lunatic.

Six

The cops were closing in. I could feel it. They knew we'd lain up in a lair somewhere close to the robbery scene. Because we'd left our stolen getaway car in the bank parking lot.

Actually, Hoboken was the next town over. We caught a bus moments after we left the bank.

But the cops were getting closer for sure. Sniffing the pavement for the scent of our paranoia.

Back on the sixth floor without Alice, I was always in a pissed-off mood.

Eric didn't have cable, so I couldn't watch old movies on TCM. I tried reading, but I could never get past the first sentence. "The first time I laid eyes on Terry Lennox he was drunk in a Rolls-Royce Silver Wraith outside the terrace of The Dancers..." I'd close the book and stare at the ceiling. There was an old water stain that looked something like a hog's scrotum.

"You need to get out more," Marge opined.

"Leave me the fuck alone!"

"Tsk, tsk. No one likes a grouch."

One day Tunes left for parts unknown and Marge flipped out too. Pacing back and forth for hours in stony silence. Stripping down her .357, oiling it and putting it back together again five times a day.

I figured pretty soon we'd be at each other with knives or razor blades.

Then came September first. My birthday. I stayed in bed with the covers over my head until noon. By then I was sweating like a Greek in a gay bathhouse.

Someone knocked on the apartment door.

"It's the cops," yelled Marge. She skimmed her gun off the coffee table and dove behind the sofa.

Wrapped in a dirty sheet, I walked to the door and peered through the peephole. It was Alice. I opened the door.

"You never called," Alice said.

"You don't have a phone."

Alice shrugged. "What do you want from me?" She thrust a small package at me. "Here. For your birthday."

I sensed Marge behind me, gaping over my shoulder.

"Let's go down to your place," I said, stepping into the hall and pulling the door closed behind me.

"Shouldn't you get dressed first?" asked Alice.

I looked down at the sheet draped around my loins. Oops. I went back inside. But I didn't invite Alice in.

"Who's that?" Marge asked, raising an eyebrow for effect.

"Shush."

"Don't shush me. I'm your partner. I have a right to know about your peccadilloes. Your dirty little secrets."

"What are you talking about?"

"I'm talking about trust."

I jerked on a pair of Levis; scrambled for a clean T-shirt. Scooting into the bathroom, I took a leak and brushed my choppers.

Marge hung in the doorway.

"Your urine looks awfully yellow," she said. "Are you sure you're drinking enough water?"

"Let's worry about that later. I've got to go." I brushed past her. "Just hold down the fort, Marge. I'll be back."

Seven

When we got down to Alice's apartment, she had this whole birthday setup going. A chocolate-cherry cake she'd baked herself. Fruit punch that was mostly vodka. And my present. Which turned out to be one of those medical bracelets engraved with my name and blood type.

We drank two glasses of the fruit punch. The next thing we were naked. Alice turned out the lights. With the shades drawn against the afternoon sun, the room was dusky and pervaded with lust like a pornographic French novel.

Then I heard the hobnail boots of the SWAT team rushing up the stairs, their gear creaking and rattling.

Alice put a finger to my lips.

An amplified voice echoed from above: "WE KNOW YOU'RE IN THERE! COME OUT WITH YOUR HANDS ON TOP OF YOUR HEAD!"

Then Marge's shouted reply: "You'll never take me alive, coppers."

A wasp's nest of gunfire erupted, interrupted by several explosions. Boom! BOOM!

Alice pulled me closer.

A ray of sunlight burst through a rip in the old paper pull-down blinds and streaked across the room illuminating Alice's torso. Next to the areola of her right breast, a tiny black freckle hovered like a fruit fly. As I placed my lips over it, I knew I had found Goa.

Then What Happened?

Sitting on the couch with Inez, I'm using a big ass needle to dig an itty-bitty splinter out of the fleshy part of my thumb, where it's been festering all week. Inez lolls next to me. Her pale puppies cuddled up in a magenta push-up bra rise and fall like albino pomegranates bobbing on the incoming tide.

I'm clad exclusively in the South Park boxers Inez gave me last week for my birthday. It's hot as Hades in mid-July in Beaufort, South Carolina. Live oaks dripping Spanish moss, lavish sailing sloops, bygone Southern charm and rednecks up the wazoo.

Inez's husband, Dave, is away on a business trip, so Inez gives me a call. I don't have anything else going, so I show up with a twelve pack of Budweiser, on sale.

The time is late afternoon on Thursday. The TV's tuned to some 1940s black-and-white melodrama with Barbara Stanwyck as an ice-cold bitch, soon to be a murderer. She keeps flouncing back and forth across the screen talking nonsense.

Without warning the needle flies out of my hand.

I swear it isn't my fault. It's as though someone switched on a superpowerful magnet in the vacant lot next door. The needle bows outward, before taking a flying leap. The point rips through the zombie-white flesh surrounding the splinter.

"Shit!" I jam my thumb in my mouth. The throbbing subsides.

Inez looks annoyed at all this turmoil disrupting her concentration on the movie.

Gazing hither and thither across the wall-to-wall carpet, I can't see the needle anywhere. Then again, being nearsighted I couldn't spot a wildebeest until it's six inches from my nose, just before it gores me in the small intestine. When I can't spot the needle, I ease off the sofa and down onto the floor for a closer look. Next thing I'm on all fours, squinting and snorting at the orange and green shag like a trained hog looking for truffles.

Try finding a needle in a shag rug, especially an orange and green one. After five minutes I'm cross-eyed and on the verge of a tizzy.

A scream sounds. Then the loud pop of a pistol.

It's from the movie.

Nevertheless my hand grasps Inez's blue-veined foot in sudden panic.

I stare at her foot, count the hairs curling from the middle joint of her big toe. Lucky seven. My nose six inches from Inez's left foot, I've got a parrot's eye view of five slick toenails lacquered in dark cherry, verily the color of blood pulsing from a bullet wound. From the mantelpiece Dave's old brass naval clock chimes four times as I wonder whether Inez would be up for a ménage a trois. Probably not. Two fingers tiptoe up one shapely ankle to a lovely calf and beyond.

"Please, Bill," Inez says. "I'm watching this movie."

I scrunch to a seated position. In front of me are Inez's perfect knees. Her nougat white thighs ooze backward, connecting to fullish hips beneath the languid folds of a black rayon miniskirt. My nose suctions like a Dirt Devil hand vac up those thighs. Inez grows restive.

Rearing like Godzilla from the depths of Tokyo Bay, I fall forward, burying my face in her crotch. She squirms under my assault. But her legs open. The smell of Nehi Grape Soda and something else wafts up my nostrils.

Something primordial washed up by the tide.

In the next instant we're rummaging around like crazy, jettisoning all remaining items of clothing. Inez gets the giggles. My skivvies go missing.

We're hard at it, Inez puffing air like a leaky dirigible, when Inez's marmalade striped cat, Celia, decides I'm murdering its meal ticket. Without hesitation it leaps kamikaze style from the back of the sofa onto the small of my back.

Its claws flay my flesh like a penitent beneath the archbishop's lash. With a bellow of pain and rage, I leap backward. My dick flops loose, sags.

As my hands grasp for the beast, it leaps away in a glimmer of self-preservation. Saliva glistens on its fangs. Its claws drip blood. The high-pitched whine of a metal cutting tool escapes its jaws.

"Bastard cat!" I scream.

A glass ashtray scooped from the coffee table curves in a perfect collision course with the fleeing beast. At the last possible instant, Celia veers sideways. The ashtray explodes in a myriad of fake diamonds.

I feel Inez moving beneath me. I look down. A veneer of sweat covers her body like the glaze on a Christmas ham. When she opens her eyes, her baby blues exude that shell-shocked, why-the-fuck-did-you-stop-now look.

"What's happening," she moans.

But I'm totally bent on wrecking havoc upon the cat, nailing its worthless pelt to the garage door with a titanium sashimi knife.

"Yaaaaahhh," escapes my lips as I leap after the witch's familiar.

Celia shoots under the dining room table, its paws spinning on the slick surface of Saltillo tiles, and disappears into the kitchen. Charging full-bore, I vault a dining chair hooking one corner of the chair back. The chair spins wildly away as I collide with the kitchen doorframe. Fooomph.

When I yank out the knife drawer, it comes completely out, falls, scattering razor sharp blades in all directions.

"Don't you dare hurt Celia," screams Inez behind me.

I grab a knife. A long pointed one with a serrated edge.

"Fucking cat tore up my ass," I yell. "Signed its own death warrant."

"If you touch a single hair, I'll kill you, Bill."

She doesn't really mean that, I think. Though Inez is hard to read. She picked me up two weeks ago in the vegetable department at Piggly Wiggly where I'm checking out the baby eggplants and radicchio for the grill. Right after we fuck that first time in the bed of my pickup, she tells me she's going to shoot her husband. She has a long list of grievances.

97

I've always been attracted to volatile women. I like the edgy feeling of never knowing where you stand.

"Don't get all bent out of shape," I yell back. "It's only a fuckin' pet."

Slowly I creep toward Celia, where it's backed into a corner by the trash compactor and the back door, its eyes rotating like spinning marbles. Maybe that's what I'll do: jam the thing into the trash compactor. Slowly squeeze it to death.

One hand wrapped in a dishtowel for protection from a swipe by Celia's claws, knife in the other, I'm ready to pounce.

In the stillness of that moment, the ratcheting sound of an automatic weapon being armed is unmistakable, coming from the living room.

Inez has flipped out.

Celia, judging that things are at an impasse and that it's now or never, charges directly toward me. Shoots between my legs and is gone, baby, gone.

Cautiously I approach the door leading back to the dining alcove. If Inez is armed and dangerous, I don't want to give her an excuse to open fire. The knife is still in my hand. But my hand rests non-threateningly against the side of my leg. I realize I'm buck-naked.

Inez is standing by the couch, as nude as Eve in the garden. A stainless steel pearl-handled Taurus 9mm pistol with gold accents rests nonchalantly in her grip. She looks at me. I look at her. She laughs. Then laughs some more, until tears wash down her cheeks.

"Hey, baby," she finally says. "Looks like you're putting on some weight."

I look down to where my stomach, like some old stud hog's gluttonous belly, overhangs my dick. I'm not particularly amused. But I give Inez a wan smile anyway.

"F-ing cat ripped my buttocks to shreds."

"Maybe you deserved it. You crazy cock."

Beyond Inez, Celia sits licking itself in the arched hallway leading to the bedrooms. When it looks at me, I swear the bitchin' cat has a grin on its face. Or maybe I've just been smoking too much hydro. I still want to eviscerate the critter, carve it up into cat jerky.

But everything is cool now with Inez, so I don't do anything except give the cat a death threat look when Inez glances away.

The loud click of the front door lock opening splinters the stillness of our DMZ. The door swings wide. Deep shadows haunt the entryway. A figure wrapped in chiaroscuro blunders forward.

An intruder!

Inez whirls, raises the pistol. I have a broadside view of her splendid ass. Then the 9mm barks. The noise is deafening.

The home invader crumbles forward onto the slate floor of the entry. One arm falls forward out of the shadows; a thick male hand curls inward like the legs of a dying spider. Becomes still.

"Jesus, Inez!" hisses from my lips in a susurrating whisper.

Inez approaches the body. Before I take a single step, I know it's Dave lying there, dead as a donut.

"It's Dave," she says. "He must of gotten back early."

She squats down, pokes at the body with the barrel of the pistol as though he were a jellyfish washed up on the beach.

"Dead," she says. "At least it was quick."

Suddenly my body's shaking with palsy, my legs are twin strands of overcooked spaghetti, my mouth is as dry as a sand trap at Pebble Beach. I can't believe this is happening!

If it's murder, am I an accessory? Is there a crime called not-quite-accidental homicide?

I imagine myself sitting at a poolside bar years from now recounting these insane moments to a bucktoothed blonde falling out of her bikini on the adjacent stool. It's like one of those loopy stories you stumble across in the crime docket section of the paper I'm telling her. She nods knowingly even though she never reads the newspaper.

Then I tumble back into the present.

Dave and Inez haven't moved an inch.

It was an accident I reassure myself as I retrieve my skivvies and scramble into them.

"We need to call the police," I say.

"I don't think so."

Stepping around the body, Inez closes the front door. Then she saunters back across the room and begins to dress.

"No, really," I say earnestly. "If we call the cops now, maybe they'll believe it was an accident. If we wait, who knows what they'll think."

"Forget it. Once the cops are involved, it can go anywhere. Only the lawyers make money on that."

"But Inez..."

"No, Bill. Listen up." She eases the magenta bra over her tumultuous breasts and reaches behind to secure those little hooks that are so hard to open. "Whether the cops call it murder or manslaughter or something else, irregardless, we're in the shitter."

I want to say: YOU'RE in the shitter. But I don't.

"Irregardless isn't a word," I say.

"Fuck you and the dictionary you rode in on." Her forehead creases like a Vermont dirt road in a poem by Robert Frost.

"I need a drink," Inez says.

I can't argue with that.

She strides into the kitchen where a half-empty bottle of Stoli stands like a Kremlin guard on the tile countertop.

Inez and I suck down a few pops waiting for the sun to disappear behind the pecan and magnolia trees in the old hedgerow behind her house. We sit face to face at the Formica table in Inez's retro kitchen, avoiding eye contact, fiddling with the ice in our respective glasses.

"I've always wanted to check out Mexico," Inez says, as she sips her second vodka tonic. The perfect summer drink.

"Mexico? But they speak Spanish there."

"I took Spanish in high school," Inez says. "And it's cheap to live."

"How would we get there?"

"Drive." Inez lights a cigarette. She always does after her second drink. I loathe cigarettes. A good reason to clear out, I think. As if Dave's corpse in the other room isn't reason enough.

"What about all this..." I say, sweeping my hand in an arc that includes white metal cabinets, the never-used wine cooler, the dishwasher and the trash compactor.

"Dave and I were in way over our heads," Inez says. "We got our first foreclosure notice two weeks ago. Same day I met you."

I think: Who's not surprised?

"Here's the plan," Inez says.

I can hardly wait.

"We clean out the bank accounts and Dave's wallet. Pack some clothes and a few good books in the Bronco. And off we go to olde Mexico." She stubs out her cigarette, refreshes her drink and strides into the unlit living room.

Suddenly it feels very lonely in the kitchen. I pick up my glass and follow her.

In the cave-like darkness Inez stands like a buxom cigar store Indian in the vague light coming through the big plate glass window. Out by the curb my truck has become a black silhouette against the streetlight a block away. The nearest house is three blocks away. The developer of Inez's cul-de-sac ran out of money or went to prison or swallowed a bottle full of sleeping pills and stepped off the deep end, so there's a lot of vacant land in the subdivision. All is still, like the night before Christmas.

"What about Dave?" I ask.

Inez's property includes an old shed from some bygone agrarian era when the land was actually used to grow stuff. The shed has a dirt floor. Dave ends up in a shallow grave inside the shed.

Afterwards Inez wants to fuck.

Personally I've had as much excitement as I can stand for one evening. I convey this to Inez.

Inez calls me a clandestine poof and flips me the bird. She was a communications major in junior college.

We sleep in separate bedrooms.

I don't get much sleep. Keep imagining the prison group showers.

At 7:00 a.m. Inez wakes me from a doze by beating on a cooking pot with a wooden spoon just outside the guest bedroom.

"Whatthefuck," I say.

"Coffee's ready. So move your ass, soldier!"

Inez's first husband was career Army before his fatal fall from the rim of the Grand Canyon while they were on their camping honeymoon.

In addition to coffee, there's toast slathered in butter and fried pork chops with grilled onions. Inez, nursing a cup of sugarless black coffee, sits across from me while I eat.

"While I'm at the bank, you need to sell your truck," she says. "Tell 'em your mother just died and you have to pay for the funeral."

I roll my eyes.

"But first you need to drive over to the Home Depot and buy a couple of bags of lime." She taps her cigarette ash onto the butter dish. "To keep Dave from stinking to high heaven."

"You sure you want to do this?" I ask. "We can still call the cops..."

"Bill. You need to do a reality check. Mexico is the only option."

Inez wears the pearl-handled 9mm jammed in the front of her miniskirt like a threat.

"OK," I say.

Before we leave the house Inez calls Dave's work and tells them he's come down with the flu.

On my way over to Larry's Used Autos to sell my truck, I have this urge to amscray out of town; leave Inez holding the proverbial bag. Maybe catch up with my brother in Ft. Lauderdale. I even hit the gas and bolt out Route 170 into the countryside. I pull over by a fallow field that reminds me of my worthless existence. Light shimmers off the quicksilver surface of a pool of standing water in the drainage ditch beside the road.

Next thing I see Inez in the aquatic mirror, tears in her eyes, the front of her blouse half undone. In a chocked-up voice she's telling a burley Broderick Crawford look-alike sheriff the lurid details of how I blew away poor Dave in a drug crazed rage, then forced her to perform an obscene sex act. When this vision dematerializes into the here and now, I realize that not only can't I take a powder. I can't let Inez out of my sight!

Later at Larry's they rip me off. Thirty-five hundred dollars is their best and final, though I've got less than a hundred thousand miles on her. It's a buyer's market when you have to sell in a hurry.

Meanwhile, Inez closes out the joint savings account she had with Dave. Eighteen hundred dollars. When she tries to do the same with the checking account, the teller balks, says she needs to speak to the manager. Inez tells her to forget about it.

When I first shovel lime on Dave, on Dave's face to be exact, he looks for a few moments like a dead Marcel Marceau. Then I cover the rest of him and he just looks like a cadaver covered in lime.

By a quarter to four we're ready to roll.

As I back the Bronco out of the driveway, Inez yells:

"Stop."

She jumps out of the SUV and scurries onto the little cement front porch where she pins a handwritten note to the door. I stand behind her reading it: Dave's fever is off the charts. Have taken him to his mother's.

"That should keep 'em guessing for a while," Inez says.

"Where does Dave's mother live?" I ask.

"Moved to Taos for the air. Had a stroke eight months ago. Can't speak. Hanging on by a thread."

"Ah."

I restart the Bronco.

We keep driving west until three a.m. Finally, somewhere on the Cumberland Plateau past Knoxville I tell Inez we need to stop or we'll end up as the blackened remains of a fiery crash.

She's as hyper as a born-again cicada but she agrees.

Pulling off into a rest area jammed with 18-wheelers, I take a much needed leak in the public facilities, then zonk out in the back seat of the Bronco. In front Inez chain-smokes and gazes at the stars through the sunroof.

When Inez shakes me awake, it's still dark.

"What the fuck time is it?"

"I'll drive," Inez says.

"Then why the fuck did you wake me up?"

At the next exit, Inez swerves off the Interstate. She looks over at me, but I don't say anything. Just raise one eyebrow.

"We needed to get off the Interstate," she says defensively. "THEY always look there first."

Inez is in meltdown.

"Relax," I say. "It'll be at least three days before someone finds Dave. Unless, of course, a hunter with a dog walks by the house."

Inez's month twists into a knot of strawberry saltwater taffy. She's not buying it.

"And while we're on the subject of second-guessing our getaway plans," I say, "we should have taken my truck, not the Bronco. When they find Dave, they'll be looking for the Bronco."

"We needed the money from your truck. This piece of shit's totally worthless."

"Oh, yeah, I forgot."

The day is coming on, sunny and hot. Did I mention that the Bronco's air-conditioning is broken?

Inez switches on the radio. Carly Simon belts out a plaintive tune of love betrayed. The landscape we're passing through is rugged and heavily wooded. Inez pushes the speedometer past 70 on a two-lane county road.

"Let me drive," I say.

"Everything's cool, man," Inez says.

" I know it is," I say. "But a cop's going to bite our collective ass if you keep driving this fast."

Inez squints, as if she's trying to read the small print of a legal opinion. Then I realize she's focused on the gas gage. Its little orange pointer points at EMPTY.

"Shit!" says Inez. "We need to get gas."

Miraculously a lone gas station appears around the next curve.

There's nothing else around. No houses, no trailers. Not even a body shop. At first I think the gas station's closed. But when Inez pulls up to the pumps, a lit green neon sign that says OPEN hangs in the window of the darkened office.

A hand-written note taped to the single set of pumps states: Paye afore ye pump. Are these words meant to be a joke? Or have we entered a time warp back to the 18th Century?

"Shit!" Inez said.

Inez swears a lot.

She jumps out of the Bronco, leaving her door wide open, and strides toward the office, a wad of bills in her hand. I walk over to the edge of the woods to take a piss. I wonder if I can buy a cup of coffee or a candy bar inside.

Just as I zip up, Inez bursts from the office and jogs toward me waving her arms. I make a dash for the Bronco and climb into the driver's seat. Inez jumps in the passenger side and slams the door.

"What happened!" I demand.

Inez is panting. Too many cigarettes. Finally she screams:

"The fucking attendant tried to rape me."

"And ..."

"I shot him."

"O, Jesucristo."

As we bolt from the parking area, leaving behind a spray of gravel and a settling dust cloud, a Dodge Viper going back toward Knoxville passes on the roadway. We shoot directly in front of him. He veers off the tarmac, horn blaring, brakes squealing. Through the rearview I watch him flail through a patch of high weeds and then swing back onto the blacktop.

"Was he dead?" I ask.

"I have no fucking idea. I didn't wait around to check." When she looks at me her eyes are little black currents of fear and loathing. "When I came in he was seated at a desk wearing some old work shirt. Looked like your normal hick. When he stood up he was naked from the waist down, with this huge nasty thing pointed at me. I dropped the money."

"You dropped the money?!"

She nods.

"And you pulled out the Taurus and shot him?!"

She nods again.

I slap my forehead. "Jesucristo."

"But I remembered to pick up the money. And took another eighty dollars from the cash drawer."

"So your prints are on both the drawer and the office door handle." Inez sits back and crosses her arms.

"And if the guy isn't dead, he can identify you in a lineup."

I'm driving at a normal speed. But inside my head I'm riding a typhoon. We, repeat we, are in ultra deep doo-doo. My stomach is in fast spin cycle. Acid burns my throat. I consider asking Inez for a cigarette. Or pushing her out the fucking car door.

When we come to a four corners, I turn left. A sign for the Blue & Gray Motel points in that direction. I have no idea where we are. Somewhere between Knoxville and Chattanooga. Maybe we should check into a motel. Hide the Bronco in the woods. Lay low for 24.

In the seat next to me Inez is hyperventilating, sucking in great gouts of air and blowing them out again. Suddenly she stands up on the seat, thrusting her head and upper body through the open sunroof.

"I can't breathe," she croaks from above.

Up ahead a low tree branch sticks part way into the road. I swerve the Bronco and hit the gas.

Ka-thwapp.

The rest of Inez's body flies out through the sunroof. She lands on a sandy embankment and rolls down to the edge of the road.

I pull up in front and watch her in the rearview. She lies completely still. A raven flies out of the woods and lands near Inez. He hops this way and that, eyeballing the body. When he jumps on her head and starts to peck at her nose, I open the driver's door and scramble out. The raven takes flight.

When I reach Inez, one side of her face is a wreck of torn and bloody flesh. Her eye is missing. I kneel down, feeling for a pulse.

The sound of a tire slowing on the gravel edge of the road causes me to glance over my shoulder.

Ten feet back a Crown Vic with a police flasher on top comes to a stop at the roadside. An archetypal law enforcement moron climbs out. The officer, dressed in quasi-military khakis and cowboy boots, thick leather belt and holster, shades, regards me with keen interest.

Inez isn't breathing.

Slowly I stand up, my empty hands held wide and open in what I hope is a non-threatening pose.

"Howdy, officer," I say. I nod my head at Inez's cadaver. "Woman here is in need of some serious medical attention."

An Orphan's Tale

1947

I murdered my mother. Hemorrhaged to death giving birth to yours truly. Three months later my father in a fit of the Devil's ennui drove to N.O. and got himself stabbed six times in a girly bar in the Vieux Carre. R.I.P.

Hence, I became an orphan. Name of Easter.

Up until age fifteen—my second year of high school—I resided at the Rankin County Home for Displaced Girls. That's in Rankin County, Mississippi. My best friend was named Geneva. This is what happened.

Every Monday, Wednesday, and Friday we left school early to attend choir practice with Mr. Nesbitt at the Circle of Fire Baptist Church. It didn't matter whether you could hold a note or not. Choir was a mandatory activity. In case you died and went to Heaven.

I could tell right away Mr. Nesbitt was a pervert. He had this way of twisting the hairs of his mustache when he got nervous. Which was whenever he looked at me.

My breasts had recently started to expand exponentially. My legs were smooth and muscular from running cross-country in middle school. I had adopted this sunburned waif look, with lots of freckles, dirty blond ragtag hair and flower print cotton dresses that left my legs mostly bare.

In fact, I was quite the little number.

On the break during our third rehearsal, Mr. Nesbitt called me into his office. He was drinking a bottle of grape Nehi. The room smelled of cigarettes and old dry rotted prayer books.

Mr. Nesbitt came around the desk to where I stood looking back though the door at my friend Geneva. He put his sweaty hands on my shoulders and turned me around, his eyes ogling my chest. I thought for a moment that he was going to touch my breasts, even though the door was wide open and Geneva was standing there, the perfect witness.

But he just stripped me down to my skin with those cottonmouth eyes of his. His creepy hands were still on my shoulders, so I turned my head and bit him as hard as I could, right where the thumb connects to the palm.

"Aaaahhhh!"

His wounded hand flew back to slap me, but I ducked and ran out of the room.

"Jeepers," Geneva said. "You really ticked Mr. Nesbitt off."

I didn't say anything, but I knew there'd be more trouble.

That evening at dinner—we all ate in a big high-ceilinged hall, kind of like nuns in the Middle Ages—I got into a fight with Loretta Lee, a girl two years older than me and a psychopath. She got a black eye. I got a tanning delivered by Miss Beech herself and sent to bed without dessert. Miss Beech, an old lesbo with a buzz cut, had been head mistress at Rankin House for eons. It was whispered she wore leather undergarments on the weekends.

I cried, but only after lights out. Miss Beech would get hers.

The next day, Saturday, right after breakfast cleaning day arrived in the dormitory rooms and vast hallways of Rankin. Orphans running up and down, helter-skelter with brooms, mops, and feather dusters. In the chaos, Geneva and I snuck down to the duck pond for a smoke.

I'd just taken a first deep drag on the dried-out Lucky I'd cadged a week ago from a traveling drummer, when there was a great rustling and commotion amid the swamp milkweed and honeysuckle that loomed over the water hyacinth choked pond. Next thing the weeds parted like the waters of the Red Sea and two men broke into the spider webby clearing where we were crouched down with our cigs.

Tall and slim and as bent over as a late-summer green bean, the first intruder was tucked in faded overalls and a pale green collarless shirt. A slug-white scar slashed across his forehead. Notwithstanding the September heat wave, the other intruder sported a black wool suit, white shirt and namby-pamby tie. Both had white handkerchiefs tied across their faces like comic book bandidos.

Despite this attempted disguise, I instantly recognized the shorter rounder marauder as Mr. Nesbitt. Who wasn't surprised?

I didn't know the other man. But his scared demonic visage reminded me of the villain played by Boris Karloff in The Body Snatcher, which I'd seen at the cinema in Jackson on a school trip.

"Jeez Louise! Run!" Geneva shouted, dropping her cigarette and bolting for the open lawn that undulated down in front of the three-story red brick edifice that was Rankin House.

"Wait for me!" I yelled.

But I was too slow. Mr. Nesbitt's accomplice wrapped me in his arms while Mr. Nesbitt covered my face with a washrag steeped in some sweetly nauseating chemical. Recollecting a tooth I'd had pulled the year before, even as my brain began to spin down the rabbit hole I realized the chemical smell was chloroform. Darkness met me halfway.

When I came to, I was surprised I wasn't stark naked. After all, isn't that the point of being abducted by a sex maniac?

Nope, I was still wearing my purple violet print dress, Sears Roebuck panties, and black sensible shoes with brown socks.

A rat poison headache pounded behind my eyes, so I closed them again. I was lying across the leather backseat of a Ford automobile. The smells of old leather and road dust danced in my nose. I felt the automobile cavort and pitch and yaw and shimmy over the rough roadway.

When I opened my eyes again, I found myself staring at the back of Mr. Nesbitt's bald head. Little tufts of hair clung like bats above each ear. The rest was a pinkish expanse of tightly pulled skin strewn with warts, birthmarks, moles, and dimples. Ugh.

I had to escape!

Leaping up I thrust my hands in front of Mr. Nesbitt's eyes, nails clawing into the surrounding skin. The auto lurched sideways as Mr. Nesbitt shook his head, trying in vain to dislodge my grasping, blinding fingers. In the next instant the automobile shot across the shoulder and pitched into the ditch, bouncing and bucking, oil pan scraping and sparking on the hardscrabble earth.

Desperate, Mr. Nesbitt swung his right arm backward like a cudgel, catching me in the side of the head and sending me tumbling, while his body thrust forward against the steering wheel, sounding the horn in a long plaintive howl. The automobile jerked to a sudden halt in a tangle of scrub pine, witch alder, and dwarf palmetto. Dust settled over everything.

Mr. Nesbitt's red face glared feverishly over the seatback at me where I lay wedged in the leg space between the backseat and the front seatback.

"You little dimwit. You almost got us killed."

"Better that than what you intend," I spat back.

"Shut your trap."

His hand smashed into my cheek. My eyes welled with tears. I lay motionless on the sticky rubber floor mats, listening to my heart. Suddenly I was afraid for my life.

Mr. Nesbitt got out of the automobile and walked around it, surveying the damage.

"Damn! The whitewalls are ruined. And look at the front bumper."

I leaned out the window.

"Your career's ruined, Mr. Nesbitt. You'll never teach choir again. Or Bible studies. In fact I bet they put you in prison and throw away the key."

He gave me another if-looks-could-kill look.

Next thing I knew he'd taken some rope out of the trunk and trussed me up like a turkey for Thanksgiving. At first I squirmed and kicked. I might have been naked for all the modesty this entailed. Finally Mr. Nesbitt threatened to smack me again if I didn't cooperate. At which point I gave up.

I ended up in the trunk. It was a rough ride for a while, flopping around like a bass in the bottom of a dinghy, arms and legs banging into the jack and other loose tools, retching at the astringent smell of heavy motor oil. It was hot as Hades in there. My lips soon grew dry and cracked.

When the ride smoothed out, I figured we'd entered the main road that ran from Meridian to Jackson and on to Shreveport, a place I'd never been to.

After awhile Mr. Nesbitt pulled the automobile onto the shoulder and stopped. Maybe he got nervous that I would suffocate or expire from the heat. The wheels scrunched on sand. The car door opened; then slammed shut. He must have been standing right next to the trunk when he spoke.

"You ready to get outa there?" he called.

"You gonna kill me now?"

"No. I'm not going to kill you. We need to come to an accommodation."

"Like what?"

"If you calm down and behave like a young lady, I'll let you sit in the passenger seat next to me."

"How do I know you won't do something nasty?"

"Like what?"

"Like expose yourself."

There was a long silence.

"You'll have to trust me, just like I'll have to trust you."

Thus we reached agreement on the terms of my de-incarceration.

Mr. Nesbitt opened the trunk and untied the rope holding my hands. I managed to climb out and, with my feet still fettered together, hobbled around and climbed into the passenger seat. When Mr. Nesbitt got in and started the engine, I pulled the hem of my dress down as far as I could. In his eyes I was as naked as a jaybird.

Ignoring his chameleon scrutiny, I flipped open the sun visor on the back of which was a vanity mirror and, using a spit-dampened Kleenex, began wiping off the oil and dirt from my face. Nothing could remove the black shadow of the bruise where Mr. Nesbitt had hit me.

I wondered if Geneva had sounded the alarm. Whether there was a posse out looking for Mr. Nesbitt and me.

When I looked over at Mr. Nesbitt, he was staring at my bare calves, as if I was some kind of Greek statue. Pervert par excellence. So was our French teacher. If you messed up your verb conjugations, an oak switch was applied to bare buttocks after class. But after all, this was the Deep South.

"Where are we going?" I asked.

"My brother has a hunting cabin in East Texas."

"Can we stop in Shreveport? I've always wanted to go to Shreveport."

"We don't have time."

"We could rent a hotel room right downtown, with Egyptian cotton sheets and a private bathroom with a claw-foot tub. Order room service, have sex for days."

Mr. Nesbitt's eyes did some somersaults and stuff.

"Isn't that the point of kidnapping me?" I asked. "To enjoy the fruits of your labors?"

"I think you should be quiet."

His eyes promised endless pain.

I decided to shut my trap.

One arm resting on my open window ledge, hair ruffled by the wind, I gazed at the boring piney woods and counted the mile markers. On the one hand, I just wanted him to get it over with. I was tired of being a virgin. On the other hand, I wondered if it would hurt. And what if I liked it? Would that mean I was a nymphomaniac?

The thing that worried me the most was Mr. Nesbitt. He had nothing to lose. Once he'd had his way with me, he might just kill me and head down Mexico way.

Mr. Nesbitt's eyes kept flitting like berserk cicadas between me and the road ahead. He spat out the window as if in disgust with the entire universe.

"You've ruined me," he said.

"Me? Ruined you? What about my life? Ravaged, then murdered and buried in a shallow roadside grave."

He didn't even hear what I was saying.

"I have a wife," he said. "Civic responsibilities. Then you come along, like Satan's candy cane and it all goes up in smoke."

"You could have controlled your urges," I said. "Besides, I could be your child."

"That's the horror of it. The horror!"

He commenced pounding his forehead against the steering wheel. The Ford veered into the opposing lane. Luckily there was no other traffic.

"Jeez, Mr. Nesbitt, don't have a crack-up."

"Don't you understand," he moaned. "I'm crazy about you. Forty-one years old and crazy about a fourteen-year old Jezebel."

"Fifteen," I retorted. "And I'm not wicked, just hardened by circumstance."

Mr. Nesbitt's hands strangled the steering wheel as if it might be my neck, so I went back to staring out the window at the passing scene, which was mostly pine trees and the occasional weathered clapboard house with a yellow dog sleeping in the dusty front yard.

A sign announced: Jackson 3. That's the state capital.

On the outskirts we passed a fried chicken joint. I was starving. So apparently was Mr. Nesbitt because at the last second he turned the Ford into the gravel parking area. The lot was empty except for us. A motorcycle leaned at a rear corner of the building. The cook's?

Before he got out of the car, Mr. Nesbitt retied my hands with the rope, then looped it through some part of the car under the dashboard, pulling my hands into my lap.

"Be good," he said.

He didn't show me the gun or knife or razor hidden in his pocket. Just his hands rubbing together like nervous gerbils.

I speculated that after our late lunch, it was likely Mr. Nesbitt would rent a cabin at some wayside motor court. Buy some local bourbon. Then the fun would begin.

Posse or no posse, I needed to vámonos sooner rather than later. I watched him disappear through the screen door of the chicken shack, which closed with a bang. He hadn't even asked me what I wanted to eat.

F— him!

Just then four high school seniors in a Tweety Bird yellow Buick coupe scrunched across the gravel and parked next to the Ford. The driver flapped an eye closed, then open. He was handsome in a football quarterback sort of way. Sandy hair, blue eyes, white teeth, square clean-shaven chin.

"Comin' or goin'?" he asked.

"I've been kidnapped," I said.

All four of them were looking at me now.

"Kidnapped," said the dark-jawed, tanned bully in the front passenger seat.

"Kidnapped; kidnapped," echoed the red-haired Irish twins in the back seat. Tweedledum and Tweedledee.

Just as the driver stepped out of the Buick, Mr. Nesbitt stuck his head out through the screen door and got me in his sights. A sparrow caught in the hypnotic gaze of a snake.

"Half dark, half light okay with you, Easter?"

The boys immediately shied away. I was running out of options.

"Go fuck yourself, Mr. Nesbitt," I said.

The good-looking driver turned and stared at me, then at Mr. Nesbitt, who was now completely outside the screened-in dining area of Schubert's Chicken 'n Catfish Shack and striding toward us.

It's hard for a short, roundish middle-aged man to look threatening, but Mr. Nesbitt looked threatening.

"Look," I said to the football star, "He's got me all tied up. I'm his sex slave."

He gaped at my rope-bound hands, his eyes bugging out.

Then Mr. Nesbitt was standing right next to him, his suit jacket spread open and the butt of a revolver visible tucked into his waistband.

"Something bothering you, kid?"

"Well ... just ... the woman ..."

He hitched his thumb in my direction.

"How come she's tied up?"

"Crazy as a loon. In transit to the Piney Woods Facility for the Criminally Insane," Mr. Nesbitt said.

One hand pushed his suit jacket wide and back to dramatically expose the revolver. "That's why I carry this."

"He's a liar," I said. "He's going to rape and torture me. We just stopped to get something to eat first."

115

Mr. Nesbitt's hand was around my throat.

"You'll have to excuse me," he said to the quarterback.

"Sir…"

Before he could utter another word, Mr. Nesbitt, using the pistol barrel, smashed the quarterback across the face once, twice, and once again before he sagged to the gravel, rivulets of blood painting his face. Or what was left of it.

One of the Irish boys started to cry. The bully backed toward the chicken shack. The screen door squealed open and the cook leaned through.

"What's goin' on here?" he asked.

"Is my order ready yet?" demanded Mr. Nesbitt.

"Hold up there…" The toothpick-mouthed cook riveted his eyes on the unmoving body lying in the gravel. "What's wrong with that boy?"

Mr. Nesbitt shook the revolver like a shaman's rattle. "We've got to get going. Bring me my chicken order!"

The screen door slammed behind the retreating cook. I figured he was going for a weapon, shotgun most likely. So did Mr. Nesbitt.

We shot out of that parking lot like a bat out of Hell, gears grinding, gravel flying. When we hit the highway we sailed directly in front of two cream-colored convertibles packed with armed deputies coming up fast. The posse. Better late than never.

A roar of emotion erupted from the lead convertible. They had recognized Mr. Nesbitt's automobile.

Gritting his teeth, Mr. Nesbitt floored the gas pedal. We sped forward. But the posse soon began to close the distance. Mr. Nesbitt's eyes danced a crazed jitterbug.

"Cut me loose," I said. "I'll drive. You shoot out their tires."

To my astonishment Mr. Nesbitt extracted a pocketknife from his jacket pocket, opened the blade with his teeth and cut the rope binding my wrists. In moments I was free. We changed places, the car swerving wildly.

Was I nuts? Had Mr. Nesbitt brainwashed me?

Not a Chinaman's chance.

So why did Mr. Nesbitt cut my bonds? Maybe because he was in a tizzy. Or on the verge of a nervous breakdown.

Regardless, even as he leaned out the passenger window and began shooting, I twisted the Ford onto a topsy-turvy dirt road that tumbled down to the bank of a wide sluggish river. The Pearl.

Mr. Nesbitt gripped the door handle and cursed a blue streak as we plummeted ass over elbow down the steep and rugged incline. At the bottom we hit a slight rise at the top of which we became airborne, landing twenty feet ahead with a tooth-shattering, bone-snapping jolt. Instantly the automobile bounded into a series of flips. Dust swirled. The driver's door flew open; my hands were torn from the wheel. I somersaulted from the churning wreck into a shallow backwater overgrown with alligator weed. Taking a quick inventory I found no broken bones or other major injuries.

A great roar deafened me, as the Ford automobile plowed into the trunk of a cottonwood and burst into flames. Above, at the edge of the highway, members of the posse milled about watching the blaze.

Bye-bye Mr. Nesbitt.

It suddenly occurred to me that there was no way I was returning to Rankin House. I was done with that part of my life. Simultaneously I sank deeper into the alligator weed infestation and moved stealthily toward the open river.

In no time I was riding south with the current, hidden by a pine log that chance floated by.

I had decided to seek my fortune in New Orleans.

Amazingly, I was still a virgin.

But not for long.

On the Lido

I take my morning walk as usual: down to the vaporetto docks, turn right along the promenade overlooking the dung-brown lagoon and the antique spires of Venice in the distance, then back up along a narrow, man-made canal used to anchor motorboats in the summer. The canal is undergoing major renovations at a snail's pace. Stacks of paving stones litter its banks. A few burly men in thick sweaters bend over and examine them, mumbling perhaps in Romanian or Turkish. Occasionally they take a stone and set it in place.

Exactly on schedule a berserk schnauzer appears on the balcony of a modernist house with gray shutters that overlooks the canal. When the schnauzer sees me, it starts to bark. The house is large and made of stucco with iron railings on its numerous balconies.

The man who built the house is surely dead. I imagine a slim, dark-browed army officer who successfully transitioned into black marketeering and intimidation after the Italian surrender in 1943.

I flip the schnauzer off. In a tsunami of rage, it barks until I turn the corner and head up past the old Jewish cemetery. The cemetery is haunted. I can feel it.

A fluttering of alien voices inside my head. All of them speaking in Hebrew.

I should know: I attended Hebrew school from the age of eight until I stopped believing in God.

Before moving to Venice I visited my doctor one last time. He told me I was still emotionally susceptible and handed me a script for a 90-day supply of 2 mg Lorazepam. The walking wounded from my divorce. I wonder what he'd say about the voices.

This morning I intend to pass quickly by the arched cemetery entrance without even looking in. But instead I walk up the gravel drive from the street and stand under the arch gazing at the gravestones and listening to the fog's tears drip sadly from the skeletal branches of the trees.

Six months ago this spit of sand, Venice's beach resort lapped by the Adriatic, teemed with bikini-clad nymphs, thugs, tourists, movie moguls, and middle-aged men in nylon Speedo briefs.

But now it's January on the Lido, a time of fogs and muggings.

That's why I always carry a .25 caliber semi-automatic thrust in the depths of my trench coat.

When my wife and I split up six months ago, she got the condo in Taos and the income stream from the screenplay. I got to keep my laptop, the paperback rights to the novel (maybe eight thou a year) and my wool-lined Burberry.

In the distance the caretaker busies himself around a freshly dug excavation awaiting its cadaver. In the foreground a female figure in a black wool coat and retro cloche-style felt hat fitted with exotic feathers stands before a weedy gravesite. In fact the entire gloomy cemetery is thick with brambles, vines, stunted palmettos, and the brown skeletons of last summer's weeds. When there isn't a corpse to handle, the caretaker spends his time sleeping in his chair pulled close to the gas heater.

When the woman visitor turns in my direction, for an instant I think she's an old bag of bones, stark naked under her open coat. Like photos of Auschwitz victims. Aghast, I look quickly away; two seconds later curiosity pulls me back.

In fact she's young, maybe twenty, and only almost naked. How did I make those mistakes? A pale pink cocktail dress stretches from nipples to upper thighs. Four-inch heels perfectly sculpt her legs.

My eyes follow the exposed flesh upward to a cleft chin affixed to a long, sad face. Who died? I wonder.

An affirmative nose and high cheekbones reminiscent of a Botticelli nymph dominate the midpoint of her face. Her eyes are unobservable; hooded by heavy lids, they trace back and forth across the gravel path looking for something. A thumb and forefinger tug at one earlobe. Black hair curls from beneath her hat like tendrils of smoke. Taken together these oddments coalesce into a face of astounding beauty.

For a moment I stop breathing.

An electrical current flutters around my cojones like the blue aura of a flying saucer. Testosterone pumps through my blood. My prick tightens. I must go to bed with this woman.

Then it occurs to me that I'm completely and utterly out of my fucking mind!

Start out slow. Offer to buy her a café correcto or a fine. Or lunch at Harry's Bar.

Before I can act on these thoughts the woman abandons her search and comes in my direction. Without the slightest acknowledgement, she walks past me down the modest slope and disappears through the open half of the ironwork gate. I can't speak. I'm a nervous wreck. Her eyes are green.

Asshole, I think. I take a final drag on my cigarette and grind it under the heel of my shoe. Then wracked by guilt about littering on hallowed ground, I lean down to retrieve the butt. Next to it lays a medallion-shaped gold earring. When I rub away the dirt, the profile of a Levantine naiad appears like a vision.

This is what she was looking for!

Helter-skelter I rush out of the graveyard bearing my find. The road in front of the cemetery stretches straight for some distance in either direction. But the woman has totally disappeared.

Panic ignites. I start to run back toward the canal. But that doesn't feel right, so I turn and jog in the other direction. A couple walking a Doberman appears at the next intersection. I stop, panting, blocking their progress.

"A woman..." I stutter. "A tall woman in a black coat."

To the couple I must appear crazed. I am crazed. I have to find this woman.

"We haven't seen anyone," the woman says defensively.

The man looks me in the eye.

"Calm down," he says.

He reaches out a hand toward my shoulder.

I don't want to calm down. And I still don't believe she went in the direction of the canal. She must have come this way. Are these two playing a game?

"I don't believe you! And don't touch me!"

The couple steps abruptly away from me, their eyes surveillance cameras watching my every move. The dog growls low and long. For a moment I consider shooting it on the spot, an anticipatory strike. Then I realize I'm out of control.

My face twists into a grimace of apology.

"Sorry to have bothered you," I say, holding out a hand, open palm facing the pair. "I was just released from a…a hospital. Just a little unused to interacting in the real world. But there's nothing to worry about. It gets better every day."

In fact, this is all true. I got so worked up during my divorce, when it was over I checked myself into a private loony bin for a three-month rest cure. Two days after my release, I maxed out my credit card and flew Business Class to Venice.

Before the couple can respond I skirt around them and continue jogging up the cross street toward the beach.

I decide a car must have been waiting for her outside the gate. Was her lover driving? Surely just a relative or friend. Crazy as it may sound, I'm the one who wants to be her lover.

Or maybe not so crazy. She has to be Jewish. Who else would visit a Jewish cemetery? Which means my mother would have approved. A small but important detail.

But why was she in the boneyard?

Maybe her lover died. Yes, I'm sure of it. That's whose grave she was visiting.

Two more blocks and I'm striding along the beachfront with its rows and rows of deserted cabanas like the coffins of summer stretching outward onto the flat fog-bound beach. Occasional cars zip past on the oceanfront avenue. Other than the couple I scared shitless, I meet no one. The woman from the cemetery has vanished into thin air.

I console myself with the thought that the Lido is a small place, especially in winter when most of the hotels and restaurants and shops are closed. Sooner or later I will find her.

Then I'm at the Piazzale Bucintoro intersection, beyond which towers the façade of the old Excelsior Hotel, its windows shuttered for the winter. From there I turn down the Gran Viale Santa Maria Elizabetta, heading back to my room and work.

But I can't get the face of the woman at the boneyard out of my head.

I'm writing a new screenplay, one that will make a lot of money. But today it's not going well. My laptop display shows a blank page.

A cup of tea laced with Teacher's doesn't help. I smoke another cigarette. I even try reading a novel. *The Dunwich Horror*. Next moment I'm pacing back and forth between my hot plate and the drafty windows of my rented lodgings. Ancient floorboards creak under my steps; dead flies litter the windowsill.

I can't stop thinking about the lady who vanished. Her haunting face materializes like a faded photograph in the cloud of blue cigarette smoke circumnavigating my room. She must have been freezing her ass off in that skimpy outfit with her coat hanging open, her nipples as hard as teak in the bone-chilling damp.

When I look down I have a hard-on.

I need some air.

I need to get laid.

Shrugging into my raincoat and leaving the gold earring on my bedside table, I stomp down to the vaporetto stop for San Marco. A crowd is waiting, including several attractive women. I try to catch an eye, even commenting on the arctic weather to one tart wearing a gypsy skirt and dangly bead earrings. But there are no takers. Their mothers warned them long ago to beware of gringos bearing gifts.

It's even colder out on the water, as we cross the channel from the Lido to Venice proper. But I stay on deck sucking down the salt-rimmed air.

When we arrive at the Piazza San Marco vaporetto stop, I stroll up the stone jetty to the Hotel Danieli. A grande olde dame, a former doges palace from the Renaissance, the Danieli looks across the jetty to the treacherous tides and currents of the Basino di San Marco, where the Grande Canal meets the unforgiving sea. Its unassuming dusty rose façade reminds me of a lithe older woman who answers her door wearing a terrycloth robe. Going inside is like watching her disrobe. The lobby is a vast golden whorehouse, its atrium soaring five-stories, ascended on two sides by a grand staircase. The pick-up lounge, supported by exquisitely carved columns and soundproofed by thick oriental carpets, is as vast as the Russian steppe.

Taking a Wall Street Journal from the pile at one end of the concierge desk, I sit down in the lobby lounge and order a beer. On my left two women sit close together talking earnestly in German. I wonder if they're planning the resurrection of the Third Reich. The younger, perhaps in her thirties, suddenly jumps up and runs from the lounge in tears. A domestic dispute.

Abandoning my newspaper, I pick up my glass of beer and walk over to the survivor, a woman at the end of her fifties stuffed into tight leather pants and a chocolate-brown blouse, her hair combed straight back like a man's. High cheekbones have kept her face from collapsing. But her mouth is as thin and careworn as a cheap motel room.

"Is this seat taken?" I ask.

She smiles up at me, her canine teeth glinting in the light of a chandelier, and motions noncommittally to the empty chair.

"May I be entirely honest?" I ask, leaning forward from the edge of the seat.

"If you must."

She speaks English with a heavy Berlin accent.

"You were the only person I saw when I entered the room."

"Maybe you should consult an ophthalmologist."

I take a sip of my beer.

"I like Venice in the winter," she says.

"Cold as a witch's tit out there," I say. Then: "Have you had lunch?"

"I'm afraid I've just eaten breakfast."

"Then an aperitif or a café correcto?"

"I'd like to get some air."

"Have you been to the Lido?"

Outside she lights a cigarette.

"Can you float me a loan?" I whisper, nibbling her neck. "A hundred and fifty euros."

Holding the cigarette between her lips, she rummages in her gaudy chain-draped designer bag the size of a small suitcase, hands me a wad of currency. I slip it into my money clip without counting it.

"You're American," she says.

"Does that make a difference?"

"Not so long as you profess your undying hatred of George Bush."

I clutch her arm and start down the quay toward Piazza San Marco.

"Not the vaporetto," she says. "Let's take a water taxi. So much more intimate."

Who am I to object? It's her nickel. Though I don't see what's so intimate about having the two-man speedboat crew gazing lustfully at her ass whenever it sways in their direction.

Her raccoon-collared bomber jacket goes well with her mannish haircut. Just before we board the water taxi I buy a paper cone of roasted chestnuts from a street vendor. We stand in the open cockpit of the motor launch scarfing them down and throwing the shells overboard.

"Why was your friend crying?" I ask.

"That's none of your business."

"Then make something up." I take a long swig from my flask before offering it to her, which she declines. "Or tell me your life story."

After a pause she says: "My father was an officer in the Waffen-SS. He was stationed in Venice among other places."

"That's weird." I gaze off across the turgid lagoon. "My dad worked for J. Edgar Hoover."

"He was thrown in prison when the Reich fell. They wanted to bring him to trial and execute him. But he had too many friends. After awhile all charges were dropped and he was released. Then he met my mother and here I am."

"The key to this game is attention to detail," I say. I pull a photograph from my wallet. It shows J. Edgar Hoover and another man standing on the steps of the Supreme Court. "That's my father," I say, pointing at the other man in the picture.

She laughs.

"I guess your old man did some bad shit during the war," I say.

But she's not in a confessional mood.

"I'll have that drink now, if you don't mind.

We don't talk for the rest of the crossing.

From the docks we walk up Gran Viale Santa Maria Elizabetta. The café lights are on. The fog seems to be rolling back in.

"Let's stop for a coffee first," I say.

"No," she says. "Let's buy a bottle and take it up to your room."

In no time we're naked, sitting cross-legged on my bed drinking shots of slivovitz and doing high fives. The steam radiator is actually giving off heat and I'm getting excited looking at her plush, slightly-gone-to-seed body.

"Look." She points. "Your thing is sticking up."

"My thing? You mean my cock."

Next moment she's sucking on it like it's the holy grail of lollipops.

It's the beginning of the end.

An hour later my German frau, sated, snores contentedly. I realize I don't even know her name. Nor does she know mine, unless she glanced at the unopened letters on my night table.

Curious, I open her handbag. Amid an assortment of feminine debris, I find a leather cardholder containing a MasterCard and a German personalausweis card. They bear the same name: Sabrina Bauer.

Her name has an alliterative crispness like an ice-cold melon with prosciutto. But it doesn't matter because soon she will be dead!

Jesus! Where did that thought come from?

For a flash moment I see her nude body, twisted by death, sprawled across my bed. A scarlet stain defaces the white linen sheets.

Then I'm thrown back amid the living, where I stagger backward, collapsing into the chair at my writing desk. Frau Bauer snorts and turns over onto her stomach. Her sex peaks provocatively beneath the crevasse of her buttocks.

But I'm no longer interested. The lust that drove me to the Danieli is back again but Sabrina Bauer's charms are not the solution.

My armpits pool with sweat. My head throbs. My ears ring with a siren's song.

It's the voice of the woman I witnessed at the cemetery. I'm sure of it, even though I've never heard her speak.

Pulling the blankets around Frau Bauer's bare shoulders, I grab my coat and the not quite empty bottle of slivovitz and slip out quiet as a mouse. By my watch it's only four o'clock when I leave my stuffy Victorian rooming house but the day has already sunk in deep despairing evening.

Feverishly I tramp up and down the Gran Viale Elizabetta searching for my graveyard naiad in the half dozen cafes still open.

Nada.

Then I decide to go back to the graveyard. Why? It's lunacy to think the woman I'm searching for would return there at this miserable hour. But I go anyway. On the way I stop at a pharmacy, with its glowing green cross, and buy a flashlight. The back street route I take is devoid of passing cars, of any human appearance.

When I slip through the narrow opening left in the wrought-iron cemetery gate, light streams from the windows of the caretaker's apartment. Giuseppe is smoking a cigar. An espresso pot steams on the stove. I knock on the door and enter, holding up the bottle of slivovitz.

Giuseppe's eyes light up.

"My friend, my friend. You are just in time for coffee."

He pours two cups. To each I add the last of the slivovitz in equal parts.

"Do you know the woman who was here early in the morning?" I ask.

"What woman?"

"The one in the long black coat."

Giuseppe still has a blank look on his face, though this is not an unusual condition.

"Come on! Don't be a jerk." I finish my coffee in two gulps. "She was standing looking at one of the gravestones on the middle path."

"No woman," says Giuseppe. He winks at me; taps his forehead. "You need woman?" he asks in English. Giuseppe is trying to improve his English. I wonder whether he's considering pimping his sister to me. A country girl, buxom, olive-skinned, and brainless.

"Of course there was a woman. She was wearing a black coat. Under the coat she was nearly naked. You should remember that."

Giuseppe shakes his head.

"No woman," he says obstinately.

Whatever. My nerves prick me to my feet. Giuseppe rises and grips me around the shoulders. As I leave he says:

"You drink less slivovitz." Then, as an afterthought: "Fuck more."

A stupid grin splits his face like a knife through a cantaloupe.

My flashlight piercing the pitch-blackness like a Cyclopean eye, I walk up into the cemetery and stop at the third headstone on the middle path. It's a cheap, unpolished stone with just a name and dates. Aliza Paolozzi 1924 – 1944

Was Aliza Paolozzi a relative of the woman I'm so desperately seeking? Based on the dates, was the deceased a victim of some Nazi atrocity? Or just an unfortunate death at a young age? Brought down by cholera, typhoid fever or some other malevolence.

There are no clues to even begin to answer these questions. But a new possibility rises in my head. My mystery woman and the deceased might share a last name. It's a long shot, but tomorrow I'll ask my landlady if she knows any families with the name Paolozzi.

Mist congeals like oil and drips down my collar as I slog back toward civilization. My feet are wet and turning blue. But my mind is revved-up.

I'm loco with desire. If it's the last thing I do, I must find this odd, beautiful, nameless woman and take her to bed. It's how Adam must have felt when he came upon Eve in the Garden.

Walking through the treacle-thick fog shrouding the Lido, I realize I've made a wrong turn somewhere. The Gran Viale Elizabetta with its beckoning cafes should be just up ahead. But it isn't. Only another empty street overarched by the blank looming facades of mausoleum-like houses. The only sound is the reverberating echo of my own footsteps.

Around a curve I find the Snack Bar Gogol. A long narrow room with a bar down one side. Dim lights. A guy polishing a glass, moving the stale panini and tramezzini around in the flyblown display case.

And there she is, my bone yard seductress who set my cojones on fire. She sits sideways in a booth toward the back, her bare legs thrust outward in perfection. The tabletop in front of her is empty. Of course she is alone.

When I enter the Snack Bar Gogol she stares at me with her unearthly seaweed green eyes. A black nausea twists my stomach. I've never been so frightened. I want to run for my life. Those eyes know the inside skinny on Hell. Have been there and back.

Then a gunmetal coin drops like a sluice gate and she's the world's finest hooker, an innocent's first love, and the girl from Ipanema, all rolled into one. The air reeks of her perfume. She's been waiting for me for a while.

"Two araks," I say to the bar guy.

I carry the drinks over to where she's now sitting up straight and ease down opposite her.

Her hand strokes the inside of my leg. I'm going crazy.

"Who are you?" I ask.

"I need you to help me," she says.

"Do you live on the Lido?" I ask.

She puts her finger on my lips.

"I don't have much time," she says.

The arak goes down like burning acetone.

"I want to make love to you," she says. "But first you must promise me. To do the one thing that I ask."

I hold up my right hand with two fingers crossed.

"My mother and father died at Auschwitz. I watched their prison train leave Venice. I should have been on that train. Instead I slept with the local SS Gruppenfuhrer. He treated me like a pet monkey. But I was alive. One day in a rage he pulled out his Lugar and shot me dead. After I had already given him my soul."

"That's a great story," I say. "My dad worked for J. Edgar Hoover."

When she stands up, she's wearing a glove-tight black dress. Against the fabric her skin is as white as bleached bone. Walking toward the cesso, she looks back, motions to me with one finger. When I follow her in, she locks the door of the pissoir and grabs for my cock. I assume the role of a roué in a French porn novel. There's barely room for two people, so my seductress rests her ass on the edge of the tin sink jammed in one corner. Her dress rucked above her waist, her legs point to the ceiling. I'm thrusting away like an Olympic swimmer in his final race.

Except it's not just me. Two mirrors, one behind the door, the other over the sink, project in either direction a hundred me's having it off with a hundred murdered Jewish women. No. There must be a thousand thrusting and roiling images stretching toward infinity.

But all the women have different faces and bodies!

It's as though I'm shtuping a chorus line of exotic, wildly enthusiastic shtetl maidens all at the same time. How does that work exactly?

After a while I have to slow down.

"What is it you want me to do?" I gasp.

Next thing I know I'm coming to on the piss-reeking floor of the cesso. At first everything is black & white. Then colors bleed in. The only trace of my seductress is her fading perfume. Staggering to my feet, I tuck away my frazzled dick.

Back in the bar, it's just me and the bar guy. My skin prickles, as if someone has beaten me with nettles. When I pay for the araks, my hands shake so badly I can barely count out the coins. I'm geared up. I can do this.

Outside I immediately go into a jog. Up down. Up down. Up down. Then I turn and head up the street. At the next corner I'm on the Gran Viale Elizabetta, back in familiar territory. I'm running flat out now. The few people out and about turn to look as I race by. My cigarette-destroyed lungs wheeze and gasp for air.

I bound up the steps of the boardinghouse where I live. The front door crashes open. I bowl past my landlady Signora Ricci, knocking her on her ass, and bolt up the stairs.

When I throw open the door to my room, Frau Bauer sits up in a fright, just as I rest the barrel of my .25 caliber pistol against her forehead and pull the trigger.

No one in here believes me. That I was intimate with a ghost. Of course, I produce no evidence to substantiate this claim. I don't tell the doctors about the gold earring that I hide under my tongue whenever any of them or the hospital attendants are in the vicinity. If I told them, they would confiscate it.

Yes, I tell them. I fucked a ghost. The ghost of a Jewish woman murdered in 1944 for no reason at all. Murdered by Waffen-SS Gruppenfuhrer Heinrich Bauer.

Shark Bite

The twelve-foot tiger shark moved effortlessly beneath the undulating, silvery surface of the sea. Having risen from the frigid depths, she felt pleasure from the warmth of the sun stroking her body. At the shallowest portion of her run, the sunlight drew her hulking shadow across blank patches of open sand.

After the long winter she was pregnant again. Which put her in an ill humor. She wanted to pick a fight with an air dweller; rip him to bits.

Hunger surged through her gut. She flicked her tail angrily, her fin breaking through the barrier between water and air in a white-edged cleaving, like a scar.

Through the rolling lens of the sea, the air dwellers walked at the edge of the beach, stood looking out to sea, splashed in the shallows. But none came further into the water then where the waves broke on the shallow sandbar, well away from the deep drop off where she circled.

The day before she had chanced upon an air dweller flailing pathetically across the sea's pulsing surface. Sweeping up from below, drawn inexorably by the air dweller's thrashing movements, she struck the swimmer. Her teeth chomped through muscle and bone. Amid a crescendo of desperately splashing limbs, she drew the air dweller under, leaving a wake of spreading blood and torn fragments of flesh.

The day after the swimmer ran out of luck, a shark hunter drove out from town in his cowboy-red F-150 pickup. He sported a waxed mustache, cold blue eyes, and a faded cap bearing a crescent moon and palmetto. Along the calf of his right leg a jagged slug-white scar marked a long ago encounter with a denizen of the deep. An inflated two-man Zodiac flopped in the truck bed.

Armed to the teeth, the shark hunter and his assistant pushed the Zodiac through the surf and scrambled aboard. The surfers, playing it safe, waved from their stools up at the snack bar, holding their long necks aloft in mock salute.

"Piss on them," the shark hunter said.

For hours they cruised the Zodiac back and forth, hither and yon, on both sides of the shark nets anchored 200 yards offshore. They ran Blue Runners and Jacks as bait, dumped sheep's blood in the water, drank a case of beer, cursed and swore a blue streak.

But no shark fin sliced the undulating gunmetal surface.

When the sunlight ebbed, they put into shore.

Sitting in the cab of the F-150, the shark hunter, his nose sunburned, his knees stiff from kneeling in the Zodiac, reached under the seat and found the bottle of hooch. "No fuckin' way am I comin' out here on Sunday," he said to his partner.

He took a long pull on the bottle.

Then started the engine and headed back toward town.

As he glanced in the rearview mirror, the lights at the snack bar flickered and went out. The engine roar of the last departing surfers rose and faded as they revved a deuce of decked-out Harleys and razzooed into the night. The pickup passed two campers lolling on canvas and aluminum deck chairs in front of their tent pitched by the roadside, working their way through a screw-top bottle of wine. The glow of a gas lantern set on the table between them kept the darkness at bay.

The waves glowed phosphorescent in the starlight.

After forty years of cruising the seven seas, the tiger shark was wise to the ways of air dwellers. When the roar of the Zodiac's engine reverberated in her head, she dove deep and swam silently, her mind awhirl with thoughts of the coming metamorphosis. After four hundred million years, it was time to fight back against the pillagers and despoilers of the seas in a new way. Every shark she met over the last circle of time as she swam through the oceans and seas, the bays and inlets and harbors, had repeated the same mantra. The transformation was coming. Soon it would be here. Soon.

As she swept through the deep, she felt strange forces tugging and remolding her essence, transmuting her very being into something else, something new and frightening and unbelievable.

When the light from above began to fade and the pulsing echo of the Zodiac's engine ceased, she rose from the stygian deep. As the million dots of milky ancient light appeared, glinting off the glassy cusp between water and air, she knew the time had come. The moment of evolution had arrived.

She felt herself grow lighter. Every second growing lighter and lighter. Up and up and up she came, faster and faster. At last exploding out of the sea, climbing into the air.

The wheels of the Sheriff's pearl-colored Escalade crunched on the sandy shoulder of the coast road, some fifty yards south of Earl's Snack 'n Beer. The Sheriff slammed the truck door and walked toward Deputy Smith. Bobbi E. Lee Smith, in a Clemson T-shirt, jeans, and a tan windbreaker, was seriously out of uniform. But after all, it was eight a.m. on Sunday morning.

"What the hell is this, Bobbi?"

"Some jogger called it in. It's bad. Real bad."

It was a fuckin' massacre is what it was.

Blood soaked into the shredded remains of a canvas tent. Aluminum tent poles twisted and snapped in two. Fragments of flesh clinging like odd ornaments to the glossy leaves of a rhododendron thicket.

"Reminds me a that movie Saw played over at the Starplex," Bobbi said.

The Sheriff's boot struck something that rolled away like a soccer ball. Except it wasn't a soccer ball. It was a human head! The Sheriff leaned over and gagged. Somehow he kept his breakfast down.

"Jeezus."

His hand rested on a heavy metal signpost sunk into the sand. The oblong sign at the top of its eight-foot height had been viciously twisted to one side as if struck by an immense force. A row of jagged punctures ran up the sign's center.

"Those bullets holes?" the Sheriff asked.

"That. Or teeth marks."

"Son of a bitch! You're not tryin' to tell me that mother-fuckin' shark has grown wings?"

"You might could say that."

In between the holes and sheered off paint the Sheriff could still make out the words on the sign. It read: NETS NOT SHARK PROOF.

Mexican Standoff

Mistah Kurtz—he dead.

Neiderbaum is the bane of my existence.

I pull aside the tent flap. Rain whips down in acid sheets, making the night as black as the inside of my stomach. The area around my tent is a quagmire of mud not unlike the winter trenches of the Great War.

Ten yards away, secure on a stone platform, Neiderbaum's tent glows like an alien spaceship. It's made of some new hi-tech translucent cloth. Backlit by a gas lantern, two silhouettes, one on top of the other, hump wildly, the old el dick-a-roo slamming away at la pussy with utter disregard for anything but its own pleasure.

I'll kill the bitch! is what comes to mind as I watch this shadow play. At the same time I've got a hard-on.

Correction. I'm going to kill Theodore Neiderbaum.

It all began six weeks ago in Cal Western State's Archaeology Department, the last day of the spring semester. I'm the junior lecturer. Neiderbaum is Vice-Chairman. I'm standing in the departmental office making small talk with the new typist Brenda, a buxom little thing with a cherry blossom complexion and myopic eyes. A chest-high counter divides the room in half. On one side sits Brenda and the departmental files. I'm on the other side leaning over the counter.

"You're sure you won't come for a drink?"

"Gee, Alex...I mean, Professor Silverman, my boyfriend would be pissed," says Brenda. "I don't want to get a black eye."

"If he threatens you, you can always sleep at my place. On the couch."

"He killed a man once in a bar fight."

"Frankly, I don't understand why you would take up with someone who's clearly a psychopath."

"Who can explain my trailer trash urges?" she says blithely.

At that moment Neiderbaum in garish tweeds walks by. His thick hairy fingers pluck the printout of my trip reservation from my hand resting on the countertop. His eyes scan the page. His tanned brow wrinkles like a plowed field.

"Where is it you're digging this summer?" he asks.

"Zetehux, down in the Puuc Hills. A four-hour drive south of Merida. The last two on dirt roads.

"A third tier site, isn't it?"

"We're the first team to dig there. We're hoping to find a bunch of shit the grave robbers missed."

Neiderbaum refolds the itinerary and slaps it back and forth across my nose. Brenda giggles. My face goes Tabasco red.

"Maybe I'll see you down there," he says.

Like Hell! I think.

The itinerary leaves his hand. I grab for it. But it swooshes away through the air, grazes the countertop, slips over the edge and nosedives into the crack between Brenda's desk and the half-wall supporting the counter.

"I'll print you another one," Brenda says, still laughing.

Neiderbaum is now walking away.

"See you later, Teddy," Brenda calls after him.

My team for the dig at Zetehux consists of three graduate students, Mary Beth, Chip, and Fawn, and four locals.

Mary Beth is pudgy and enthusiastic. Chip is thinking about dropping out of the program and applying to business school. Fawn is trouble.

Five-six-ish, jet black hair swept back from the an unsullied brow and tied with a rubber band, neon blue eyes set a tad too close together on opposite sides of a petite upturned nose, lush lips cast in a pout, small but assertive chin, and a raging pair of knockers designed by God himself. She favors tight T-shirts and baggy cargo pants. A space exists between her front ivories through which she periodically spits globs of tobacco juice with daunting accuracy.

The locals are the usual swarthy malnourished lot. Extras from *The Treasure of the Sierra Madre.*

We've been in Zetehux a month, and Mary Beth's legs and arms are covered in throbbing infected mosquito bites. She's running a fever.

I stand looking down at her flushed distorted face, wondering whether I should send her to the hospital back in Merida.

Fawn and Chip are over at the dig: a mound of stones that were once a towering Mayan edifice, lying broken and hidden for centuries under a camouflage of ravenous trees and vines.

Mary Beth looks like dog crap. Pale with a tinge of yellow. Dark lemur-like circles around her eyes. Lips parched and cracked. Slow shallow breathing.

I take a stained and greasy washrag from her forehead. Finding it bone dry, I soak it with water from a jug, fold it like a blindfold and lay it across her eyebrows. Her cheek twitches. Not quite dead yet.

I think: You really need to send her up to the hospital in Merida. Chip can drive her. Except Chip does a lot of the heavy digging, as well as managing the Mexican spade crew. He's fluent in Spanish. On the other hand, with him gone, Fawn will have no choice but to capitulate.

Because of Mary Beth's illness, Fawn and Chip share a tent. As far as I can tell they aren't fucking yet. But Fawn uses him as an excuse every time I suggest a walk in the jungle or some other nonsense. My tawny eyes follow her like albino bats. She is a goddess. At Cal Western State we have a by-law that prohibits faculty-student rutting. But this is Mexico.

My random thoughts are interrupted when one of the Mexican crew bursts into the tent. His pupils are dilated. He's nervous, jittery. Is he stoned on some hallucinogen?

"What is it, Miguel?" I ask.

"Come see," he says, "Muchos dioses antiguos!"

Miguel stinks. I hand him a cigarette and fire it up with my Marine Corp issue Zippo, before lighting my own. The Corp's emblem rises from the chrome plain of the lighter's surface like an anthill on the Serengeti. I bought the lighter in a pawnshop in Fresno. The acrid smoke of cheap Mexican cigarillos drowns Miguel's stench.

Ancient gods? What is he talking about? Is it possible they've made the astonishing career-making find I dream about? A chill scuttles up and down my spine like the little pink feet of a white mouse.

I glance down at Mary Beth one more time. What the fuck am I supposed to do? Then I motion to Miguel.

"Vayamo."

We exit the tent, cross the slash-and-burn clearing and start up the path that slices through the jungle. On the left is the latrine. It and Miguel smell about the same.

As a matter of personal hygiene, I can't go for more than two days without a shower. We rigged one up outdoors just to the right of our three tents. Fawn, sipping a mescal in the early twilight, often watches me soap down my tanned and seasoned physique, then rinse off. But when I come back from dressing in my tent, she's sitting on Chip's lap.

Around the next bend in the trail, a sudden tree-covered hill blocks out the sky. The Mayan temple we're excavating. At a propitious spot we've sunk a trench into the side of the ruin. So far the only results are a few worthless shards of pottery.

At the moment Chip and two more of the Mex crew, Juan A and Juan B, squat in a half circle at the mouth of the trench. As Miguel and I come up to them, I realize they're passing a jay. Chip hands me the reefer without looking up. I take a long pull, closing my eyes and letting the smoke slither deep into my lungs.

But pot doesn't really do it for me. Just a slight veering off track, a dazzle of light in the corner of my eye.

"What's going on? You're taking a lunch break already?"

"Go take a look," Chip says, nodding in the direction of the trench.

"Where's Fawn?"

"In there."

The overcast day steeps the trench in heavy shadow. Fifteen feet into the hillside it becomes a tunnel penetrating into the depths of the pyramid, a wormhole into a long-hidden undead past.

I grab the flashlight lying at Chip's feet and head in. I have to duck my head to enter the cave-like portion of the excavation. To prevent cave-ins, a veneer of rough boards covers the walls and ceiling of the tunnel. Ahead I detect a faint glow. Scrambling over a landslide of dirt and stone, suddenly I'm standing at the threshold of an oblong room two thousand years old!

Gripped by sudden vertigo, as though standing at the brink of a bell tower, I reach out and steady myself against the wall. The only light in the room comes from a white gas lantern set in the middle of the floor. Fawn stands next to it, furiously scribbling into her notebook. I am overcome by lust.

She turns and sees me.

"Alex! We fuckin' found it, Alex." She waves her hands in the air and twirls like a dervish into my arms. "Look at this place."

We're hugging. I nuzzle her neck. She throws her head back, laughing. I go for a breast. Nibbling the nipple through her T-shirt.

Suddenly, she breaks away; strides back to the center of the room.

"Not here!" she says. "It'd be like doing it in church."

"I'd like to do it in a church."

She ignores me, gazing around the ancient room. "So, Alex, what do you think the twisted fucks were like who painted this place?"

But I'm already staring at the mural-covered walls. Kings and queens and high priests, warriors and their prisoners, sacred animal totems, gods and goddesses. Many of the images are familiar from other sites. Except they're all engaged in wild fornication of one form or another. Each panel is a Mesoamerican version of a Paul Avril etching. The tongue of a squat toad creature laps a princess' nether regions. Choc, lord of storms, rains semen down upon a dozen maidens. The aged fertility god, Itzamnaj, toothless and gnarled as the bark of a cottonwood, spryly partakes of plump poontang. We've discovered the fucking Mayan Kama Sutra! The Pompeii of the Yucatan!

I'll be rich is the first thought out of the gate. Followed by and famous. The Fawns of this world will be lining up outside my door.

Three hours later my mind has had enough of Mayan porn. Too many whips & chains and beheadings. Snuff porn.

"We need to go back to camp and think about all this," I say. "Besides I could use a drink."

"Me too!"

"Whatever," says Chip, who gave the Mexican crew the afternoon off. "I think we should lock this place up."

"There isn't a door, dingbat," Fawn says.

"We should make one," Chip says. "I'm concerned about how the peasants in the nearby villages may react if they see this stuff. It's creepy."

"Relax, Chip," I say, "this discovery is going to make us millionaires."

"Take me to your mescal," Fawn says, pushing me toward the tunnel. I hope she'll grab my cojones from behind, but she doesn't.

Back at the camp, I take a quick check on Mary Beth. She's awake and smiles weakly up at me. Petrified that I'll catch whatever it is that's devouring her alive, I place my hand on her forehead. It's burning up.

"How do you feel?"

"Like dog shit."

"Interesting..."

"Oh, my God!"

Mary Beth leaps out of the cot, dives through the door, and makes a beeline for the latrine.

I turn and walk to our makeshift clubhouse, a rough-hewn table, and four aluminum and canvas camp chairs under a canvas fly. Chip hands me my first mescal of the day.

"Bad news," I say, tossing my thumb in the direction of el latrino, or whatever they call it down here. I drink the mescal in one gulp, wince at the burn, then continue: "Chip, you'll have to drive Mary Beth up to Merida. To the hospital. I'll give you a list of things to bring back."

Chip purses his lips and nods sagely.

"Lot's of bad news comin' down. I stopped by the kitchen to get a fresh bottle of hooch. Looks like the spade crew have given us the finger. Disappeared without a trace, as they say."

"You're kidding. Why would they do that?"

Chip shrugs.

"Fuck if I know." He taps the mescal bottle on the lip of my empty glass; then pours in a double, while I hold it steady. "Drink up," he says.

By five o'clock Chip and Mary Beth are in the Mitsubishi, ready to go. Mary Beth, in the passenger seat, has the shakes now. She's wrapped in an old hand-stitched quilt, her eyes shimmering pools of fever, her teeth chattering.

"I envy the fresh sheets you'll be sleeping in tonight," I say to Chip.

"I'm not sure who's getting the better deal out of this," Chip says, gazing at Fawn where she sits in the clubhouse.

"We'll see you in a couple of days," I say.

"You hope."

Even when Chip screeches his wheels, Fawn doesn't look up from the novel she's reading. Her hand automatically reaches out to her fourth mescal cocktail resting on the tabletop and draws it to her lips. As I long to be drawn.

A cloud of dust erupts as the Mitsubishi jolts and farts up the laterite streambed that pretends to be a road in these parts.

I sit down opposite Fawn. As I pour another drink, my eyes rake from her nose to her toes and back again. She squirms in her seat. But she knows she can't postpone the inevitable.

I flash into consciousness like a bat diving from its perch. The squeals and hee-haws of a four-wheel-drive vehicle thumping and sliding its way down the rough roadbed disrupt the undertow of the jungle. It can't be Chip, I think, unless I've been asleep for two days.

As I scoot from bed and slide into jeans and a T-shirt, I realize Fawn isn't next to me in my doublewide canvas cot. On the wood crate next to the bed sit two half-full glasses of Mexican rotgut, a torn foil condom wrapper, and the Chester Himes thriller I'm reading.

I poke my head through the mosquito netting, then the tent flap.

Coming down the hillside is a very expensive Mercedes all-terrain vehicle. And gripping the wildly lurching wheel is none other than Teddy Neiderbaum.

FUUUUUCK!

When he sees me, an array of white teeth glint from ear to ear. I know I'm about to be screwed twelve ways to Sunday. I should have listened to the alarms ringing in my subconscious, retrieved the .38 pistol from under my pillow and put the asswipe out of business. Instead, as Neiderbaum climbs out of the still rocking vehicle, I say: "What the hell are you doing here?"

We circle each other like strutting fighting cocks looking for an opening.

"I told you I might show up. My other plans for the summer went to Hell in a hand basket. Anyway, I haven't been on a dig in years. Need to get back in shape."

Suddenly the door of the latrine bangs open. Fawn walks toward us, looking fresh as a daisy.

"Professor Neiderbaum. What a surprise."

"Teddy. It's Teddy. Came down to give Alex a hand. Beneficiary of my years of experience. Brought a case of 10-year-old Canadian whiskey too. Box of Cohibas. Do you smoke cigars, Miss…?"

"Fawn."

"Miss Fawn?"

"Just Fawn." She spits a bullet of tobacco juice into the dirt half an inch in front of Neiderbaum's ostrich-skin cowboy boots.

Neiderbaum is a big man, a fact I never fully appreciated before. 6-3. Face like a bulldog on steroids. Barrel chest. Arms thick as smoked Virginia hams. Eyes seething with quicksilver emotions.

For the rest of the morning, he works like seven devils hauling wheelbarrows full of rock and gravel from the dry streambed to a slight rise opposite our campsite, constructing a stone platform on which he pitches his tent.

I'm sitting in my canvas chair drinking mescal sunrises and wondering what the hell Neiderbaum's really doing here.

I throw Fawn an ironic glance, but she remains distant and unresponsive as she goes about her camp chores. She looks sumptuous in short shorts and a fitted linen safari shirt.

After lunch we take Neiderbaum to the excavation. He is appropriately dazzled by our discovery, teetering like a drunk from painted panel to painted panel, gaping at the panoply of Mayan perversions revealed by the beam of his flashlight.

Then Neiderbaum makes his own discovery: in one corner a low narrow doorway obscured by a cave-in of stone and sand. Grabbing shovels we clear away the debris.

On the other side is a small airless room with rows of shallow niches running down two sides. Each niche contains its own special accoutrements. Ceremonial rattles, obsidian knives, incense burners, weed pipes, stone animal totems and fired-clay figurines, and a hundred and one other pieces of Mayan ceremonial tsatske. It's the storage closet of the high priests of Zetehux.

Unbelievably a giant phallus, five feet long, eighteen inches in girth, leans nonchalantly against the room's back wall. Its details are spare, the work of some avant-garde minimalist who lived a thousand years ago. Yet it's unmistakably a dick, painted a lurid red color.

Close up it turns out to be carved out of wood, with a hollow interior. Easy to move. At Neiderbaum's insistence he and I lug it into the main room. Fawn goes into hysterics, slapping her knees, falling to the floor where she rolls from side to side gasping for breath. Finally she recovers from her giggle fit, only to catch sight of the twelve-inch marble dildo Neiderbaum found in the storeroom and thrust into the pocket of his cargo shorts.

"Is that a banana in your pocket?" Fawn asks, breaking into fresh howls of laughter.

We carry the big wooden dick out into the open air. Dark rain-heavy clouds torment the heavens. Neiderbaum's pupils have shrunk to shimmering black currents behind which madness dances. His lips are caked with dried spittle. When he thinks I'm not looking, he mutters gibberish to himself. Is he on drugs? Suffering from sunstroke? Going insane? But he is Vice Chair of the Department, so I don't make a fuss.

"What are we doing with this?" I ask, indicating the gargantuan prick.

"Taking it over by my tent, so I can examine it later."

I flip my head skyward toward roiling thunderheads.

"Better put it under the clubhouse fly. You don't want the paint to wash off when it rains."

We end up putting it in Neiderbaum's tent.

Exhausted by all this activity, I collapse to the ground. My shirt is completely sweated through. Fresh blisters on each hand throb and ooze. My head is pounding from the pressure of the incoming tropical depression.

Neiderbaum pours Crown Royal into a pair of glasses. But I can't drink it. Next moment I'm on my knees retching bile into the dirt. I hope I'm not coming down with the same bug ravaging Mary Beth's interiors.

"I need to lie down," I say. "Take a nap."

"Up all night tomcatting?" asks Neiderbaum.

I don't bother to reply. Neiderbaum heads back to the excavation. I take four aspirin and a sleeping tablet and sack out.

The waterfall of Fawn's laughter draws me awake. She and Neiderbaum are having drinks in the clubhouse. Her safari blouse is nonchalantly disheveled. One of her legs rests sideways across the arm of her camp chair. Neiderbaum's fingers trip the light fantastic across the bare stage of her thigh.

Rage and jealousy savage my brain like ravenous wild dogs gnawing a corpse. Have they been getting it on down at the excavation? How could Fawn betray me like this? I'll castrate Neiderbaum and mail his balls to the Smithsonian!

Tamping down my chaotic emotions, I stroll nonchalantly over to the clubhouse.

"Anyone for dinner?" I ask.

A month-old sports section from the Caribbean edition of the Miami Herald and an open can of peanuts form two-thirds of an odd tableau on the tabletop. My Marine Corp ashtray, in which two fat Cohibas smolder like burning turds, constitutes the final element of this inanimate melodrama.

"There's some baked beans sitting in a saucepan on my Coleman stove," Neiderbaum says. "Add a can of cocktail franks, reheat and you're golden."

"Golden?"

"Oh, please," Fawn says. "Don't start."

I jerk her to her feet; pull her against me.

"What about last night? Doesn't that mean anything?"

"Get a life, Alex."

Neiderbaum leaps up and with a baroque flourish presses the barrel of a pistol to my head. My brain spins like flushed water in a toilet bowl. The situation is completely and irrevocably out of control!

"About those beans and franks," Neiderbaum says.

I release Fawn. She picks up the limp sports section of the Miami Herald and slaps it back and forth across my face. Then she turns and walks toward Neiderbaum's tent. Jumbo drops of rain plummet from the sky. Moments later it becomes a raging downpour.

"Night," Teddy says. His testosterone bulk, an evil troll from a Grimm's fairy tale, splashes across the clearing.

I'm left with the peanuts and a half empty bottle of Crown Royal. I feel an inescapable need to kill someone.

Watching them fuck behind the veil of the tent wall is both a turn-on and a hugely deflating bummer. I remain transfixed until Fawn screams for the third time and kicks over the white gas lantern. With a tinkle of broken glass, Neiderbaum's tent turns pitch black.

The pouring rain of the storm despoils the night. My forehead throbs with fever, sweat dripping like 3-in-1 oil down my neck and chest. It feels as if someone's red-hot fingertips are searing into my shoulders.

I need to go back to sleep. Knit up the raveled sleeve of care. There'll be plenty of time to shoot Neiderbaum in the morning.

The sound of drums roots around in my head like a pig searching for truffles and at last nudges me awake.

Drums?! You must be shitting me. It's the fever.

But it is indeed drums. Two to be exact, calling and answering each other in deep somnambulistic tones.

When I poke my head outside the tent, the sun is burning the edges of some feathery clouds, the remnants of last night's storm. The effect is like grilled cheese sandwiches sliced open with a filleting knife. The beat of the drums intensifies.

A crowd of straw-hatted and shawled peasants stands in front of Neiderbaum's tent on its raised platform of stone and gravel. The crowd sways left and right to the rhythm of the drums. Among the gathered flock I see at least two men from our excavation crew.

As the light thickens, the wooden cock becomes apparent, rising like a giant's middle finger in front of Neiderbaum's tent.

In the next instant, Neiderbaum, entirely nude, steps from the tent just as the sun breaks like a burning wave over the jungle canopy and sweeps across the shadowy slash and burn clearing where we're camped. Neiderbaum's tanned flesh turns to burnished gold. Half his face is painted a sickly green color, the other half bleached flour white. His eyes burn as brightly as blood diamonds caught in the white-hot glare of an arc lamp.

A leather harness encircles Neiderbaum's buttocks like a spider its prey. This contraption holds in full erectile display the marble dildo that had sent Fawn into hysterics the day before.

My mind reels. What is going on here? It's as if I've stumbled onto the set for a Tarzan remake directed by Larry Flint.

Then Fawn appears, draped in a blood-orange robe that glints in the sunlight. A pair of loin-clothed acolytes draw her toward a wooden bench in front of Neiderbaum. She stumbles, sways, rolls her eyes. She must be drugged to the gills.

Her robe falls away. Stark naked she is guided to the bench, where she sits, then rolls onto her back. A patchwork of black and red Mayan glyphs have been painted on her body, defiling the perfection of her flesh.

Neiderbaum and the whole bunch of them are totally bonkers! Seduced by a dark spell emanating from the room beneath the ruined pyramid. Caught in some Mayan black juju. And Fawn is their sacrificial victim.

No fuckin' way, pal!

I wave my .38 revolver in the air.

"Stop!" I shout.

The drums cease. All eyes turn toward me.

"Alex," Neiderbaum says. "What a surprise."

"Let her go."

I walk through the crowd, which separates in front of me like flesh beneath a surgeon's blade, and step up onto the stone and gravel platform. I look out upon the faces of the surly peasants.

"The show's over," I say. "Everybody go home."

Neiderbaum pushes me sideways. We stand facing each other.

"You don't understand," he says. "What you've discovered here at Zetehux is the doorway to a new world order in which there are no limits, no boundaries."

I'm holding the revolver; Neiderbaum grips an obsidian sacrificial knife. Our eyes are locked in cold fury, but neither of us is prepared to make the fateful first move.

With a Herculean effort of will, I break out of the Mexican standoff. Die, asshole!

My finger curls around the trigger and pulls it back. But the firing pin clicks on an empty chamber. I've forgotten to load the fucking weapon.

Neiderbaum lunges with the knife.

We struggle, teetering wildly back and forth, a ganglia of intertwined arms and legs. Somehow my hand encircles the marble dildo. Its harness gives way and the phallus comes free. Even as his teeth sink into the muscle of my shoulder, I bring the striated stone schlong crashing down again and again on Neiderbaum's skull. Bone and brains transmogrify into pulp. Neiderbaum's teeth release their grip. He groans; crumples to the ground. Rivulets of blood cover my hand and forearm.

A cry of dismay rises from the crowd of peasants. Then a great stillness descends, as though a Victorian bell jar has been lowered over the clearing.

But the sharp scent of danger snakes up my nose like ammonia arising from a broken ampule. This is no time to take a break and consider the existential dilemma of my sorry-assed existence.

Fawn stands; stumbles toward me, hands outstretched like a sleepwalker. For a moment I think I see Mary Beth and Chip among the crowd of peasants. Then I realize it's their heads impaled on wooden spikes, bobbing up and down as the crowd equivocates. Am I hallucinating?

A swarm of peasants bent on revenge rush toward the dais, their faces distorted by rage.

"Don't leave me behind," Fawn begs.

For a moment I think: Sorry, baby. You should have thought twice before you betrayed me for Neiderbaum. You're on your own. Then I have a change of heart.

Scooping Fawn up in my arms, I turn and sprint toward Neiderbaum's Mercedes parked a dozen feet away behind his tent. She's as light as a Styrofoam casket. Just as I reach the vehicle, the forefront of the crowd pours like a flood over the stone platform.

As I clamber into the driver's seat, a stone strikes me behind the ear. My fingers touch the wound, feel the warm rush of blood. A larger stone slams into the back window; a web of cracks spreading from its epicenter. Fawn curls in a ball on the passenger side.

When I yank down the sun visor, Neiderbaum's keys tumble into my hand. The gods are with us!

The engine turns over on the first try. I blast out of there with a spray of gravel and mud. The air-conditioning flips on automatically, chilling me to the bone.

Five miles down the road I arrive at a four corners. A hand-painted sign in front of a tumbledown shack offers beer and tacos al carbon. On the front veranda a woman lolls in a hammock nursing a baby.

An ancient and dilapidated autobus is stopped in front of the taqueria while the driver is off in the bush taking a piss or a snort of coke. Two boys offer an iguana for sale to the passengers. They walk back and forth beside the bus, holding their prize aloft to the array of open or missing windows. A desperate Indian woman dressed in black hawks slices of pineapple and mango dusted with chili powder to the bus travelers. Armed with a machine gun, a soldier guarding the crossroads gazes at the passing scene with a worried expression.

Sitting in the stationary SUV taking all this in, I realize my hands are shaking uncontrollably, overcome by palsy. Swirls and droplets of dried blood cover them. Neiderbaum is dead. Mary Beth and Chip too. All dead. The beat of the drums pounds relentlessly in my head like the undecipherable thoughts of an idiot savant. But I know one thing for sure. One thing.

There is no going back.

Fawn uncurls her sinuous and luxuriant form. She finds an old shirt in the back seat and puts it on. Her eyes are glassy; her lips as dry and dust-covered as used sandpaper. But she's still a fucking goddess!

"What happened back there, Alex?" she whispers. "What are we going to do?"

I run down my side window. The sudden intake of warm moist air fogs the windshield. I motion to the two boys holding the prehistoric iguana.

"Que direccion es Guatemala?"

One of the youths points.

Even as I toss out an assortment of peso coins, I steer the Mercedes down the rutted byway designated by the iguana seller.

We're heading south into uncharted territory.

In seconds, the fecund wall of the jungle closes in on either side, shutting out the sky.

Samurai Avenger

I am the samurai avenger.

By day I work as a performance cook in a Japanese steakhouse.

I'm on my break in the back by the service entrance when I see two men robbing a woman in the parking lot. I recognize her. For the last hour she sat alone at my grill top and polished off a shrimp and chicken combo special, two dry martinis, and an Asahi Black. She is one of those half-pretty women who always seem slightly out of focus. Her fitted gray pinstripe suit makes her look corporate and malnourished.

Back in the parking lot one of the thugs holds a high-tech Beretta against her forehead. She's on her knees, giving him a blowjob. When he comes he almost pulls the trigger.

The second felon rummages through her Balenciaga handbag, finds a fat wad of cash. The bag and its other contents decorate the pavement. Next he yanks the woman to her feet, throws her over the fender of the dark blue Impala parked behind her and fucks her like a porn star.

She falls to the gravel-covered tarmac. The two sociopaths bound into the Impala, back over the woman twice, then blast out of there, spraying a comet's tail of gravel in their haste. At the last moment one of the men leaps out of the passenger side and fires a bullet into her head.

My cigarette gripped between my vengeful lips, cigarette smoke burning my eyes, I write the license plate number of the Impala on the palm of my left hand. Then I go back to work.

My shift ends at 11 p.m.

By then my friends on the Internet have given me the name and address of the Impala's owner. I shed my work clothes and don the leather samurai outfit I keep in the trunk of my car. My razor-edged sword leans across the passenger seat within easy grasp. Before I start the car I chomp down a couple of breath mints because you never know whom you may run into. An old girlfriend. The girl of your dreams.

When I get to the address, it's a vacant lot.

Maybe I wrote the license plate number down wrong because of the smoke in my eyes. Maybe my friends on the Internet fucked up. Maybe. Maybe. Maybe.

Life is full of excuses.

I drive around for a while, but nothing turns up. A couple of loners out walking their dogs. Everyone else is hunkered down behind locked doors and drawn shades, masturbating on the living room couch, tripping on shrooms, passed out in a pool of vomit perchance to dream.

Passing a cluster of strip clubs, I consider going in and looking for the two killers. These are the kinds of places where guys like that normally hang out killing time. But the management will look askance at my samurai outfit. And they'll never let me in carrying my sword.

A dull orange light seeps over the eastern hills. It's getting late.

Flummoxed, pissed off, aced out, I head back to my neighborhood. The neon beer signs in the windows of Randy's Tap are turned off. Not even a tomcat is strutting the streets.

I park in my usual slot next to the dumpster. Stash my samurai suit in the trunk. In my apartment I brush my teeth, urinate and hit the sack. Tomorrow is a workday.

But I am the samurai avenger. Justice will be done.

Blue Fin

Johnny Ito came awake like an insect. One moment suspended in total stasis, drifting on a current of time, the next wired into the universe, every sense, eyes, ears, nostrils, dry turgid tongue, jittery fingertips, searching the blankness of the night for danger. The soft sibilant noises of the building's infrastructure tickled the hairs in his ears. Then the far-off thupping sound of a traffic helicopter taking the pulse of the predawn Monday wove a pattern of mundanity.

Another Tokyo day had begun.

Effortlessly, Johnny sprang spider-like from the bed and padded across the tatami mat to the bathroom. His fingers found the wall-embedded rheostat switch and flicked on the bathroom's recessed overhead lights. A raw metallic light suffused the room, glinting off the pearl-white surfaces of molded plastic that formed walls, floor, and ceiling of the modular living space.

As he splashed tepid water on his face, the rustle of Egyptian cotton sheets and a tiny moan of pleasure or dismay came from the bedroom, announcing Momoko's return from fairyland. Grabbing a towel, Johnny leaned in the doorway wiping his face and observing Momoko's dreamlike beauty, as pale and unblemished as a perfect moonflower. Her narrow high-cheeked face wrapped in a punkish bramble patch of raven-black hair rested amid a tumble of oversized pillows. A long supple neck descended to angular shoulders. The ragged line of the bedsheet dissected her body at waist height, leaving her torso bare. Her small conical breasts confronted him like twin interstellar ray guns.

One almond-shaped eye opened and fixated on him.

"Don't you ever sleep?" Momoko asked.

"Time waits for no man," Johnny said with a harsh snicker.

"Come back to bed and fuck me to oblivion," she pleaded.

"You're making it awfully hard for me to go to work."

Johnny smiled but remained resolute, dressing quickly in jeans, Converse All Star lo-tops, a Ting Tings T-shirt, and black pigskin leather jacket. The sleek German coffee machine on the kitchen counter spat out a double espresso thick enough to stand on its own two feet. Johnny downed it in two sips. The caffeine hit his blood like a typhoon. Seconds later he stepped into the elevator and plummeted the thirty-seven floors to street level.

At 4:00 a.m., darkness still draped the high-rise core of Tokyo's Shinjuku neighborhood. A half hour away, the summer dawn waited in the wings. The air was thick with humidity and cancerous particulates.

The chrome-encrusted navy blue Cadillac Eldorado Baritz convertible circa 1959 that Johnny had rescued from an El Paso, Texas, used car lot hummed at the curb. The white canvas top was new; the blue and cream leather seats still the original. When he saw it parked like this, the word shark always came into Johnny's head. Or Batman.

Swarthy complexioned Tio Tepo, also from El Paso, hunched behind the wheel, his rough-hewn hands calmly in control of the supercharged V-8 engine. He had been Johnny Ito's driver for the last three years, ever since Johnny returned from an around-the-world tour and opened the Silverado Country-Western Sushi Bar on the trendiest street in Roppongi. It was a lot safer way to make a living than running dope from Ciudad Juarez.

Across the street a group of citizens moved in slow motion accord, hypnotically acting out an inscrutable array of tai chi movements designed to reduce the stress and high blood pressure of life in a megalopolis of 35 million highly competitive gooks.

Johnny eased into the passenger seat. He and Tio Tepo exchanged a resounding high five.

"Let's go get us a big fat bluefin," Johnny said.

"You got it, amigo."

Tio Tepo stomped the gas pedal, and the Eldorado leaped away from the curb like an enraged water buffalo in high lust. They sped through the almost empty predawn streets, dazzled by a silent display of flashing, spiraling, and skittering neon signs.

As the Caddy squealed around a corner, Johnny retrieved his iPhone from the front pocket of his jeans and dialed Otani-san.

"Mushi-mushi," came Mr. Otani's oily voice.

"What have you got for me?" Johnny asked.

"Times are very bleak," Mr. Otani lamented. "Not like the old days. The giant bluefins are disappearing. Eating whale is considered barbaric."

"Don't give me a history lesson," Johnny said. "Jack Nicholson's throwing a private party at my place. I need the finest tuna money can buy."

"There is only one fresh tuna worth buying today," Mr. Otani said. "But the price is too high; over a hundred thousand dollars."

"Buy it."

Johnny deep-sixed the call to his wholesaler and, leaning back in the cream-colored leather seats and closing his eyes, watched a rerun of Momoko lying in bed masturbating while he dressed.

In minutes the Eldorado entered an underground garage on the edge of the vast Tsukiji Fish Market. Mr. Otani waited for them at a small coffee bar just outside the main auction hall. The smell of the sea and its denizens pervaded everything, wood, cement, tile, clothing, skin, like a thick oil.

They exchanged obligatory bows. Tiny porcelain cups of steaming coffee and shots of Yamazaki single malt whiskey sat on the oak bar. Johnny picked up one of the shot glasses; sniffed; then drank its contents in one gulp.

"That'll knock your socks off," he said. Johnny was a cognoscente when it came to American hardboiled slang. "So what's the deal?"

"Razu Takizawa wants the prize bluefin."

"That yakuza asshole?"

"The same."

"But you bought it, right?"

"Yes. Legally, the tuna belongs to you. But..."

"Then fuck him!" Johnny inhaled another whiskey; then spun around and gripped Mr. Otani around the shoulders, drawing him close. He could feel Mr. Otani cringe under this personal contact. "Okay, pal. Show me this fish that's costing me a fucking fortune."

Crossing an alley they entered the auction hall. The reek of decomposing fish grew instantly stronger. In the vaulted warehouse space, rows of frozen tuna carcasses displayed on wooden pallets competed for the attention of restaurant owners, wholesalers, and the digital cameras of meandering tourists. Fish market workers in overalls and knee-high rubber boots, cigarettes hanging from their lips, watched the passing scene with hostile eyes. The dissonant clanging of a handheld bell announced the beginning of the new auction.

Mr. Otani led the way into a quieter room where the corpse of the exquisite giant bluefin lay in a coffin-shaped wooden crate. Even in the spare industrial light the fish's silver-blue skin shimmered and coruscated, calling to mind some wondrous mechanical creature that had crossed over from a realm beyond human imagination. Its mouth gaped in a silent scream of protest for its ignominious fate. A single white sightless eye stared at Johnny with all the animosity of things of the deep for those who live on dry land.

As Johnny Ito gazed at the once grand creature, a tear crept into the corner of his eye. He brushed it away.

At that moment a short, powerfully built man in black trousers and T-shirt emerged from the shadows. His arms were covered in garish tattoos depicting the highlights of his yakuza career: kidnappings, extortion, gangbangs, murders, beheadings.

Behind him stepped two longshoremen thugs. One, in a bloodstained sweatshirt bearing the words University of Tokyo, held by his side an evil-looking steel hook used for lugging fish carcasses hither and yon. The other maggot, his head as bald as a beach swept by a tsunami, rhythmically slapped a wooden bat against the calloused palm of his other hand.

"It's been a while, Johnny," said the man in black, his eyes glinting like two rough-cut rubies lit from within. "I heard you were back in Tokyo."

"Razu. How the fuck've you been?"

For a moment their eyes meshed, wrestling for position.

"I'll pay you seventy-five thousand for the fish."

"Your offer's way below fair market price."

"Fair market price is in the eye of the beholder. Besides I'm letting you live."

"But I'm not selling."

In the same instant, Johnny's Converse clad foot slammed into the crotch of the hook-wielding sleazeball. The gangbanger's brain short-circuited from the sudden intense pain, his eyes rolled up, and he collapsed to the floor, moaning.

Tio Tepo rested the barrel of his nickel-finished Colt Python against the cheekbone of the other head-butter, who froze instantly. The only sounds were the ratcheting noise of the Python's firing hammer being drawn back and the clatter of the wooden bat hitting the floor.

Johnny blinked.

"Sorry, pal. But I need this fish to make a very important client happy."

"It's my mother's birthday," Razu said. "She'll be very disappointed."

"She'll get over it."

Razu spread his hands in a gesture of equanimity.

"I'll see you later, Johnny."

He turned his back and walked away.

"Not if I see you first," Johnny called after him. Then twisted around to find Mr. Otani, who had been trying vainly to fade into oblivion. "Get some guys to put the tuna in the back seat of my Caddy," Johnny said to him. "I'll take it to the restaurant myself."

As it turned out, the bluefin was too big to fit crosswise on the back seat of the Eldorado. Instead they put down the convertible top and set the coffin-like box upright jammed against the transmission hump. Driving into the Tokyo dawn, it was as if the bluefin was leaping into the air in a last desperate attempt to escape. A ray of sunlight glinted off the fish's gunmetal hide in a biblical moment.

"Razu will be back," said Tio Tepo.

As he spoke, a pair of Subarus, one red, one silver, separated from the curb and swam behind them like two moray eels. The streets were still relatively empty, though delivery trucks were starting to take up curb space, guys with hand trucks carting crates and boxes and bales through storefront doorways. The overhead expressways were jammed; traffic moved like dark sluggish rivers.

In front of them, a string of green lights blinked on in receding succession, an impromptu runway cleared for takeoff.

Tio Tepo went for it, pushing the Eldorado's speedometer past 80, screaming around a half-ton noodle delivery truck that backed suddenly into the street, leaving the Subarus in the proverbial noodle dust. To avoid slamming into the delivery truck on whose side appeared the smiling face of a typical Tokyo housewife happily slurping from a bowl of noodles and fish broth, the driver of the silver WRX steered sideways and crashed the customized street racer into the curb, destroying the right front wheel and axel. By the time the red WRX squeezed past the noodle truck, the navy blue Caddy with the dead tuna in the backseat had made three turns and was nowhere to be seen except by an orbiting civilian spy satellite or the ever watchful eyes of the yakuza's network of street informants.

Razu, sitting in the deep leather backseat of a spit-polished midnight-black Mercedes the length of half a city block, signed into his account with GeckoGraphic, owners of a civilian spy satellite network. Even as GeckoGraphic's Asian area satellite located Johnny Ito's speeding Batmobile wannabe on a street grid beamed to Razu's iPhone, a small-time heroin dealer visiting a customer at a corner steamed-dumpling-and-coffee joint called Pop Eye's dialed Razu's iPhone to report the identical location of Johnny Ito, Tio Tepo, and the sacred bluefin.

Tio Tepo glanced sideways at Johnny.

"Wish that tuna could talk," he said. "Hard to imagine what kind of stories it would tell. Wild stuff, I'm sure."

"You're not getting sentimental on me, are you?" asked Johnny. "Twelve hours from now that baby is going to be nothing but sashimi garnished with a perilla leaf and a side of shredded turnip."

Tio Tepo gestured wildly in the direction ahead.

"If we live that long."

Ahead a gargantuan waste management vehicle painted to look like a giant squid burbled from a side street, turned, and bore down on them at ever-increasing speed. Twenty tons of inexorable steel driven by an apeshit yakuza samurai.

"Yikes!" Johnny shouted.

To the right a stone stairway descended a small hillside to an ancient and serene Shinto temple, its hand-hewn columns and eaves painted in exotic colors. Tio Tepo headed for the staircase. They pitched and yawed and bounced down the wide but shallow steps. Johnny's teeth and organs shook as if caught up in the long-predicted giant quake. Blood oozed from a cut lip. He grabbed the tuna's coffin, which was showing signs of wanting to fly into the bushes.

Hang in there, fish, he thought. We need you. I can think of a lot worse fates than ending up as Jack Nicholson's dinner.

When the waste management truck started down the stairs, it instantly destroyed a stone banister, several prewar street lamps, and a small shrine honoring the woodland deity guarding the temple. As the stairs ended and the Eldorado ripped pell-mell across the greensward in front of the temple, Johnny looked back in time to see the garbage truck plow into a bronze lion seated halfway up the steps.

The lion, no match for the full-throttle 20-ton waste management vehicle, exploded into a dozen jagged pieces. At the same time the garbage truck became airborne. Listing to one side it flipped ass over elbow into a punishing barrel roll. The driver's head penetrated the front windshield and instantly turned to mush. The passenger, catapulted through an open side window, was impaled on a brass lawn ornament, and bled to death. The giant squid rolled to a halt in a bamboo thicket. The woodland deity smiled.

"Thank you, fish!" Tio Tepo said.

"Don't be ridiculous," Johnny retorted. "The fish had nothing to do with it. The yakuza asshole behind the wheel had no fucking idea how to drive that thing."

Tio Tepo stopped the Caddy and waited while Johnny ran up the steps of the temple and emptied his pockets of coins and bills in front of the altar. He even took off and left as an offering a diamond pinky ring Momoko had given him.

Over the rising blare of sirens, a numbers runner standing at the top of the steps relayed to Razu's iPhone the gory details.

"Fuck! Fuck!! Fuck!!! Why is it I always end up having to do every fuckin' thing myself?"

"I don't know, boss," said the bald-headed driver with shoulders twice as wide as Elizabeth Taylor's ass.

"It was a rhetorical question, asswipe."

Razu squeezed out a glop of imported French hand cream and began rubbing his hands together.

"Let's meet them at the Silverado." Then he added: "And make it snappy." A line he'd heard in some gaijin gangster flick.

Meanwhile Tio Tepo found a back entrance to the shrine, drove back onto the street and turned in the direction of the pleasure district of Roppongi. From the backseat, the bluefin gazed cross the flared blue-and-chrome fins of the Eldorado at the passing scene.

Johnny Ito's mother lived in a two-bedroom apartment on the second floor across the street from the Silverado Country-Western Sushi Bar. When she opened the steel apartment door, Razu pushed past her into the apartment. Following behind him his driver quickly subdued, bound, and gagged Mrs. Ito. Razu opened a front window. Across the narrow street and up a little bit the Silverado's awning hung over the sidewalk. He checked his Heckler & Koch 9mm semi-automatic. Then told his driver to wait in the alley and be ready to grab the bluefin.

Moments later Tio Tepo pulled the Eldorado up to the front door of the Silverado. Razu started firing. Tio Tepo and Johnny crouched in their seats. Tio Tepo returned fire.

Unbeknownst to Razu or his driver, Mrs. Ito had been a famous escape artist. She had once even opened for David Copperfield in Vegas. In seconds she made mincemeat out of Razu's driver's tie-up job.

As Razu leaned out the window blasting away, Mrs. Ito charged into the living room and rammed a mop up Razu's ass. Even as he squeezed off another shot, Razu, thrown wildly off balance by this ass attack, pitched out the window, rolled across a narrow awning and fell to the street.

The last bullet Razu fired was dead on, hitting Tio Tepo in the upper chest, but missing his heart. Thrown backward, Tio Tepo's foot, caught at an odd angle under the dashboard, drove the gas pedal to the floor. At the same moment his hands mesmerically shifted the automobile into reverse. The Cadillac shot backward like a bat out of Hell.

Razu struggled to his feet, shaking the stars from his head. His pistol was nowhere to be seen. He turned and started to lope toward the alley. He was ten feet from the entrance when the blue fin of the Eldorado pinned him to the wall, crushing him like a bug. Seconds later the Caddy burst into flames.

Johnny Ito escaped the inferno with minor burns. Momoko came to visit him in the hospital and immediately took off her clothes and leaped into Johnny's bed. Tio Tepo was also pulled to safety. His bullet wound not fatal. But the magical giant bluefin was broiled to a fare-thee-well.

What the Fuck Was That?

When I leaned down into the bathroom sink to slurp a drink of water from the tap, this black nightmarish thing slithered out of the faucet and right up my nose.

It happened in a flash, even as the cool rush of water spilled over my parched lips, and I gazed blurrily at my distorted image in the bathroom mirror. My nose was maybe half an inch from the faucet mouth, my maw agape, sucking at the stream of ice-cold agua.

Next instant, this low-slung mat-black outer space insect creature emerged like a mini stealth bomber from the end of the nozzle and launched itself across the gap. Grappling onto the longish hairs protruding from my proboscis, which I systematically neglected to clip to my wife's eternal disgust, it bolted like a gun shot up my nasal passage.

I jerked backward, a trail horse shying from a coiled canebrake rattler. My fingers grabbed onto my nose, I snorted wildly.

"What the fuck was that?!"

Was I hallucinating? A psilocybin flashback harking back to my misspent youth? Or had an errant dust mote momentarily settled across my eye's cornea, creating the illusion of an invading alien slug? Or was it only the fragmentary residue of the nightmare that moments before had roiled me from the depths of my afternoon nap?

I ran a finger down each side of my nose, feeling for some irregularity or protuberance where the thing had lodged itself inside. Nothing.

But when I sniffed, one nostril felt clogged as though someone using a Popsicle stick had jammed a cotton ball as far as possible up the passageway.

Pinching my nose between thumb and forefinger, I leaned over the sink and blew fiercely. Nothing happened. The left nostril still felt blocked. Had the little bugger used its razor-sharp teeth to attach itself like a lamprey to the soft membranous tissue of the nasal wall? A wave of panic susurrated across my nerve endings.

"Stay calm," I said.

Leaning close to the mirror, I tilted my head back and gazed at an odd angle up twin black holes like the barrels of a sawed-off shotgun.

What I needed was a flashlight.

Frantically I scrounged through the drawers and shelves of the bathroom cabinets. A pack of multi-colored condoms. Several depleted tubes of toothpaste. Matches. A rusted pair of tweezers. A partially smoked jay. Hairpins. But no flashlight.

Lighting a match, I grabbed the tweezers, using them to hold the tar-stained roach to my lips, to which I then applied the flame and sucked greedily. The pungent resinous smoke swirled deep into my lungs. Just what the doctor ordered, I thought. A little ganja to calm my overwrought nerves. A veritable balm of Gilead.

Abruptly I recalled a newspaper article I'd read the week before about brain-devouring amoebas that frequented the sluggish waters of mud-bottom lakes. Mud bottom were the only kind of lakes we had down here in Texas.

Holy shit! I thought. The thing that went up my nose was for sure one of those brain-chomping critters. I was a dead man!

I had to see my doctor immediately.

Without bothering to leave a note for Cecily, my wife, I hauled ass out of our garden apartment down to Austin Street where my doctor, Dr. Joseph Wang, practiced general medicine on the fourteenth floor of the Amicable Life Insurance Building.

I blew past the nurse/receptionist and burst like a Comanche into Dr. Joe's office, where he sat poking distractedly at a plate of shrimp lo mein and sipping a martini. At the hubbub of my entry, Dr. Joe leaped to his feet and went into a defensive Choi Kwang Do stance, chopsticks held like killer nunchucks.

"Ray," he said. "What the matter you?"

He shifted into an offensive position, chopsticks thrust menacingly forward.

"You watch out, cowboy. I break your nose. You go home. Take cold shower."

"NO. Doc. You don't understand. You gotta help me. You know those killer amoebas? I've got one. Went right up my nose."

"WHAT you say?"

"A killer amoeba just crawled up my nose. I'm a dead man. You've got to help me."

He cocked his head, considering the situation.

"You want me fix?" he asked.

"Si." I nodded my head vigorously. "Si, si."

The rasping sound of a garbage truck grinding its gears announced the presence behind me of Dr. Joe's nurse/receptionist, Soledad, clearing her throat.

"Come with me, Ray."

In Dr. Joe's examination room, Soledad took my weight, temperature and blood pressure.

"You need exercise," she lamented. Then: "Get undressed except your underpants. Lie down on the examination table."

These preliminaries had diddly-squat to do with treating my killer amoeba infestation. But you didn't argue with Soledad. Five-eight and brawny. She sprinkled steroid powder on her Grape Nuts and worked out at Gold's twice a day, before and after work. A ballbuster.

Luckily that morning I'd put on a fresh pair of Merona-brand boxers, green and magenta checks with skulls.

A sheet of brown wrapping paper that crinkled and scrunched when I climbed up covered the examination table. I lay on my back, sweating like a dying bass, imagining the amoeba feasting on my cerebellum.

Dr. Joe stepped into the room followed by the dog-breath odor of steamed bok choy. A huge snarling Doberman materialized in front of my face, drool foaming from the black edges of his jaw. It must be the pot, I thought. The thing couldn't have started eating my brain yet.

Or had it.

The newspaper article never said how long it took the little fuckers to get down to it after they'd zipped up your snozzle.

When I blinked, the Doberman morphed into Dr. Joe. His leering face stared down at me, white teeth glinting like the incomprehensible thoughts of a psychopath. Dr. Joe's eyes glowed Chinese red, like ripe lychee nuts. Had he already been taken over by aliens?

"Where hurt? I take rook."

Out of nowhere he jammed the black plastic spout of an otoscope as far as it would go into my left nostril.

"Ow!" I yelled, trying to squirm backward.

Dr. Joe's forearm and fist slammed into my chest. "Hold still, preeze."

Air burst from my lungs like an exploding vacuum clearer bag. I couldn't breath. My lungs were nonfunctional. I was drowning in air. My eyeballs bugged out. Tears flooded down my cheeks. Bile seared my throat.

Dr. Joe lay across my chest, knee thrust against my privates. One eye was pinched shut; the other squinted into the otoscope. The herbal essence of Sen-Sen wafted from his lips.

As air reentered my chest, a high tremulous voice I didn't recognize asked: "Do you see it?"

"Something in there. Berry serious."

Dr. Joe stood back, his head nodding up and down.

"Need take drastic action."

"What do you mean?" I sputtered. "What kind of drastic action?"

With a cacophony of clanging metal, Dr. Joe yanked open a drawer in the instrument table close at hand. He held aloft a surgeon's scalpel. Its steel blade gleamed in the florescent light.

"Wait a minute." I held up two hands, my heels digging at the brown wrapping paper surface, trying to push away from Dr. Joe's immediate vicinity. "You could hurt somebody with that. How about you just shoot some water up my nose? Flood the fucker out of there!"

Dr. Joe edged toward me, scalpel held at shoulder height. I scrunched backward until I was squatting like a Mexican peasant on the pillow end of the examination table.

"Miss Soledad," Dr. Joe called out. "Please to assist with unruly patient."

Next moment Soledad, wearing the bloodthirsty smile of a cannibal at a beachside cookout, swooped toward me grabbing one ankle and trying to pull me back flat on the table.

Fuck this! raged through me brain. My other foot shot forward in a wild kick, catching Soledad in the neck. She gagged. GAAAAAAA! And fell sideways.

Leaping past Dr. Joe, I scooped up my clothes and made for the exit.

"You pay for this!" yelled Dr. Joe behind me. "I call cops."

Riding down in the elevator, my brain fizzed and popped like a defective string of firecrackers. But by the time the doors opened onto the lobby, I'd reached the following conclusions: Dr. Joe was one of them, an alien mastermind. His plan was to incapacitate me by severing my prefrontal cortex, turning me into a zombie. Zombified and a prisoner in his offices, the flesh-eating space aliens could feed on my brain at their leisure, copulating and reproducing until the signal to infiltrate was beamed from the mother ship.

Or maybe I'd been drinking a bit too much lately.

Regardless, I'd escaped Dr. Joe's clutches by the skin of my teeth. But the little black bugfucker was still resident somewhere in my sinuses. I knew what I had to do. I had to drown the thing.

Still carrying my bundle of cloths and boots I scampered across the lobby and leaped into my El Camino resting on an expired meter. The police officer who had just slipped a ticket under the wiper blade followed me with hostile eyes.

"Hey, pal, you can't run around naked like that."

"Sorry," I said. "Gotta go."

I tore away from the curb, narrowly missing a UPS truck, and aimed for the storm-swollen Brazos six blocks away. In seconds I parked on the verge, ran with reckless abandon down the riverbank and threw myself into the muddy current.

As I sank into the thick chocolate-colored stream, too late I remembered I'd never learned to swim. The swirling waters closed over my head and darkness fell.

The next thing I remembered was a downward jerking pressure on my chest, repeated again and again. Water trickled from my mouth.

When my eyes fluttered open, I gazed upon the face of an angel. Soft honey-colored skin, cheeks like passing clouds, a brow as placid as a bayou backwater, tapered nose leading to lips holding the promise of a ripe mango, eyes blue and storm-tossed, all this curtained by golden shoulder-length tresses. And, lest I forget, a pair of hooters to rival the great pyramids of Egypt.

Even as I accepted this dream, this heavenly vision, she leaned down, placed her mouth over mine and blew bursts of air down my esophagus.

When she drew back to a sitting position and resumed pumping on my chest, I saw the thing, sleek, charcoal black, and sinister as an arachnid refugee from the pits of Hell, resting on the soft curve of skin just above her lips. For a moment it clung to the blonde fuzz that edged those lips; then sprinted up one of her nostrils.

At the same moment the emergency medical tech saw that my eyes were open. She smiled.

"Welcome back from the dead."

"You don't know the half of it," I said.

It was her problem now.

No Way, José

Chapter 1

The pick-up bounces over a curb and comes to a jolting halt. I'm ready to die, the man who calls himself Alberto thinks. For, as it is written, this life is but a sport and a pastime. Sitting in the truck bed, back to the wind, he lifts his head and, after a moment of meditation, opens his eyes.

They're parked next to a gas pump in the shade of a metal awning. The oblong shadow cast by the awning covers a row of eight gas pumps, except for the last, which is in the blazing sunlight. A sign reads: Czech Stop.

Is this a security checkpoint? Alberto wonders. His fingers begin to tingle.

Should he make a dash for the hedgerow? And then...the bullets ripping his flesh. The end.

In fact, it's just a gas and kolaches stop-and-go along the Interstate, the nearby town having been settled by Czechs a hundred years back.

The driver, Bill Cody, sloe-eyed and rough-hewn, clambers out of the cab and gets the gas flowing into his tank. His fingers find a toothpick in the flap pocket of his cowboy shirt and he plunges it between two teeth.

"Better get somethin' ta drink," he drawls at Alberto. "Still got a couple more hours ta Dallas."

Alberto's lips are as dry as a seven-year drought. He tries to speak. At last:

"Dallas still two hours?"

Bill wrinkles his forehead.

"Where'dja say you were from?"

"Corpse us Christi."

Bill's frown deepens. "No fuckin' way, José. Not with that accent. You're a God damn illegal. And not from south of the border."

The nozzle clicks off, and Bill hooks it back in the pump and twists the gas cap shut. He walks across the tarmac to the cinderblock store, offering, among other delicacies, beer, soda pop, bags of deep fried pork rinds, and a dozen or so varieties of kolaches.

Alberto stares after him, trying to parse out the meaning of Bill's words.

Inside, Bill pays for the gas, a 16-ounce Dr. Pepper, and a bag of rinds. He isn't a big kolaches fan. Waiting for his change, he thinks: Shit, they don't pay me enough to worry about illegals on my day off.

At the last moment he grabs a bottle of water for the hitchhiker.

They're back on the Interstate, moving at about 75 m.p.h., when the right front tire disintegrates. The pick-up swerves onto the verge, then swings sideways the other way into a passing semi. Alberto, gripping his nylon carryall, flies over the tailgate into a honeysuckle bush. The 18-wheeler, gouts of black smoke spewing from its brakes, shimmies back and forth, catching a fender of the spinning pick-up on the rebound. Ahead, the driver of a monster RV glances into her rearview and panics, wildly twisting the steering wheel. Out of control, the RV clips a road sign, then flips sideways a dozen times down an embankment. No survivors.

When the dust settles, the pick-up is topsy-turvy at the bottom of the same embankment. The steering wheel pins Bill Cody like a moth in a specimen box. With seven broken ribs, a collapsed lung, internal bleeding, and serious liver and spleen damage, the prognosis ain't great.

Gasoline, leaking from a rupture to the intake pipe, pools next to Bill's open window.

Alberto leans down and looks in Bill's eyes.

"I'm sorry," Alberto says. "But you know who I am."

Bill doesn't say anything, but his eyes fill with murder.

Alberto lights a match. Cupping it in his hands, he squats down, holding it toward the puddle of gas. When he drops it, flames leap in a dance macabre.

In protest a pair of ravens take flight from the power line above.

Alberto climbs from the ditch to the service road. Just ahead a single blacktop lane runs perpendicular into the countryside. In no time Alberto is lost from sight down that Texas capillary.

Chapter 2

Lydia Floodway wrenches the old Bronco into gear. It shoots out of the driveway like a bat from Hell. Or maybe a pterodactyl. A comet's tail of pea gravel spews behind.

As they turn up Grandview, Zeke, Jr., in the backseat, thrusts his hand sideways, pushing his fingers under his sister Maud's bare thigh.

"PERVERT!" she screams and digs her nails into his hand.

"Ow!"

"Leave your sister alone, Zeke, Jr."

Under cover of the seatback, Maud gives him the finger.

"Mom. She just cursed me," he says.

"Maud. Don't be throwin' gasoline on the fire."

Maud is sixteen going on twenty-six. Maud is jailbait.

Zeke, Jr., is fourteen. He's drilled a spy hole through the shared wall separating their bedrooms, so he can watch his sister undress. Maud is well aware of the hole. Zeke, Jr., wants to be a cop when he grows up.

The Bronco's oversized wheels scrunch on gravel. A chain-link fence separates Taylor Street from the playground, where Mr. Bates, the science teacher, surveys the scene of potential mayhem with tungsten-hardened eyes. Glancing street-ward at the arrival of the Floodways, he nods at Lydia. He'd once made a pass at her at the annual Founders Barbecue. No way, José.

Zeke, Jr., and Maud exit through opposite doors.

"Allison'll pick you up at three," calls Lydia.

Maud stops and squints back at her mom. "Don't you remember? I'm going over to Jane's. To study for the history test."

"Oh. Right."

Zeke, Jr., is already in the playground, his arms locked in a wrestler's tussle with his pal Andy, their heads bent close together, feet shuffling for position in the dirt.

Lydia drives away from the school; then a hundred yards further on pulls over next to the Seventh Day Adventist hall to light a cigarette. She puffs desultorily, thinking about Brian Beetle, the lawyer.

When he's naked he looks like any other man, she decides. With his stupid dick pointing at the ceiling. Nothing special just because he's a lawyer. Afterward he lies there on the damp sheets, watching her dress. It's creepy, him looking at her like that, his eyes heavy from sex.

Maybe I should end it, she thinks.

A wild itch runs helter-skelter across her crotch. She scratches herself vigorously.

Time to get to work. On that note she throws the smoldering butt out the window, stomps on the gas and swings into the street without looking. Luke Riley's pick-up swerves to avoid the Bronco, his horn blaring.

"Look out, you crazy bitch!" Luke hollers as he accelerates down the quiet residential street. By the time he gets to Main, he's doing sixty. Runs right through the red light.

Pointlessly, Lydia flicks him off.

Chapter 3

These days Dietz mostly doesn't give a shit.

In less than twenty-four hours, he and the Dallas PD will part company for good. Early retirement it says in the paperwork. His attorney worked it out, after the video of Dietz, or someone who looked exactly like him, beating the crap out of a homeless junkie aired on the ten o'clock news.

He has a place already picked out in Ft. Lauderdale. Big enough for him and his mom. And a security job with a cruise line.

Except now even the future is pretty much fucked.

Because Dietz's mother's as dead as a dodo. Lying in a pool of blood with a letter opener sticking out of her eyeball.

Detective Larry Santos, slim and dark as a cheroot, kneels by the body. He moves the head from side to side.

"Right through the brain," he says.

"Huh," Dietz says. "Didn't have much of a brain left."

He sighs. His haunted eyes gape from a booze-swollen face. Gray stubble sprinkles his cheeks like fake fairy dust.

A hundred-watt bulb in a shade-less ceiling fixture floods the room with acid light, exposing the thrift store dreariness of a nowhere life. Charlie Frampton, another homicide Detective, strides in from the kitchen.

"Your mom keep money in the house?" he asks.

"Whatever she had woulda been in a marmalade jar in the cupboard next to the stove," Dietz replies.

"Looks like they found it." Frampton says. He holds up a triangular shard of pottery bearing the letters Mar.

Detective Santos gives a low whistle.

"Look at that," he says. "They cut off her finger." He points to where the ring finger of Dietz's mom's left hand is missing, except for a bloody stump. "Must have been after a ring."

Frampton leans over to look, hands resting on his thighs.

Dietz slams his fist into the wall, making an indentation in the plaster. Blood oozes along his split knuckles.

"Damn! Fuck!"

He squeezes his eyes closed to hide the tears that suddenly cloud his vision.

"Bastards. I'll fuckin' cut their nuts off."

Frampton comes over and wraps a beefy arm around Dietz's shoulder. "Take it easy, man. We'll get 'em."

"It was my dad's wedding ring," Dietz says. "He won it at a poker game. Mom started wearing it after he died."

"Anything special about it?" asked Frampton.

"It's a rattlesnake's head with a two-caret diamond eye."

171

"We'll get it back," Santos says. He walks outside and stands on the falling down porch breathing in the damp night air. Some forensics guys come up the front walk, nod to Santos, and disappear inside.

Dietz comes up behind him.

"Larry," he says. "My mom didn't deserve to die that way."

"Nobody does."

"When you get them, I want...I want to interview them. Alone."

"No way, José."

"You owe me."

"That was a long time ago."

They each stare in a different direction into the night. The glow of the city illuminates rolling banks of clouds, the remnants of an earlier thunderstorm.

"Your mom have a car?" asks Santos.

"'89 Chrysler Le Baron. Burns oil like a motherfucker. But she loved the fact it was a convertible. Made her feel young."

"Looks like they ripped it off." Santos gestures at the empty driveway. "Which means they're probably headed out a town."

"Sombitches won't get far in that. Over a 150,000 miles on that baby. On her last legs. Mom only used her to go to the grocery and the liquor mart."

"Give me the license plate number. We'll put out an APB."

"I hope it fuckin' blows up."

Chapter 4

Brian Beetle places his thumb and index finger alligator-clip-wise around Lydia Floodway's protruding nipple and squeezes.

"Ow!" Lydia jerks free and bounds out of the bed.

"Awesome," Brian says.

"If I did that to your dick, you'd be screamin' your head off." Standing at the window, she pulls back the lace curtain an inch or two and gazes at the street hammered by the two o'clock sun.

"Come back over here, baby. Let me kiss it all better."

Lydia leans down to retrieve her Wal-Mart panties from the stained carpet.

"I've got to get back to work."

"Oh, come on. One more ride for the big fellow." Brian shakes his semi-hard penis, as though it were a godsend.

Lydia hooks her bra; then fiddles with the buttons of her blouse. "I've really got to stop doing this, Brian. Zeke's bound to find out. Then what am I going to do. I've got two kids, a mortgage, a shit job..."

"Life's full of risks."

"What if I divorced Zeke and we got married?" This one comes down the alley toward home plate like a wild-assed spitball. Brian steps back from the plate, letting it fly by. The ref calls a strike.

"No way, José. Marriage is NOT my thing, darlin'."

"No. Of course not. How foolish of me to bring it up. A big shot criminal defense lawyer like you. A commitment other than to the aggrandizement of your ego just doesn't play."

"Darlin', you know when we started this, I told you it was just for fun. I like you a lot but..."

Lydia buttons her almost-too-tight slacks and slips on her sandals. She looks at him one last time. His penis is now little more than a breakfast sausage. His brow furrows with concern that she might do something crazy, like pulling out a pistol and blasting away.

Instead she opens the door.

"Kiss my ass!" she says and walks blithely out and down the stairs.

Chapter 5

"Call me Alberto."

He holds out his hand but the driver ignores it. "Thanks for pickin' up. Hot. Very hot."

"Hot as Hades," says the driver.

He's still eying Alberto up and down, expecting him to morph into evil incarnate. Or at least a bayou vampire. Alberto smiles.

"Nice truck."

Out of some wayward sense of duty, Mason Barrow always picks up hitchhikers. But that doesn't mean much. He distrusts anyone he hasn't known for at least twenty-five years. And he hates liars. His truck is thirteen years old and looks like shit.

Ain't nobody going to vouch for this pilgrim, he thinks. Maybe I should just shoot him and leave 'im by the side of the road. Course some would call that murder, a flaunting of one of the Lord's commandments. On the other hand, aren't our finest sons toiling in the killing fields of Iraq? Moral ambiguity's like a slow-acting poison. Either you cut through the bullshit or slip into a coma and die.

He shifts his F-150 into gear.

"Where ya headed?"

Alberto smiles.

"Not too smart to be out walkin' in this heat," Mason says to fill the gap. "Easy to die of sunstroke."

"Hot."

"You can say that again. So, where'd ya say you was goin'?"

"Going? Yes, going to Dallas." Alberto smiles again. "You take me Dallas?"

"No way, José."

Barrow concentrates on his driving. Sun-burnt fields, some with a smattering of cattle or goats, almost dry mud-bottom creeks lined with cottonwoods, and the occasional ramshackle farm pass by outside the insect-spattered windshield.

"You took the wrong runway to get to Dallas, pal. Next town up's Defoeville. That's where I'm goin'. Have ta drop you there."

His passenger nods his head.

"They've got a nice café. Get yourself some lunch."

But Alberto's eyes are already closed. Behind the curtain of skin, his mind replays Bill Cody's death by fire.

Do not surrender to your emotions, he tells himself. You have sworn to bring down the great glass towers of Dallas, home of the Cowboys. Many will die. But none of them are innocent. The blood of your family is on their hands.

The flames in his mind no longer rise from Bill Cody's crumpled truck. He dreams of a ruined house in a Baghdad suburb, destroyed by Hellfire rockets from an American attack helicopter. The screams are from the seared lips of his two brothers and a sister.

Chapter 6

"Zeke. I'm starving. Let's knock it off and get us a feedbag."

Zeke Floodway, in farmer's dungarees and a flannel shirt with its sleeves ripped off, jumps down from the kitchen counter where he's been bolting cabinets to the wall. A scruffy beard and unkempt shoulder-length hair tell the story of a hippie lad now past forty but still puffing on the old hookah in between shots of Jim Beam. Sawdust and dirt streak his sweated forehead. He pulls out a red bandanna and swipes his brow.

"Where ya wanna go, Elmo? How 'bout a burger down ta Edgar's?"

"No fuckin' way, José, am I gonna eat lunch at that dump and risk gettin' a dose a E. coli. Somebody oughta put Edgar outa his misery. An' bulldoze the place."

"Okay, then. Wherever you want to go."

"I've been meanin' to try that new gent's club opened downtown. Somebody told me they've got a free lunch."

"Ain't no free lunch, Elmo. You'll end up blowing you profits on a pair of tits and ass."

Elmo's mood changes like quicksilver.

"Let me worry about my profits," he snaps. "You just worry about stayin' on my good side." His narrow eyes stare at Zeke, until Zeke looks away.

"Whatever, bro."

They cruise down Main Street in Elmo's van. The front end makes a scraping sound, as if they're dragging a body.

Main Street is a sad ghost of its former distinction, back when being the county seat meant something. Now the old courthouse is haunted by a bunch of third-rate lawyers picking over the bones. The twenty or so Jewish families, and anyone else with an ounce of vision or some unencumbered cash, have long since decamped to Austin or Dallas or El Paso. Lots of empty storefronts with sun-faded For Lease signs in their windows. The rest are taken up with insurance, mattresses, lawyers' offices, rip off appliance rentals, and spurious antique parlors.

"Hey," Elmo points. "Ain't that Lydia's Bronco?"

"Might be." Zeke recognizes the license plate number. It's Lydia's.

"Ain't the place where she works way on the other side a town?"

"Could be."

"What's the matter with you, man? Might be. Could be. You need to get some conviction."

"All I'm sayin' is, that Bronco might be hers or it might not. Lot a old Bronco's around."

"And if it is Lydia's, then what in heck is your little honey pot doin' way over here at..." Elmo glances at his Sanyo sports watch. "At 1:30 on a Thursday afternoon?"

Zeke lets the question hang there like the corpse of a child molester.

Elmo pulls his truck into a slanted parking space in front of the old Griswold Hotel, at eight floors the tallest building in Defoeville. Its main dining room is now The Night Owl Lounge – A Gent's Club. A hand-painted cardboard sign says: Free Lunch 11 – 2 weekdays.

When they exit Elmo's truck, the sun batters down on them like the blows of a ball-peen hammer on a tin roof. It's enough to shrivel any anticipation of what might await them inside.

Elmo pulls open one side of the fake-suede-covered doors. When it swings closed behind them, they're in freezing cold pitch-blackness. From nowhere a cigarette girl in a snow-white bra and panties swooshes up to them. Besides cigarettes, her tray holds mints, gum, exotic condoms, and religious pamphlets in English, Spanish, and Arabic.

"There's a five-dollar cover," she says, holding out her hand.

Elmo gives her a ten. So much for a free lunch, Zeke thinks. But keeps his mouth shut and follows Elmo and the girl from the foyer into the main part of the lounge. It's nothing like the Motel 6 ambience of the Korean whack shack out by the Interstate.

The size of the room is deceiving, as it's painted black, walls, ceiling, floor—all black. Psychedelic posters of naked women are illuminated on the walls by special lights. A narrow stage struts into the room. There's a bar down one wall. The rest of the space is taken up with rows of tables facing the runway.

On the runway a woman on her knees eats out another woman lolling in a hammock.

Two half-hammered lawyers, one young, the other mid-career, sit at the bar making comments about the culinary qualities of the show. Otherwise the place is empty.

The cigarette girl motions Zeke and Elmo to a table up close to the stage. Elmo orders two beers, which are also extra. The two women change places.

Elmo is mesmerized by the action. Zeke walks over to the buffet table at the side of the room. It's slim pickin's: a few slices of limp ham, chips and salsa, a bowl of pretzels. Instead, Zeke goes into the men's room.

Standing at the urinal, Zeke's mind travels backward in time. To Lydia's Bronco parked at 1:30 p.m. in front of the old Bockman Block, a nest of storefronts inhabited by lawyers and related vipers.

What the fuck's going on here, Zeke wonders.

He shakes his member in confusion, zips up, and walks back into the club. One of the naked performers lounges in Zeke's seat talking to Elmo.

Zeke just keeps walking 'til he's back out in the burning sunlight. Standing at the curb, he looks back up to the next block, but the Bronco is gone. The street is devoid of traffic. Of any movement at all. Is Hell hot or cold? he wonders.

Chapter 7

The Jolene brothers are a walking catalog of opposites. Fat and skinny, squat and tall, dumb and less dumb, angry and cool, a preacher's black suit versus slacks and a golf shirt. Ray is the tall skinny one in black with an Associates Degree from Inez Junior College down in the Rio Grande Valley and the imperturbable demeanor of a mahatma. Sociopathic eyes gaze sadly from his chiseled face. Warren is the other brother. He wears his hair in an archaic flattop.

They stand at the edge of a pasture, looking down at the Le Baron where it sags into a drainage ditch at the side of the road, its front axel cracked like a peanut shell.

"I hate foreign cars," says Warren, kicking up a fan of dust. "Made by a bunch a gook ass-wipes."

"Le Baron's a Chrysler product, right out of Detroit," replies Ray, his thin fingers toying with his goatee.

"No way, José. Why's it called Le Baron, then?"

"How the fuck should I know. Some marketing guru made it up."

Warren turns and stares at a clutch of cows that have meandered up to the barbed wire fence to get a better look at the newcomers.

"Fuckin' cows!" he blurts. "I hate the country. Makes my skin crawl. All the bugs, pollen, rodents."

"Take it easy, Warren."

"Yeah, genius brother. An easy boost, you said. An old lady with a mattress stuffed to the gills with cash." Warren pauses to unzip his pants. Extricating his schlong from its place of residence, he pisses in the direction of the cows. "How much did she have? Forty fuckin' bucks in a jam jar. Then the old bag goes for a gun. Good thing I grabbed the letter opener."

"Yes. A wonderful piece of luck. Now we're up for capital murder."

"Don't sweat the small stuff, brother. Where the fuck are we, anyway?"

"Sign back there said two miles to Defoeville."

"Far fuckin' out. Just what I wanted to do: take a stroll in the country."

Warren walks over to the Le Baron, yanks open the driver's door, and pushes the seatback forward so he can reach underneath. He stands up holding a steel-gray Saturday night special, which he slips into his trouser pocket.

"What 'ave you got in your other hand?" demands Ray.

"It's the old biddy's ring. And the finger it was on."

"No. Goddammit! What you've got is evidence that'll tie us directly to the old lady's murder. Give it here."

"You can have the finger. But I'm keeping the ring."

"You wait and see. They'll be injectin' our asses down in Huntsville before this is over."

Ray takes the appendage and throws it as far as he can into the field. Turning away, he walks up the road in the direction of Defoeville. For a long moment Warren's eyes follow the trajectory of the finger; then he starts after his brother.

Chapter 8

At 12:49 p.m. Maud sprints across the tiled hallway of Millard Fillmore Memorial High School and slides into her front row seat in Mr. Bates' General Science class. Mr. Bates is writing formulas on the blackboard, but turns in time to catch a fleeting glimpse of Maud's talc-white thighs before she snaps her legs shut.

Maud puts her fist face down on the desktop, the middle finger extended. She smiles like a coquette, all the time thinking how awful it is being sick, the upchucking and the fevered nightmares. The next moment she leaps from her seat, steps into the hall and throws up.

Several passing students scoot out of the way. Mr. Bates looks on with disgust. When she's done, he steps to the door and hisses:

"Better go to the nurse. I'll come by later."

She's shivering, her skin as splotchy as a sow's stomach. The nurse gives her Tylenol and tells her to rest on the daybed. Lying on her back behind the metal and cloth screen, her eyes won't close. It's just nerves, she tells herself. We always used a condom.

The last thought in her head before she falls asleep on the squishy daybed is: maybe I should buy one of those pregnancy test kits.

Mr. Bates' lips on hers draws her out of a swamp of fervid dreams. His hand is on her crotch. She pushes it away.

"No way, José," she says. "If we do it here, we're sure to get caught."

"Maybe it would be worth it."

"You mean the head rush of fucking in the nurse's office or being indicted for child molestation?"

Bates pouts. But stops groping her.

"What time is it?" she asks.

"Two fifteen."

"God." She closes her eyes and puts her hand to her forehead. It feels cold and clam-like. Her neck is stiff. "I feel like shit."

"Maybe you should go home."

"Nobody's there."

"I could drive you."

She reaches up her hand and jerks his head down toward her. Her lips fasten upon his like a leech. Her vomit-bitter tongue entwines with his.

To hell with going to Jane's to study for the history test, she thinks. I could go to fucking jail, he thinks.

Chapter 9

Sergeant Earl Petty, Texas Rangers, Company "F," Waco, Texas, considers the coating of dust on his black cowboy boots. Taking a monogrammed handkerchief from his back pocket, he leans down and buffs until the spit shine returns.

The dust is from the walk down the embankment and back to get a last look at the remains of Sergeant Bill Cody, ditto. More like a napalm atrocity than a dead Texas Ranger.

When Earl turns at the thud of a car door closing, Lieutenant Giles Truluck shambles toward him. Weather-stained Stetson, cowboy shirt with pearl buttons and a bolo tie, black pants and cowboy boots. Two wood-handled .32 caliber Smith & Wesson revolvers are holstered at his hips.

"At least his wife's run out on him and his kids are grown up," the Lieutenant says, grasping Earl in a hug.

Earl extricates himself and blows a wad of spit between his front teeth.

"Highway Patrol got here first. Driver of the semi..." He flicks his head to where it's parked a little way up the highway. "Says Bill's truck suddenly just lost control. Driver didn't see the RV go over cause he was tryin' like hell not to flip himself."

"At least it was quick."

"Bein' burnt to a crisp can't be much fun."

The Lieutenant looks up at the vast blue sky, his eyes glisten. He's at a loss for words. Then:

"Think it might rain?"

"No way, José."

The line of vehicles passing on the left have slowed to 30 m.p.h., looking for blood or a zipped body bag.

"Here's the odd part," Earl says. "Truck driver thought he saw someone walk away from Bill's pick-up just after it went up in flames."

Chapter 10

Zeke walks up Main Street until he comes to the empty parking slot where the Bronco had been. On the glass storefront opposite it reads: Brian Beetle Attorney at Law. A black velvet curtain blocks any view into the interior. He thinks about going inside, making an appointment. Then just walking past the secretary and shooting the guy at point blank range as he sits behind his desk.

Christ! Zeke freaks. What's the matter with you? It's all in your head, jerk-off.

But he can't let it go.

At the far end of the Bockman Block, Zeke steps from bright mid-afternoon sun through the door of Carl's Tap. Inside, it's dark and beery. An ancient air-conditioning unit wheezes in the background. The Tap is barely cooler than outside.

A bar runs the length of the long narrow room. There are no tables. A stuffed chihuahua with a sneer on his lips sits on top of the cash register near the front door. The chihuahua's name is Carl. John, the owner, nods.

"Shiner," says Zeke.

"No way, José. Barrel's empty. It's either Budweiser or Bud Light. And I guess I know the answer to that one."

John draws a pint of Budweiser and sets it in front of Zeke. There're four other guys drinking in the Tap at three in the afternoon on a Thursday. Zeke knows all of them.

Defoeville, it goes without saying, is a small pond.

"Hey, Wendell." Zeke nods to the man standing next to him. "How's it goin'?"

Wendell nods back. "Doin' okay."

"Got a cigarette."

Wendell pulls a pack of generic smokes from his shirt pocket and shakes one loose. John provides a match. Zeke blows a cloud of tobacco smoke toward the ceiling. It tastes like burning shit. He read somewhere they use dried shit in India for cooking fires. He stubs the cigarette in an ashtray bearing the likeness of Arnold Schwarzenegger.

"Give me a shot of Jameson," Zeke says.

"If you weren't gonna smoke it, what'dja take it for?"

"Wendell, you're an asshole."

Wendell roils forward like a tsunami, an out-of-work nobody who's been looking for an excuse for a fight all afternoon.

Zeke hits him straight in the stomach and twice across the jaw. Wendell shakes his head, trying to break free of the blows. His hand goes for the pocket of his pants.

"Look out!" yells John. "The SOB's got a razor."

Zeke knees Wendell in the nads. He crumples like an old wrinkled shirt. On the way down his chin meets Zeke's upwardly mobile steel-toed boot, and his head nearly flies in the other direction. A tooth comes loose and rattles like a sex-crazed June bug against the cheap wood paneling.

"Sombitch been lookin' for trouble since he got here," John says.

"I'm in the same boat," Zeke says.

A fellow drinker with a clerical collar pipes up: "Is he dead?"

"Not even close," John says.

"Then he won't be needing absolution."

Hands under Wendell's shoulders, John starts to drag him toward the back of the bar. He glances up at the patrons: "Well, don't just stand there..."

The priest and another man each take a leg and in no time Wendell is history. Zeke throws a five on the bar and goes out the way he came in.

Chapter 11

A day earlier, down the road a piece at the Piney Woods State Facility for the Criminally Insane, an in-patient named Maurice A. Vende hides in the false bottom of a laundry cart and is pushed to freedom. His escape isn't discovered for twelve hours. By then it's too late.

"Shouldn't we notify Austin?" Dr. Jatarji, the Assistant Director, asks.

"No way, José," the Director replies. "M. A. Vende killed and ate his parents, three siblings, four neighbors and a cat before he was caught. I'm not going to ruin the golden years of my career trying to explain to a bunch of Austin bureaucrats how he got loose. Maurice never existed."

The Director picks up M. A. Vende's file and starts feeding the pages into a heavy-duty paper shredder. Dr. Jatarji, suddenly afflicted with a massive headache, flees back to his office where, drawing the blinds, he sits in semi-darkness doing deep breathing exercises.

Chapter 12

Gravel crunches like granola beneath Sheriff Sonny Troop's boot soles, as he rocks back and forth, like a Jew at the Wailing Wall, on the narrow shoulder of the road. He's six-five, with a face as stiff as a gale-force wind.

"What'cha got, chico?"

Deputy Ned Ritter taps his hand nervously against his trouser leg. His eyes are blue and hardboiled. His nose bulbous and misshapen. His sunken cheeks pocked with old acne scars.

"Le Baron in the ditch with a broken axel."

"I can see that. Tell me somethin' I don't know."

A smirk plays across Ritter's face like a late night rerun.

"License number's the same as that APB out of Dallas. Murder suspects, armed and dangerous."

"Damn, boy! You know how to get the blood goin'." The Sheriff purses his lips. "Where do ya think they're at?"

"No blood in the car. Engine's cold. Hard to say how far they've gone. Mighta even caught a ride. I thank we oughta call the state troopers."

"No fuckin way, José, am I lettin' some buzz-cut state boys in mirrored shades take the photo op for bringin' in these asswipes. Are we on the same page, Ritter!?"

"Seems like a high risk situation, sir." Ritter picks up a handful of gravel and starts pinging it off the Le Baron's fender.

"Ritter! Don't go turnin' into some pissant pansy on me, now."

Sheriff Troop pulls out his .357 pistol and fires off a single shot, shattering the front window of the Le Baron. Ritter, his face bright red, looks up at the endless blue sky.

"We'll play it however you want, Sonny," he says without conviction.

"Okay then. Let's assume these bad guys went toward Defoeville. We'll start lookin' in that direction."

They head back to their respective vehicles.

"Hey, Ritter. Better take the safety off your weapon," the Sheriff calls out. He slams the door of his Crown Vic and runs the wipers to clean the dust off the windshield. A dashboard indicator tells him he's low on washer fluid.

As the Sheriff peels out, Ritter, sitting in his Impala with the door open and one booted foot still on the ground, flips open his cell and dials. At least I can get some Dallas cops in on this, he thinks. He knows Dietz from a police workshop two years before.

After some bleeps and sizzle noises, a voice breaks through the static: "Dietz here."

Chapter 13

Maud Floodway runs her fingers up and down Bates' black-trousered thigh. The outline of his circumcised thingamajig throbs against the cheap fabric. His forehead and armpits are awash in sweat. He can hardly breathe, let alone drive the car. But he keeps going.

This is crazy, he thinks. Looney-tunes.

On the main streets he tells her to slump down in her seat, so she's invisible from the sidewalk. Soon enough they cut through a riprap of back streets in the black section of town, past rattrap cottages and shotgun shacks.

Passing a gas station with rap music blaring from a pair of speakers, Maud says:

"Let's get some potato chips and beer."

"No way, José" is Bates' reply.

She pouts and gives him the finger. He guns the engine. The car spins, almost, but not quite, out of control.

They turn down a narrow blacktop road. Maud's is the last house before the road meanders off into the countryside. It's a rambling two-story job, with a Dutch colonial feel and a porte cochere. Her father's inheritance. The stucco is gray and weathered, the wood trim rife with dry rot. The windows are blind eyes.

"My mom doesn't get home before 4:30," volunteers Maud.

"Risky," Bates says. His watch says 2:45. Somehow he knows that today Lydia Floodway will come home at three.

Then Maud puts her hand on his penis and all is lost.

He parks his Chevy Malibu on the verge; they hurry up the driveway like a pair of burglars. Maud finds the key under the backdoor doormat.

Inside, Bates surveys the kitchen, as if expecting a plague of paparazzi to burst from all sides, cameras flashing. But it's just a worn old kitchen, linoleum curling at the edges, cabinets painted so many times it's like another dimension.

Maud comes up behind him.

"Boo!"

Bates: "I don't think I should..." Maud fiercely smooshes her lips against his, forestalling further laments. Her tongue in his mouth recalls the fingers of the dental hygienist he goes to twice a year. Déjà vu.

Maud: "Let's go up to my parent's room."

Bates wants to scream: Are you out of your fucking mind!? Instead he lets her lead him through a dark mold-smelling hallway and up a steep stairway that squeaks at each step like a riot of rats.

Maud's parents' bedroom is about half an acre big. There's a stone fireplace at one end and a vast white-sheeted, maple four-poster. Maud slips behind Bates and closes the door, the ancient latch making a loud metallic click like a gunshot.

Chapter 14

A stand of bamboo lines one side of the road. From within it comes a sudden rustling, snapping and swaying. Warren Jolene goes into attack mode, legs apart in a front to back V, chest slightly forward. He holds the old lady's .22 caliber Saturday night special in front of him like a dousing wand.

"Who the fuck's there!"

A gaunt gray-skinned man in hospital scrubs emerges from the bamboo thicket and commences dancing to some internal tune. He's barefoot. Rivulets of blood run from hand and foot wounds, where he's scrambled through brambles and hedgerows.

"Stop that and answer my question. Who the fuck are you?" demands Warren.

"Looks like a nut case," Ray says. "Somebody around here keeps him in the attic. They musta forgot to turn the latch."

"Maybe I should put him out of his misery."

"No way, José. It's bad luck."

"And we already got enough a that, right?" For a moment Warren thinks about shooting Ray right between the eyes. Instead he says:

"But he might tell someone he saw us."

"Who's gonna believe a Goddamn goofball?"

"You mean screwball."

"Whatever."

Ray scratches his chin.

"Let's go," he says, and starts trudging up the road.

Warren turns back to the nut case: "You never saw us. Got that?"

M. A. Vende rolls his eyes up into his head until only the whites show. "I can be very discreet," he says.

"Yeah, right."

Warren hurries after his brother who's disappearing around a curve in the road. Through the trees he can see a water tower in the distance. That must be Defoeville.

After a few strides Warren catches movement in the corner of his eye and whirls around. M. A. Vende, a half dozen steps behind, teeters along the edge of the tarmac, carefully placing one foot in front the other like a tightrope walker. His wide-flung arms flap up and down for balance.

"Don't be following us, now," Warren says in a stern voice.

M. A. Vende's flipped-out eyes glide up to meet Warren's. "Yes sir, no sir. I won't get any closer," he singsongs.

Warren, though he's a murderer several times over, can't look into those eyes for more than a few seconds. He turns away and starts moving in a light jog to catch up with Ray.

Maurice drops back, following them like an anorexic coyote hoping for scraps. Or a Lecter lite looking for a wet work opportunity.

Chapter 15

"Wadaya mean, the house is on fire! No fuckin' way, José." Mason Barrow screams into his cell phone. He glances over at Alberto. "Hold on a second," he says into the phone.

He swerves his truck into a gas station and shimmies to a stop.

"Sorry buddy," he says. "I've got to drop ya here. My old lady's burnin' down the house. I gotta get back home."

He leans across Alberto to unlatch the passenger door. It sways open and Mason urges the hitchhiker to climb out. Vamonos.

Alberto stands in one of the gas portals watching the disappearing license plate of the pick-up amid a blast of burning oil. Behind him the pounding rant of gangsta rap explodes from loudspeakers mounted over the door of the cashier shack and mini-mart. Its hypnotic beat is not that distant from the imam's chanting of the daily prayers.

He enters the premises, where a young black man with suspicious eyes and a Rasta do stands with hands below the counter. A loaded sawed off is just a grab away.

Alberto smiles. His stomach churns with hunger.

"Which way Dallas?" he asks.

"Whadja say, man?" scowls the attendant.

"Dallas. Which direction, por favor?"

"You talk funny, man. This here's Defoeville where you at."

"Only which way Dallas, please."

"If ya want directions, ya need ta buy somethin'. Ain't no free lunch, if you get my message, bro."

"Buy food?"

"Whatever whacks your wick, man."

Alberto walks up and down the aisles, grabbing Twinkies, Doritos, beef jerky, a Kit-Kat bar and more. He sets the armful of junk food on the counter. The attendant runs each item past the scanner.

"Twelve dollars and 84 cents."

Alberto fumbles in his sports bag and comes up with two fives and two ones.

"Ya still owe me 84 cents."

Alberto gives him a blank look.

"Gimme another dollar, peckerwood." He makes change. "Now listen up." He turns and points through the flyblown window. "See that road over there? That gets ya to the Interstate. From there, Dallas be about an hour an a half."

The attendant puts Alberto's cornucopia of junk food in a plastic sack and pushes it across the counter. Alberto nods and smiles. It's all coming together. Soon I will be in paradise, he thinks.

Chapter 16

At 10 minutes past three o'clock Lydia Floodway grovels before her supervisor, Tom de Silva. His sallow complexion reminds her of a drainage ditch, his eyes are scaly. She could never sleep with him.

"This headache's about drilled to the center of my brain," she says, hand resting on the doorframe of Tom's office. Her sleeveless blouse reveals wisps of wiry underarm hair, bearing witness to Lydia's slacker bohemianism. She's the banker's wild daughter, before he shot himself on the eve of his indictment for grand theft and embezzlement.

Tom folds his hands on the desktop and studies her with an intense lacertian gaze. He'd just as soon fire her as look at her. He knows she won't ever fuck him.

"You've used up all you sick days," he says.

"It's after three, for Christ's sake."

"There's no fuckin' way, José, that Jesus needs to be a participant in this discussion."

"What I mean is, the day's shot."

"You took a two-hour lunch."

She gives Tom a shitass smile.

"I had to run home, check on Zeke, Jr.," she lies through her choppers. "He's running a fever. In fact, I'm probably gettin' what he has. Could be one a those tropical fevers movin' north cause a global warming. Like in that movie..." For the life of her, Lydia can't remember the name of the movie. "The one where everybody dies at the end."

The words DENGUE FEVER flash on and off at the back of Tom's eyeballs. He has the urge to jump up and slam the door in her face. Rush to the men's room and wash his hands.

"Get your ass outa here, Lydia. You can work extra hours tomorrow."

Lydia grabs her purse, slams her desk drawer, and is out of there.

At three-thirty traffic is light, except for the gravel trucks passing through to some new construction by the Interstate. An outlet mall according to the Cottonwood County Times Herald.

She stops at Malone's for a dozen cold Shiner longnecks, spaghetti, Paul Newman's spaghetti sauce, hamburger, the fixin's for garlic toast and a bottle of vin rouge from Lubbock. Her headache is gone.

Back in the Bronco she twists open one of the Shiners and drinks half of it in one swallow. It's funny how boffing at lunchtime always makes me thirsty, she thinks. The longneck ends up in the ditch. She opens the glove compartment to get a Kool and finds Brian Beetle's business card. Crumpled, it arcs after the beer bottle.

A Lyle Lovett tune twangs on the radio.

After her father killed himself, her mother took to bed and was eventually institutionalized. Not a great gene pool. But men find Lydia enormously attractive. Skin buttery as aged white cheddar. Heavy milk-and-honey breasts. Hairy crotch. Trim but not boney.

The fact of men's unquenchable hunger for the rut both pleases her and pisses her off. Sorting through these emotions, she drives too fast through the black neighborhood, past children walking home from school and the Gas and Go, with its rap rhapsodies blaring. A grizzled black man with a Day-Glo yellow vest and handheld stop sign motions for her to slow down. She doesn't see him.

In her head Lydia makes a list of the 69 things she can do on her Tuesday and Thursday lunch hours after she dumps Brian. Maybe Zeke'll buy her a bowl of chili.

Next Tuesday she'll tell Brian it's fini, as her grandmother used to say. I hope to hell he doesn't throw a hissy fit, she thinks, grinding her teeth.

Suddenly she's aware of a man walking down the road in front of her. The Bronco's moving way too fast. She swerves, runs through a shallow culvert and up a slope to the edge of a cotton field, then back down again to the blacktop, where the Bronco jerks to a stop. Sitting, head bent, hands grasping the wheel, she drinks in goblets of air. She's afraid to turn her head or even glance in the rearview, imagining a blood-spattered corpse splayed across the macadam.

When she finally looks behind, the man is standing at the edge of the road starring at her. An athletic bag hangs by a strap from his shoulder. Slim, nut-colored, conservative in black pants and a peach-colored dress shirt. Hispanic? There's something different about him, she thinks.

"Sorry," she calls too loudly through the already open front passenger window. "Lo siento."

He makes no response.

"Where ya headed, streak?"

He steps toward the Bronco. "Going to Interstate. To Dallas."

Funny accent, she thinks. Not Latino. Looking into his eyes, she finds nothing there. No fear of dying. No anger at nearly being run down on some two-bit Texas byway. No expectations or recriminations. Nada.

"Interstate's a couple a miles. Jump in an I'll give ya a lift." It's the least she can do.

Seconds later they pass Lydia's house. She glances at its distinctive and reassuring profile. A curtain moves aside and Maud, naked, stands in one of the windows of Lydia's and Zeke's bedroom.

What the hell!? Lydia thinks.

She looks at the stranger, who's mumbling to himself, his lips moving soundlessly.

"You'll have to excuse me," Lydia says. "But I've got to stop at the house. You can have a cold drink."

Chapter 17

From Carl's Tap, Zeke makes his way two blocks up and two over to the Double Bubble Lounge, an oblong cement-block bunker painted burnt umber. Against this background wasabi green bubbles effervescing from a wasabi green champagne glass spell out the bar's name.

Inside, the action is slow, the barman sullen. A couple of aging goodtime gals sporting frizzy perms and freeze-dried facelifts are entertaining two off-work truckers, the four of them tucked away in a maroon-vinyl booth near the toilets. Shrieks of inebriant laughter ricochet off the stained ceiling tiles like the bleating of sheep bound for the abattoir.

All Zeke can think about is Lydia lying beneath the grotesquely heaving flesh of some anonymous male with a JD degree and an uncircumcised dick.

He chugs his beer and leaves.

Outside the light and heat assault him like a two-by-four across the brow. He shields his eyes with one hand. Suddenly, his nerve-jangled stomach retches and he spews sour beer into the weeds of the vacant lot next to the Double Bubble.

Recovering his composure, Zeke heads for the sanctuary of the Elks Lodge, one flight up in the Elk's Block. A poker game's starting up in the front room, but he declines an invitation to join. He has no interest in cards, even when he's sober.

But the well drinks at the Elks are cheap and he settles in, hunching over the bar in savage silence. Merle, the 74-year-old barman, keeps up an incomprehensible banter. Something about a nephew down in Beaumont born with six toes. Or is it a frog with wings?

The shots of Tullamore Dew go down easy, pumping up Zeke's anger, until he wants to rage on home and beat the shit out of Lydia 'til she begs for forgiveness. For that, he needs a ride back to his truck.

As luck would have it, Reardon Greene, ex-fire chief and ex-mayor, humps onto the next stool and orders a vodka tonic with a twist. He puts a hand on Zeke's shoulder.

"How's it hangin', Zeke, old buddy?"

"Get your paws off me, man," snarls Zeke.

"Touchy. Touchy," mocks Reardon. "You never could hold your booze like your old man."

"Fuck my old man. And the horse he rode in on."

"My, my. We are having a bad day."

"Reardon. There are eight bar stools and five tables in this room and all a them are empty except the one I'm sittin' on and the one next to it. I'd be obliged it you'd plant your butt somewhere besides in my face."

"No way, José am I moving one lousy inch. This is the last free country in the world. So I'll sit where I damn well please."

Reardon grins and takes a long gulp on his drink. Though he's sixty-five, he's still as mean as a stud bull and always ready for a scuffle. He looks sideways at Zeke, considering his bleak and furrowed gaze.

"If I was to take an educated guess, I'd say your rat shit disposition is due to one of two factors. Either you're short of cash or that wife of yours is actin' up. A wild Irish girl, if there ever was one."

"If you don't leave it be, I'm going to cram this stool down your throat."

"An idle threat, if ever I heard one." Reardon downs the dregs of his drink and nods to Merle for a refill. "Listen to me, young Floodway. In my day I've had my share of gash. When the heat gets 'em restless, the best you can do is beat the crap out of 'em."

"Thanks for the advice, daddy-o."

Suddenly Zeke wants to be home before Lydia comes in from work, waiting for her in the musty shadows of the old family kitchen. Fuck her right there on the kitchen floor, ripping off her clothes and plunging his love pump deep inside her 'til his seed spews out like a river and she screams for him to never stop.

The infusions of eighty proof pot-distilled whiskey racing through Zeke's capillaries make him stagger as he dismounts from the barstool. For an instant the floor races upward to smash into his face. Or is it the other way around? When he puts one hand on the bar, the room stops gyrating.

"You gonna be alright?" asks Reardon.

Zeke draws his face back and tries to focus on Reardon.

"Be fine," he says. "Just need to get to my truck. Out on the Old Dixie Road."

"I'll give you a lift," Reardon says. "Got nothin' better to do than take care of wayward drunks." He winks at Merle.

Chapter 18

Deputy Ned Ritter shuts off the Impala's engine and, reaching for the six-pack of Tecate in the passenger seat, pulls a can free from its plastic holder. Beyond the open car windows, the road dust is already settling. When he presses open the beer can's spout, carbonation fizzles forth like a miniature fart.

Ritter takes a deep drawdown on the 12 oz. The taste is ice cold and bitterly refreshing. Draining the can, he tosses it on the passenger-side floor.

From where he's parked, the land tilts down to a mud embankment above the sluggish channel of the Upper Big Sandy River. An ecosystem of pickerel weed, coontail and giant bulrushes rambles along the water's edge.

No way, José, am I getting involved in a shootout with a pair of mass murderers, Ritter thinks. They're all yours, Sonny. He hoists his second beer in mock salute to his boss. Hope they don't blow your pecker off, like in that Hemingway book.

Exiting the police cruiser, Ritter moseys down the shallow grade to the river's edge, holding the remaining four beers by an empty plastic ring. He halts in the shade of a hackberry. A dragonfly flits by like a pinprick of blue neon light.

The rumble of a souped-up car engine coming up the river road devours the stillness of the declining day. From out of a dust cloud, a white Camaro with a blonde female driver heaves into view, bouncing like a jack-in-the-box on the rutted road.

Parking next to the Impala, Brandy St. Pierre, buxom and blowsy in a white tube-top and pink short-shorts with the word juicy spelled across her butt, bounds forth and makes a beeline for Ritter. Ritter already has a hard-on.

Chapter 19

A wad of cigar phlegm floats in the back of Dietz's throat like a wet Go stone, but there's nowhere to spit cruising 80 m.p.h. on the southbound Interstate. Dietz squirms sideways and extricates a cloth handkerchief from his back pocket. Cupping it in front of his mouth, he gags up the glob of mucus.

Jimmy Cuervo, in the passenger seat, makes a face. Jimmy is Dietz's neighbor in the one-bedroom across the hall. Four days a week Jimmy works as a security guard at Northpark Mall.

"Hey, Jimmy," says Dietz. "Gimme the pint of Dickel in the glovebox."

No way, José, Jimmy wants to say. Drinking and driving just isn't cool. Instead he complies with Dietz's request.

Dietz takes a swig. His lips purse with satisfaction.

Jimmy re-stows the bottle on top of the .38 caliber police special and stares out the side window at the monotony of pastureland and scrub windbreaks whizzing by. Dietz shifts back into a comfortable driving position, one elbow thrust through the open window of the ancient Volvo. A warm wind blows through the interior, scurrying among the old magazines and other crap strewn in the back seat. The air-conditioning is history. A passing sign reads: Defoeville Next 4 Exits.

Swinging off at the second exit, they pass through a mixed neighborhood of shacks, trailers, and prewar brick cottages. At a blind intersection, a gravel truck bounds around the corner at high speed, airbrushing the front bumper of the Volvo. The truck driver waves.

"Fucking maniac!" screams Dietz. He leans across and flicks open the dash-box. For a moment Jimmy thinks Dietz intends to grab the .38 and let loose with a barrage of lead. But he only wants the bottle of Dickel. The spinning sound of the metal cap unscrewing echoes loudly in the aftermath of the almost collision.

When Dietz hands the hip bottle back to Jimmy, there's maybe a shot left in the bottom. Jimmy finishes it and throws the bottle out the window.

They enter Defoeville's old business district, looking for the Sheriff's Office. Again Dietz dials Ned Ritter's cell number. For the umpteenth time, the call jumps directly to voice mail.

"Fuck! Fuck! Fuck!" Dietz interjects.

A plate-glass window catching the last blistering waves of sunlight announces:

Sheriff's Office. Inside, a uniformed female bull holds sway.

"Gents. How may I help you?" Annabel Lee inquires, leaning back in a standard issue gray desk chair, New Balance-shod feet at rest on the desktop.

"Tryin' to hook up with Sheriff Troop...or Deputy Ritter. Can't seem to raise him on the blower."

"For starters," she replies, "there'll be no hookin' up around here. Cause this ain't no Turkish bath. Second, Ned Ritter's AWOL, as usual. Third, the Sheriff's cell phone is turned off, as usual, so I have no f-ing idea where he is."

"Can't you go through the phone company, trace him somehow. It's a FUCKING EMERGENCY!"

"It's a felony to threaten a police officer."

"Okay, okay. Deputy Ritter called me earlier today about two fugitives traced to your jurisdiction. The same ones who murdered my mom last night up in Dallas. Drove a letter opener into her brain. I busted ass to get down here to give a hand in apprehending these armed and dangerous dickwads. If Sheriff Troop thinks he can take these two down by himself, he's likely to get his ass in a sling. So Jimmy and me..."

He grips Jimmy with one arm and draws him close. "So Jimmy and me need to hook up, excuse me, meet with Sheriff Troop ASAP."

"Best I can do is leave a message for the sheriff in his in-basket. What motel you stayin' at?"

Dietz stares at her in disbelief. Then twirls and walks out.

On the street Jimmy catches up to Dietz and pulls on his arm. "What're we gonna do now."

"Fuck if I know."

Chapter 20

For an instant Maud's eyes meet those of her mother passing by out on the road, staring up at her from the Bronco's open driver's side window.

"Holy shit, piss, and fuck," Maud says.

Behind her Mr. Bates sprawls across the bed, naked except for a pillow pulled over his face. His thing is red and distended. A scrunched-up condom lies at the edge of the bed like a crushed flower. A hog-like snort escapes from beneath the eiderdown bolster.

Maud leaps onto the bed, shaking Bates wildly. When she yanks the pillow away, his sex-besotted gaze falls upon her with the weight of a lead-lined x-ray apron. Desperate, Maud grabs a flower vase from Lydia's vanity, drops the bouquet onto the floor and throws the algaeous water on Bates. He explodes from the bed.

"What the hell!"

"My mother's home," Maud says from a bent-over position, as she ties her Pumas. Otherwise she's still naked. Mr. Bates laughs. Ha, ha.

"No way, José."

"I shit you not."

Like some religious zealot touched by God, Mr. Bates eyes glaze over. He starts to nod, slowly, then faster and faster. On the bed behind him, snake-like, the heavy end of the condom eases over the edge and falls to the floor with a tiny plop.

Maud grabs Bates' clothes and pushes him out of the bedroom and down the hall to a large tumbledown bathroom with wintergreen and mauve tiles dating back to the time of Bonnie and Clyde. Maud longs to surrender to her hopelessness, drop to her knees before the antique toilet bowl and puke her guts out. Instead she takes two deep breaths and slaps Bates across the cheeks.

Be of good cheer, she thinks. Things are bound to get better.

"Get dressed and come down stairs," she orders Mr. Bates. "I'll tell Lydia you came by to help me with my science fair project. You were just using the bathroom, while I went to change out of my school clothes."

"She'll never believe you."

But Maud is already racing down the stairs, two steps at the time.

Chapter 21

The man calling himself Alberto follows Lydia up the back steps, through the enclosed rear porch, and into the kitchen of the rambling Floodway homestead. Her impromptu invitation recalls to Alberto the image of Americans from school: brash, open, uninhibited. For an instant he doubts that Lydia is a murderer.

Quickly he brushes away this heretical thought. No! he berates himself. The endless killing in my country is because of you Americans. All of you. My sister's murder is on your hands. Soon the circle of revenge will be complete.

Lydia steps away from the sink holding a glass of water. Motioning for Alberto to sit at the kitchen table, she sets the glass on the gaudy vinyl cloth hiding the old oak beneath.

"Please sit here. I'll be right back. I have to talk to my daughter."

At that moment, with the high-pitched squeal of sneakers on burnished wood floors, Maud appears in the kitchen doorway. She looks at Lydia, flashing the shitassed grin of the utterly guilty. Then Maud sees the stranger and everything changes.

Lydia hisses at her daughter. "I need to talk to you in the other room."

Maud walks to the sink and runs herself a glass of water. She takes a long drink; then turns and looks at Lydia again. "What's up?" She nods obliquely toward Alberto.

Alberto is stunned by the turn of events. He wants to cry out, beat himself with sharp briers, grovel before the madness of existence. The young woman standing by the window, the daughter of the woman who almost ran him over, is the identical image of his sister Azza! As if she has risen from the dead!

His eyes rake over Maud's miniskirt and fitted top. Except my sister would never have dressed like you, he thinks. Not like a harlot.

Unable to hold herself back, Lydia snaps at Maud:

"You were standing naked in my bedroom window."

"Mother!"

"Are you here by yourself?" Lydia's lips overlap in her eagerness for an instant answer to this question.

"Mr. Bates..."

"Mel Bates, that scumbag? You're sleeping with Mel Bates?"

"I'm not sleeping with anyone," Maud says, setting down her water glass and crossing her arms under her breasts. Maud suspects Lydia is cheating on Zeke. So what's the big deal? "He's helping me with my science project," she says.

"Then what were you doin' naked up there?" Lydia blurts out.

"Can we not have this discussion now? In front of a stranger and all?"

Maud turns on the coldwater tap, leans down and splashes her face. Erect again, she runs wet fingers through her hair, staring out the window.

Mom's Bronco is there. But why is a man in a black suit leaning into the open driver's side window? Now he's opening the door and climbing into the cab. Holy moly, he's stealing mom's truck! she thinks.

"Mom. No way, José, are you going to believe this..."

"Try me."

Before Maud can speak again, Warren Jolene thrusts open the door from the enclosed back porch and strides into the kitchen.

"Y'all put your hands up. This is a robbery." He waves the Saturday night special. In his thick hand it's a toy, but a deadly one.

For a moment no one cries, spits, yawns, sniffles, coughs, or otherwise makes a move. Then Lydia, with her usual bravado, steps toward him. "I don't know who you are, pal. But get the hell out of my house."

Warren's hand flies out and up, slamming the steel barrel of the gun into Lydia's face. It cuts a swathe through her flesh from cheek to hairline. A wolf pack of pain and blackness howls through the winter landscape of her brain. She crumples to the floor. Her hands cover the gash in her face, her feet kick like a swimmer treading water.

"Anybody else want some of this?" Warren holds up the cheap pistol.

Maud is crying, her face bleached of color. Alberto remembers Azza's tears when their father beat her mercilessly for meeting a man, an engineer, for coffee at the university. Alberto's father is an old man now, spending his time mumbling over the verses of the Koran.

Alberto shakes his head, his eyes on the floor.

"Fantastic," Warren says in a cheerful voice. "Now everyone put your wallets, watches, cash, and jewelry on the table."

From outside the explosion of a large caliber weapon makes Warren jerk his head around. A second explosion and he's disappearing out the way he came in.

Chapter 22

Ray Jolene, sitting in Lydia Floodway's Bronco, his hand about to turn the key left in the ignition, goes into freeze-frame mode at the unmistakable click of a weapon being armed. His mind races like a hamster on steroids. The unyielding tip of a pistol comes to rest against the side of his head, just behind his left ear.

"Don't do anything dumb," Sheriff Bobby Troop says in a deadpan whisper. "Just put both hands on the steering wheel. And don't move a fuckin' nose hair."

Ray does what he's told. Where the hell's Warren got to? he wonders.

"Now, asswipe, I'm gonna open the door. Then you're gonna get out of the truck real slow and put your hands on the roof. You with me, chico?"

No way, José, thinks Ray. The Sheriff appears as a distorted stick figure in the chrome window-detail of the Bronco. A stick figure in cowboy hat and sunglasses pointing a large weapon into the shadow behind Ray's left ear. This guy's an f-ing cartoon, Ray thinks. Deputy Dawg. There's got to be an opportunity here.

Where the hell's Ritter? wonders Troop. Sombitch is never around when ya need him. Troop's Crown Vic sits 40 feet away behind some bushes at the side of the road; his cell phone's in the vanity tray between the seats. The 12-gauge pump is in the dashboard rack.

"I was just borrowing this vehicle," Ray says. "Mine's broken down and I've got a medical emergency."

"Shut up! Or you'll be the medical emergency."

Just beat this boy unconscious and move on, goes through Troop's head, 'cause there's another killer out there unaccounted for. His left hand moves to the Bronco's door handle and presses the unlatching nob. The door, out of plumb, grinds open.

Do it now! roars like a wind through Ray's synapses. He slams his body against the partway-open door of the Bronco. As the door swings wide, it catches the Sheriff in the knee and wrist. For a second or two Troop flounders. Enough time for Ray to roll sideways out of the truck, find purchase for his feet on the graveled parking area and begin a sprint toward the house.

"Freeze, scumbag," Sheriff Troop calls out in his deep baritone. He takes aim at the fleeing Jolene brother. The first round catches Ray in the shoulder and jerks him halfway around. Ray's eyes beg for salvation, even as Troop squeezes off a second hollow-point, this time punching a hole in Ray's chest. He pitches backward, dead before he hits the ground.

Warren Jolene's face peers out through the porch doorway. Catching sight of Ray's corpse near the bottom of the steps, he begins to hyperventilate. His eyes travel outward from the body, across the expanse of gray crushed stone to where Sheriff Troop stands next to the Bronco.

"Murderer!" Warren yells.

He ducks back behind the door stanchion and fires off several shots from the Saturday night special. It's like shooting at a shadow in a darkened hotel room. Nevertheless, Troop takes a hit in the arm.

"Fuck," he spits between clenched teeth. He drops into a shooting position on the ground behind the open Bronco door. Closing one eye and sighting along the barrel, he unloads the magazine in and around the back porch doorway. The third bullet nicks Warren's neck, slashing open his carotid artery. Blood spatters wildly. Warren stumbles backward, half shoving his way, half falling, through the kitchen door.

Even as Sheriff Troop opens both eyes to better view Warren's erratic moves, Maurice A. Vende creeps closer, until he's near enough to drive the end of a metal fence post deep into the back of Troop's skull.

Chapter 23

It's his third. Or is it number 4? Who gives a fuck!

Brian Beetle stands at the White Oaks, some say White Folks, Country Club bar. It's a long highly polished bar of imported teak. Around him drink the crème de la crème of Defoeville. Judge John Magnus, Jr. Reggie Cohen, Chief Surgeon at Cottonwood Country General. Salazar Ortega and the three Salter brothers, who, as a minority company in an economically distressed county, rake in gobs from highway construction contracts and other public works. Jane Cunningham, Defoeville chapter President of the Daughters of the Confederacy.

Brian nods to Judge Magnus. Jane Cunningham, drunker than a skunk, is falling off her barstool.

Brian gazes into his cloudy drink, hoping for enlightenment. His mind reprises the day. In the morning a meth dealer, recently busted, pays him five grand in small bills. A nonrefundable retainer. Buoyed by this infusion of cash, he takes an early lunch. Then along comes Lydia.

What a pain in the ass. After they fuck, she decides to call off their affair. That's the way Brian reads her parting salvo.

This prospect sends him into a nosedive. Black depression rears its hideous head.

Hence the bar at the Club. Hence four vodka gimlets. Or is it five?

Not unlike Zeke Floodway across town at the Elks, Brian staggers slightly as he pushes away from the bar. The room swirls and spins like a midway ride at the Texas State Fair.

Drive up to the Big D, he thinks. Hit the Ghost Bar at the W. See what the night brings. He taps the bar with his fist. Sounds like a plan.

Outside in the waning day, he hands his ticket to the valet attendant. Moments later he climbs into the bucket seat of a silver Mercedes C350 sports sedan. Clicking the seatbelt lock, he puts her in drive and weaves precariously down the club driveway. At the drive's end, he stops at the brink of Turner Road. Looks left and right.

No traffic.

He stomps the pedal and peels out into the deepening gloom. Moments later a red and blue flasher appears in his rearview.

"Damn."

He pulls to the verge. Lowers the window. Waits.

When Officer Baldwin, Texas State Troopers, comes up to the driver's window, Brian hands him his license wrapped in a hundred dollar bill.

The officer looks at the bribe, spits, says:

"Step out of the car, please."

What the hell's wrong with this guy? Brian ponders. No fuckin' way, José, am I getting out of my car for some pissant traffic stop.

"Officer, I'm running late," Brian offers.

"Sir. Didn't I tell you TO STEP OUT OF THE FUCKING CAR?!!"

How dare you scream at me, flashes through a part of Brian's brain. Simultaneously, inexorably, he reaches for the 9mm he keeps under his seat in the event of a disgruntled client.

Before Brian can say mea culpa, the officer rips open the driver's door, hauls Brian from his supple leather interior and slams him to the pavement. A boot grinds into his back; handcuffs sear his wrists. Blood drips from his chin, where it's split wide on the tarmac.

The officer eases his hand beneath Brian's seat and draws out the loaded weapon.

"Well, well. I'd say you're looking at attempted murder, pal," he says. Drawing back his highly polished boot, he kicks Brian in the groin. The lawyer screams.

Chapter 24

Zeke Floodway is in a maudlin mood.

"My wife's fucking a lawyer," he tells Reardon Greene.

"Better to fuck one than be one" is Reardon's laconic reply.

They're in Reardon's classic MGB. It farts and bucks through the back streets of Defoeville, as Reardon wends his way to the location of the kitchen job where Zeke's left his pick-up. A squirrel tail flies from the aerial. Mostly static buzzes from the radio, through which occasionally breaks the throbbing guitar licks and yokel vocals of Dwight Yoakam.

Zeke decides he still loves Lydia. But does that mean he should forgive her without exacting a little family violence to even the score?

"There's my truck," he calls out. Reardon pulls over and Zeke makes the arduous climb out of the low-slung passenger seat of the MGB.

"Thanks for the lift," he says.

"Hey, Zeke. When are you going to start beating your wife?"

"No way, José." Zeke slaps the fender of the MGB, which gives forth a resounding BONG.

Reardon revs the cheesy English-made engine and spirals off into the dying day in a cloud of burning oil.

Zeke climbs into his pick-up, cranks the engine, and heads for home. He drives with the ironic caution of the well oiled. He's still thinking about breaking Lydia's neck, metaphorically speaking.

Chapter 25

Warren Jolene flails backward into the kitchen, arms waving helter-skelter like a zombie attack. Blood spritzes everywhere. Fleeting life has almost fled from his leaden eyes. The Saturday night special falls from his waning grip and skids across the floor under the kitchen table.

Like a Shakespearian actor, Warren's hands keep moving, looking for something, anything, to stop the imminent exit stage left of his sorry-assed soul. They tear through his pockets, disgorging: money clip, stolen wedding band cast in the form of a diamond-eyed serpent, bone-handled pocketknife, small change, a silver locket that belonged to his mother. These objects zigzag across the room as if Warren is upside down on a funhouse ride. But it's no way, José. No magic bean, no witch's charm is found to reverse Warren's pending departure from this life.

He keels over with a thud and lies motionless, except for the blood still pumping from his neck wound. No one gives a shit.

Lydia slumps against the tongue-and-groove dado, low moans escaping her lips as Maud ineffectually offers first aid. It's a nasty cut on Lydia's face, one that will leave a long blanched scar.

Alberto hands Maud a damp cloth. For an instant their fingers touch. For Alberto, it's electric. He wants to believe this is his sister, somehow teleported from the ruins of their home in Baghdad to America. Not just some hallucinatory doppelganger.

Bates, mouth agape in shock and awe, stands in the doorway leading to the front hall.

"Waaaaagh…" Bates is incapable of speech.

At that moment Maurice A. Vende dances into the kitchen. He holds the .357 in one hand. The other is casually tucked around Bobby Troop's severed head. Maud screams. Bates faints dead away.

M. A. Vende instantly fixates on Maud, a tasty morsel.

"Young miss, give us a kiss. We'll let you live another day. Another day to run and play."

Alberto thinks: This man is totally mad. He means to kill us all. Then he thinks of his own journey, his own mission of death and he is no longer sure about anything.

M. A. Vende's mood changes from cloudy to seething black. He drops Troop's head in the sink and moves toward Maud.

"Little Miss Muffet, tough as a tuffet. We'll carve you up and boil you down. 'Til skin and bones are all that's found."

M. A. Vende's odd words send drumbeats of dread undulating across Alberto's nerve endings. Looking down, Alberto sees Warren's pistol lying on the linoleum.

Somehow Lydia struggles to her feet, standing between Maurice and Maud. "Leave Maud alone," she says.

Maurice points the .357 at Lydia. "Out of my way, madam," he says. "My friend here can be very persuasive."

Alberto ducks beneath the table, retrieves the Saturday night special, aims and fires. A tiny bullet, no bigger than a blue bottle fly, embeds itself in the center of Maurice A. Vende's brain. Lights out.

Chapter 26

Maud and Lydia stare at M. A. Vende, lying motionless on the worn linoleum, a dribble of blood staining his lips like a vampire. Then all eyes turn to Alberto. He sets the gun on the table.

"Oh my God," Maud says.

Mr. Bates begins to show signs of life. Sitting up. Rubbing his forehead where he hit a table leg on the way down.

"I'll make a pot of coffee," Lydia says.

"Don't be ridiculous," responds Maud. "Sonny Troop's head's in the sink. Let's go in the parlor and get a drink before my nerves give out." The parlor is the only room in the house where 80 proof sour mash bourbon and other alcoholic beverages are maintained.

"Shouldn't we call the police?" questions Lydia.

"No police," says Alberto.

Overriding his words, Maud says: "What police? Sonny Troop's dead."

"Well," says Lydia. "There's always Ned Ritter. Or Annabel Lee."

"Or the state cops," Maud confirms. "But let's have a drink first."

She helps Mr. Bates to his feet. "You okay, Mr. Bates?"

He nods.

Shell-shocked, in single file they leave the kitchen, pass down the shadowy hallway and enter the moody parlor, which faces onto an overgrown woodlot tangled with blackberry creepers. Lydia turns on several table lamps. Dower portraits of Zeke's ancestors gaze down from the walls, papered in a faded rose pattern. A drinks cart is parked in one corner.

The parlor lights flicker on just as Zeke stops his truck next to Lydia's Bronco. When he strides around the Bronco, he almost trips over Sonny Troop's headless corpse.

"Holy shit!" resonates through his brain like the sounding of a gong in an outhouse. He staggers backward and, leaning against a truck fender, vomits. Exhaustion overwhelms him. He wipes spittle from his mouth; then reaches behind the seat for the tire iron.

Tiptoeing like an idiot across the expanse of gravel, Zeke leaps up the two rotting steps to the front porch. A section of dry-rotted, wood-ant-devoured step crumbles and falls away behind him. He slides cautiously to the side of the front bay window. Back to the crumbling stucco wall, he bends his head sideways to glance through the nearest pane. Lydia, Maud, and Mr. Bates are in the parlor.

What the fuck is Mr. Bates doing here? is Zeke's first thought out of the shoot.

The three of them seem to be drinking and talking as if nothing's wrong. As if there isn't a headless body lying in the driveway. The presence of Mr. Bates remains disturbing. Is it evidence, Zeke wonders for a moment, of a bizarre ménage a trois?

When he taps on the window, Lydia nearly jumps out of her skin. As he comes into the parlor, Lydia, sobbing, throws herself into his arms.

Maud says: "No way, José, are you going to believe what's been happenin' around here..."

When Maud finishes the story of the shootout, she and Zeke and Lydia look around for the stranger. Mr. Bates, having gulped down two stiff drinks, is looking a little queasy. It's then that Maud realizes that the brave brief-spoken stranger never came into the parlor. She looks over at Mr. Bates and gives him a tiny smile of encouragement.

Chapter 27

The stranger, no longer calling himself Alberto, walks quickly up the road. He sees ahead the quivering florescent lights of the gas station where he'd feasted on all the famous American junk food.

When he comes within the cone of gas station lights, he can see the same attendant standing behind the counter. The speakers blare the same gangsta rap. A galaxy of gnats swarms beneath the lights.

The cashier will know about buses to Brownsville, thinks the stranger. I'm done with killing. The vision of Azza, or her ghost, is an omen. Like the flight of a dove.

An aging Volvo, its paint faded to a smoky blue-gray, pulls into the gas station. Dietz, the man behind the wheel, gesticulates through the open window.

"Hey, you," he says. "You from around here? I'm lookin' for Sheriff Troop. You know where I can find him?"

The stranger raises his hand and waves. "Sorry."

Dietz's eyes bug out. In a flash he's out of the car and frozen in a shooter's stance. Blam. Blam, blam. He walks over to where the stranger lies in a heap, an oil stain for a halo, and shoots him one more time in the head. Blam. The station attendant gets the entire thing on videotape.

Jimmy Cuervo rushes up and stands next to Dietz.

"Hope you didn't shoot the wrong guy."

Dietz points at the dead man's hand. At the ring around one finger. The ring Alberto found under Lydia's kitchen table.

When Dietz moves the hand, the diamond eye of the snake shimmers.

"No fuckin' way, José."

THE END

Acknowledgments

Some of these stories, in slightly different form, first appeared in the following magazines: "Looking for Goa" and "Down Mexico Way" in *Dogmatic*; "Ideas of Murder in Southern Vermont" and "Incident in the Tropics" in *Sein und Werden*; "Samuria Avenger" in *3:AM Magazine*; "An Orphan's Tale" and "Maracaibo" in *Plots with Guns*; "We Don' Need No Stinkin' Baggezz" in *Pulp Pusher*; and "Mexican Standoff" in *Thuglit*. "An Orphan's Tale" was inspired by two sentences in Eudora Welty's tale "Moon Lake."

I'd like to thank a few friends who helped along the way, including Barbara Wedgewood who taught me to cross my eyes and dot my T's; Jay Parini at Bread Loaf; Ben Fountain for loving "No Way, Jose"; Michael Ray for inviting me to Blancaneaux Lodge; Hannah Tinti, Dani Shapiro, Michael Maren and John Burnham Schwartz for great times in Positano; Antonio and Carla Sersale, the perfect hosts at Le Sirenuse; Susan Tomaselli, a great editor who first showed my stories the light of day; Anthony Neil Smith who first published me in the United States; my other great editors: Rachel Kendall, Tony Black, Todd Robinson and Allan Guthrie; Bill Komodore who read most of them the first time around: and Jon Bassoff who put it all together.

About the Author

Jonathan Woods is the author of five pulp noir crime books. His story collection, *Bad Juju & Other Tales of Madness and Mayhem* ("Hallucinatory, hilarious, imaginative noir."—*New York Magazine*) was a featured book at the 2010 Texas Book Festival in Austin and won a 2011 Spinetingler Award for Best Crime Short Story Collection. His other books are:

• *A Death in Mexico*: "Captures that same blend of bleakness and corruption that drives Orson Welles' film noir *Touch of Evil*." —*Booklist*;

• *Phone Call from Hell and Other Tales of the Damned*: "Cleverly written and deeply, often hilariously, twisted."—*Booklist*;

• *Kiss the Devil Good Night*: "A frenzied and sprawling masterpiece."—Jon Bassoff; and

• *Hog Wild*: "A wild glorious ride and a fantastic feast of storytelling...Mixing the gothic with the surreal, the western with pulp."—Ken Bruen.

His stories have appeared in *Dallas Noir, Murder in Key West #1, #2* and *#10, 3:AM Magazine, Plots with Guns, Yellow Mama,* and other crime fiction anthologies and literary websites. A former Key West resident, he now hangs out in Galveston, Texas.

Thank you for reading.
Please review this book. Reviews help others find
Absolutely Amazing eBooks and inspire us to keep
providing these marvelous tales.
If you would like to be put on our email list to receive
updates on new releases, contests, and promotions, please
go to AbsolutelyAmazingEbooks.com and sign up.

AbsolutelyAmazingEbooks.com

or AA-eBooks.com

For sales, editorial information, subsidiary rights information
or a catalog, please write or phone or e-mail
New Pulp Press
Manhanset House
Shelter Island Hts., New York 11965-0342, US
Tel: 212-427-7139
www.NewPulpPress.com
bricktower@aol.com
www.IngramContent.com

www.ingramcontent.com/pod-product-compliance
Lightning Source LLC
Chambersburg PA
CBHW051106030726
47504CB00006B/1817